DEAD

WEIGHT

Also by T. R. Ragan

Abducted (Lizzy Gardner Series #1)

Also by Theresa Ragan

Return of the Rose
A Knight in Central Park
Finding Kate Huntley
Taming Mad Max
Having My Baby

DEAD WEIGHT

T. R. RAGAN

THOMAS & MERCER

The characters and events portrayed in this book are fictitious. Any similarity to real persons, living or dead, is coincidental and not intended by the author.

Published by Thomas & Mercer
P.O. Box 400818
Las Vegas, NV 89140

ISBN-13: 9781612185101
ISBN-10: 161218510X

For Joe

CHAPTER 1

FREE AT LAST

California, 1989

Headed north on Interstate 5, Carol Fullerton, sixteen going on thirty, waffled between feeling a sense of boundless liberation and apprehension. The windows of the 1969 Ford Torino were rolled down.

The wind whipped through her hair: freedom.

The slight hiss of the engine: anxiety.

Although her license, complete with picture of a young girl with blonde, stringy hair and goofy expression, had arrived in the mail two days ago, she'd been planning for this day for what seemed like forever.

Click. Pssst. Sssss.

There it was again.

The tank was more than half-full. She wasn't running out of gas. Her best friend, Ellen, had sold her the car for two hundred dollars. Ellen was a year older. In a very short time, the two of them had made a lot of memories driving around Sacramento in the car they often referred to as their chariot. The car had allowed them a certain amount of freedom and always got them where they wanted to go.

But at the moment, the engine didn't sound too good.

She needed to find a gas station and have a mechanic look under the hood, but all she could see in front of her was a never-ending stretch of highway.

She pushed harder on the gas pedal, hoping to find help before it was too late. The engine whirred and then slipped as if something wasn't connecting. She was sure she was in trouble when she saw a puff of white smoke seep out from under the hood.

Pulling to the side of the highway, she shut off the ignition, exited the vehicle, and opened the hood.

The engine hissed and sputtered.

A couple of cars whizzed past. She found an old sweatshirt from the backseat and used it to wipe the dipstick so she could check the oil. It was full. Reaching through the passenger window, she grabbed a piece of Wrigley's Spearmint chewing gum and a map. She decided to give the engine a chance to rest before she tried turning on the ignition again.

She plopped down on the gravel near the front right tire and popped the stick of gum in her mouth. She looked around; nothing but wide open fields and pine trees in the distance.

According to the map, there was a national park close by. If worse came to worst, she would head that way and look for a park ranger or, at the very least, a public telephone.

CHAPTER 2

TODAY'S THE DAY

Sierra Mountains, 2010

"Step on the scale."

"No."

"You want to leave here, don't you?"

That got her attention. The woman on the bed turned her head toward him. She was not a happy camper.

"Today might be your lucky day. Your arms are half the size they were when you first came to me. Look at this," he said, holding up a summer dress with spaghetti straps. "I even bought you a dress for the occasion."

"You're never going to let me go." Her head fell back against the already flattened pillow.

He looked at the dining room table and noticed she'd eaten the salad and green beans and left the chocolate chip cookies. It was amazing what a person could do with the right motivation. He crossed the room in a few strides and went to stand on the other side of the bed so he could get a better look at her.

She wore an oversized pajama shirt that hung past her knees. Her cheekbones were more pronounced. Three chins had become one.

"Yes," he said. "You're definitely going home. You look like a whole new person."

She ignored him.

"Come on. Get up. I want to see how you look in this dress."

He helped her slide her legs to the edge of the bed. Her feet slid slowly to the floor, the long chain clinking as she moved.

She had taken three weeks longer than most to lose a measly ten pounds, but during the sixth week something must have finally triggered her to start doing the hard work because the weight had melted off from that point on.

He picked up her logbook from the bedside table and looked it over. "Good. Good. Looks like you've been following the routine perfectly. Get dressed," he said as he headed for the kitchen.

He removed the dishes from the small wood table but left the plate of cookies. She was a messy one, he thought. Most of the women who had stayed here did the dishes and kept everything nice and tidy, but Diane Kramer was a bona fide slob. She used to be a pig and a slob. One out of two wasn't bad. When he returned to the bed, which also served as a couch when she wasn't in it, he was delighted to see that the dress fit her perfectly.

Today was definitely the day.

"You look great," he told her. He raised his hand to her face so that he could brush tangled hair from her eyes.

She flinched as if his touch was revolting in some way. The idea boggled his mind. He'd been good to her. For months he'd provided her with nutritious meals, made certain she was clothed and bathed, supplied her with books to read, and gave her a journal so she could keep track of her progress. Not once had he raised a hand to her, let alone his voice.

He nudged her arm to get her on the scale. She was five feet five inches tall. When the tip of the needle settled on the nine, he was ecstatic. "Congratulations, Diane, you did it! You weigh one hundred nineteen pounds." Once he removed the chains from around her ankles, she would be closer to 109 pounds. Fabulous.

She stood before the mirror looking glum, her shoulders slumped forward, her spine curved. There was only so much he could do. Attitude was everything.

Nothing she could say or do, though, would ruin the joy he felt upon seeing such amazing results. There wasn't a human being in the world he couldn't help. He was sure of it.

He moved her away from the scale, placed his hands on her shoulders, and turned her toward the one wall in the room that she could not reach during her stay. The wall was covered with a dark, silky sheet.

It was time for the big reveal.

But first, he grabbed the comb from the bedside table and brushed the tangles from her long, dirty-blonde hair.

She remained silent, her eyes dull and lifeless.

Once that chore was done, he went to stand in front of the sheet, inhaling deeply as he turned and stared at her. Thirty seconds passed before he realized he was holding his breath. He smiled and then snapped his fingers when he realized he'd almost forgotten the most important part.

Within minutes, he returned to the same spot in front of the sheet, glad to see she hadn't moved. He held the Polaroid camera high enough so he could see her from head to toe through the viewfinder.

"Stand up straight," he said.

She hardly moved. He took the picture anyhow. Within minutes, the negative developed and he was able to compare her "before" picture with the picture he'd just taken.

"Look at this," he said. "You've lost one hundred forty-six pounds without the chains."

He pulled the sheet away, revealing a floor-to-ceiling mirror. He turned toward the mirror and waited for her reaction.

"That's not me," she said under her breath, her sunken eyes unblinking as she gazed at her reflection.

"It's you."

Her eyes narrowed and she lifted an arm as if to make sure the reflection in the mirror would also lift an arm.

At first, her reaction irritated him. She should be overjoyed. The transformation was life changing. She'd never be the same person again. And yet she looked sad. She was in shock, he decided. The transformation was too much for her. "Do you want a glass of water?"

"I don't want to be here any longer. Please let me go."

"That's exactly what I'm going to do."

He stuffed his hand deep into his pants pocket and pulled out a set of keys. He unlocked the door to his bedroom where he stayed when he had the place to himself and promptly returned with a miniature antique key. "Sit down on the bed so I can get these chains off you."

She did as he asked, her eyes wary.

It took him only a few seconds to unlock the padded shackle from around her ankle. The cuff and chain fell to the wood floor with a clank.

She didn't move, just sat there like a lump on a log. "You're free to go," he said.

"I can go?"

"That's what I said."

She stood and walked slowly to the door, surprised to find it unlocked when she turned the knob.

From where he stood, he could see that the sun had managed to break through the clouds, the sun's rays hitting the forest floor despite the regiment of trees. The porch was covered with prickly pine needles, but that didn't stop her from stepping barefoot onto the porch.

"Don't you want to put on your shoes first?"

She looked back at him, her face lined with distrust. She didn't say a word in response. Instead, she turned back toward the wooded area, flew down the porch stairs, and ran.

Confused, he watched her run through the dense forest blanketed with leaves and twigs. Did she know where she was going? She weaved her way uphill, using her hands and feet to climb and claw her way through a stand of pine trees. On her feet again, the young woman looked as agile and graceful as a deer, as if she'd been running marathons her entire life instead of sitting in front of the television with a bag of corn chips and cheese dip.

He glanced from his backpack near the door to the kitchen floor that needed to be mopped. He knew he should probably go after the woman first and save the cleaning for later, but he just couldn't do it. He was anal that way.

CHAPTER 3

DYING TO KNOW

Sacramento, August 2010

Lizzy Gardner, private investigator, ex-pencil chewer, and thirty-one-year-old woman who would more than likely always be known as "the one who got away," looked over her notes. Two days after Carol Fullerton received her California driver's license in the mail, she paid two hundred dollars for her friend's car and took off, never to be seen again.

That was over twenty years ago.

The girl's mother, Ruth Fullerton, had recently been diagnosed with stage IV lung cancer. She was running out of time, and the poor woman was more desperate than ever to find out what happened to her daughter.

With few leads and little evidence, Lizzy figured this could very well be her first and last cold case.

She tapped the rubber end of her pencil against her chin and glanced outside. It was so hot she could see the heat coming off the asphalt in waves. The streets of downtown Sacramento were empty. Whenever it hit triple digits, the crowds ran to local waterways to cool off. Many schools would not be in session for a few more weeks, which told her the American River was probably teeming with rafts and rowdy kids today.

The moment she looked back at her notes, the door opened.

Lizzy looked up. Ever since being credited with putting away Spiderman, a notorious serial killer, business had picked up.

The woman who walked through the door was tall and slender. She looked like a movie star—a young Sharon Stone. She wore a body-hugging sheath dress with a black-and-white graphic design.

Suddenly Lizzy felt underdressed in her T-shirt and jeans. "What can I do for you?"

"My name is Andrea Kramer," the woman said. "I want to hire you to find my sister."

Lizzy gestured toward the chair facing her desk and then dropped her pencil into the old mayo jar her niece had paper-mâchéd.

Andrea stepped closer, leaving the door to click shut behind her. The woman's cheeks, Lizzy noticed, looked a little too hollow, her arms a little too bony. Glancing at the pastry wrapped in waxed paper next to her iced vanilla latte, Lizzy had to stop herself from offering the woman her lunch. "When was the last time you saw your sister?"

After taking the offered seat, Andrea looked at the floor before opting to keep her giant leather purse on her lap. Smart woman. Lizzy didn't take offense. She had her priorities, and cleaning the carpets wasn't one of them.

"It's been more than six months since I saw my sister," Andrea said.

"Have you gone to the police?"

"Yes."

"And?"

"After much harassment on my part, and waiting a ridiculous number of days, they finally wrote a report. It took them three months to talk to Diane's coworkers, shuffle through the drawers in her apartment, talk to one elderly neighbor, and conclude that my sister is a runaway."

"What have you been doing in the meantime?"

The woman snorted, a dainty little noise. "A better question would be what *haven't* I done?" Andrea reached into her purse, pulled out a plastic three-ring binder, and set it on Lizzy's desk. "I've been gathering information: phone numbers of family and friends, recent photographs of Diane, anything and everything that might help *you* find her."

Lizzy took the binder. It was divided by colored sheets, complete with color-coded tabs. Neat and orderly. Lizzy couldn't help but wonder if the woman needed a filing job.

The first section consisted of a five-by-seven color picture of Diane Kramer, age twenty-eight, five foot five, 255 pounds. Without the round face and chipmunk cheeks, she and Andrea could be twins.

The next page described Diane's personality: happy, funny, and caring. Diane adored kids and worked many hours with special needs children at The Helping Hand, a K-12 school in Sacramento.

Diane was also smart: BS in biological science, summa cum laude, graduating in the top one percent at CSU, Chico.

There were sections in Andrea's binder titled Description, Hobbies, Education, Police, Friends, Family, and Miscellaneous.

The green section labeled Police was the thinnest. That didn't surprise Lizzy. Oftentimes police enforcement looked for missing persons only in specific cases. They had limited resources, and sadly, only a very few cases got the media attention they needed.

As Lizzy flipped through the pages, Andrea talked.

"As you can see, my sister is obese. She's had a weight problem her entire life."

The word *obese* had not entered Lizzy's mind. Although she could only see her face, Diane looked healthy and happy. "Did the extra weight bother your sister?"

Andrea nodded. "Gaining weight…losing weight…it's all Diane talked about. She tried every diet on the planet: Weight Watchers, Nutrisystem, Medifast, Jenny Craig, Atkins, The Zone, South Beach, and then all of the crazier diets too, like ear stapling, the cotton ball diet, and the chewing diet, to name a few."

"The chewing diet?"

"You chew each bite of food at least forty times or for thirty seconds, I forget. Then you tilt your head back and swallow any liquid you've generated from all that chewing. Everything else has to be spit out."

Gross. "Did any of these diets work?"

"No, which is why the police determined my sister gave up and ran away. But that's ridiculous. Diane would never leave without telling me where she was going. Never. She loved her job at the school where she works. The kids at The Helping Hand adore my sister."

"It says here that she talked of suicide."

"Only once. Diane and I had a pact and she never would have broken it."

Lizzy lifted a questioning brow.

"We agreed she had to call me if she ever had suicidal thoughts again. I always figured that would give me a chance to talk her out of it."

"Did she ever call you?"

"No, not for that reason. We did talk on the phone nearly every day. I have three kids and a husband and she has dozens of kids in her classes, which provides us with endless conversational material."

The binder, Lizzy decided, was impressive. "Looks like you've interviewed her friends."

"And acquaintances," Andrea said. "Ever heard of Anthony Melbourne?"

Lizzy shook her head.

"Flip over to the last red tab," Andrea instructed. "He's a motivational speaker. Some call him a fitness guru. He's been compared to Jack LaLanne and Tony Little."

That explained why Lizzy had never heard of Anthony Melbourne. Lizzy wouldn't know a treadmill if it bit her in the ass. She flipped to the red tab titled Anthony Melbourne.

"In the beginning of his career as a fitness guru he traveled around the world," Andrea explained, "but now he's concentrating on his seminars and retreats so he stays close to home. He also runs a very popular gym, which happens to be right here in Sacramento. He's been on PBS and the Home Shopping Network more than a few times selling his products."

Lizzy nodded, waited.

"Diane used to talk about this guy as if he was God."

Andrea's sarcasm was not lost on Lizzy. The woman was not pleased with Anthony Melbourne.

"My sister thought he was the most caring, sensitive man in the world, and she spent a lot of money listening to Melbourne's... umm—"

"Bullshit?"

"Yes."

"Are you saying you think this Melbourne guy had something to do with your sister's disappearance?"

Andrea thought about that for a moment. "Yes, I guess that's what I'm saying. In my other life before marriage and kids, I was a manager of a large retail outlet. I did the hiring and I interviewed a lot of people. I could tell if they were lying. I've always been a big proponent of following my gut. People have instincts for a reason. I don't trust Melbourne and I didn't believe him when he told me he hadn't seen my sister in months."

Lizzy flipped back to the Police section where Andrea had provided a copy of the full police report. "The police report says that Diane cleaned out her savings a few days before she disappeared and that her ID, wallet, and personal effects were never found, which would point to someone leaving on their own terms."

"I understand," Andrea said. "But hear me out. What if Diane was going somewhere to lose weight? What if she had taken that large sum of money and paid Melbourne in return for some…I don't know…magical pill or crazy diet program that she thought might work once and for all?"

"Did you insinuate as much to Melbourne when you talked to him?"

"Yes."

"And?"

"He laughed. But for a millisecond, he looked away. Anthony Melbourne was definitely lying: looking away, stammering, and talking in a defensive tone. You name it, he did it. I'm not saying he killed my sister, although I wouldn't put it past him. I'm just telling you that my gut tells me he knows something."

"Did the police talk to Melbourne?"

"Twice. They said Melbourne was more than cooperative, even turned over his records, which showed that my sister had purchased his DVDs, T-shirts, and every book he's ever put on the market. They also confirmed that Diane attended two of his workshops, one in San Francisco and one right here in Sacramento, only a few weeks before she disappeared."

"What about boyfriends?"

"Diane never had a boyfriend."

"Never went on a date?"

"Not that I know of."

"Girlfriends?"

Andrea pointed to the binder. "Under the yellow tab labeled Friends. Her best friend is Lori Mulcher. They met at Chico, where they attended college together. After they graduated, they both landed jobs at The Helping Hand in Sacramento."

"So everything you know about your sister is in this binder?"

"That's right."

"You feel one hundred percent certain that there was nothing your sister wouldn't tell you. For instance, did she have any unusual hobbies?"

"I'm not sure what you mean."

"Drugs, men, gambling?"

Andrea shook her head. "She would have told me."

"Or so you think. You have doubts. I can see it in your eyes."

Andrea looked to her lap and seemed to be thinking hard about something...or maybe about how much she should say.

Lizzy felt like the bad guy, like the Grinch or one of the bratty kids who wouldn't let the rabbit eat some Trix, and she didn't like it one bit. She and her therapist had jumped many hurdles over the past fourteen years, but guilt in all forms still hovered over Lizzy like a thick black cloud.

"I did recently learn that there was a man"—Andrea used her chin to gesture toward the binder—"under Miscellaneous. A man named Michael Denton who sometimes visited my sister on the weekends."

"Why would you hold back that critical piece of information?"

"I wasn't exactly holding back. I'm telling you now, and it's all in the binder, but it's embarrassing. He's not her boyfriend. The police told me that Michael Denton is what's known as a 'feeder.'" She sighed. "He likes to feed people, especially fat women. I've done some research and there's something known as feederism, where sexual gratification is attained by the mere process of someone gaining weight." She shook her head.

"And your sister never mentioned Michael in any of your conversations?"

"Never. The police tell me he's harmless. But my sister is missing. He's definitely on my radar."

"Anything else? Did your sister get any new piercings or tattoos recently?"

"No."

Andrea Kramer was overly confident, Lizzy decided. Nobody could possibly know everything about someone, even a family member. "It looks like you've not only done your homework," Lizzy said, "but you've done all of my work too."

"Then I haven't made myself clear. I came here today because I want you to follow Anthony Melbourne."

Lizzy pulled another pencil from her jar and tapped the rubber end against her desk. "You're convinced he has something to do with this."

"I'm convinced he knows something, yes. He's holding a seminar in San Francisco this weekend."

Lizzy flipped back to the section of the binder titled Melbourne. "You want me to attend his seminar?"

Andrea nodded. "I also think it would be beneficial for you to take his personal training class."

Taking this job would be like taking candy from a baby, and it just didn't seem right. Lizzy leaned over the desk and looked Andrea in the eyes, making sure the woman listened closely. "I charge an hourly rate for surveillance, and that's not counting mileage or other investigative procedures, which would all be add-ons. Anthony Melbourne travels, which means you would be paying an overnight rate if I stay the night. It could cost you a lot of money. And all because you think Melbourne is acting a little strange? I would love to help you, Andrea, but I don't think it would be wise of you to hire me."

Andrea leaned over the other side of the desk, mirroring Lizzy's every move as she looked back, unblinking, into Lizzy's eyes.

Lizzy couldn't help but feel envious of the woman's big blue eyes, high cheekbones, and perfectly sculpted lips. Some girls had all the luck.

"I've been married for fifteen years," Andrea told her. "We have three children; one is a teenager. I know when they aren't telling me the truth. I like to think of it as woman's intuition. Anthony Melbourne is hiding something, and I want to know what it is."

Hard to believe Andrea had been married for fifteen years and had three kids. The woman didn't look a day over twenty-nine.

"Diane is my only sibling," Andrea went on. "Despite our nine-year age difference, most people think we're twins. Well, at least they did before she gained all of that weight. She's my other half. We finish each other's sentences more often than not. She loves my children as if they were her own. She still mourns the death of our mother and blames herself for the accident that took her life.

I believe Diane's food obsession can be traced back to that tragic day. It's true I knew nothing about this Michael guy until I started investigating, but you must believe me when I tell you that I know Diane better than I know myself. She did not run away. She's in trouble. When Diane first disappeared, I heard her calling for me. I would wake up in the middle of the night in a cold sweat, thinking she was in the room, but she was never there."

Lizzy knew all about waking up in a cold sweat. "Are you still having nightmares?"

"About three months after Diane disappeared, I stopped hearing her voice. I still have a hard time sleeping, but no, I no longer feel her breath against my face as she whispers into my ear, trying to tell me something."

Andrea Kramer appeared credible and her story was certainly compelling. Lizzy had never met Diane Kramer, but she too was convinced the young woman was in trouble.

"I need your help, Ms. Gardner."

"Call me Lizzy."

"I need your help, Lizzy. I want to know what Anthony Melbourne is up to. If I didn't have a family to care for, I would follow him myself."

"What about this Michael guy?"

"If you want to check out Michael Denton for yourself, go ahead, but if you decide to take this case, I want ninety-five percent of your billable hours spent on watching Anthony Melbourne. Money isn't a problem. If you cannot take this job, I'll be forced to sign with Jon Peterson."

Jon Peterson was as sleazy as they come, and judging by the coy look in her eye, Andrea Kramer already knew that.

CHAPTER 4

SOME THINGS NEVER CHANGE

Hayley Hansen sat on the curb across the street from the house where she and her mom had lived all of Hayley's life. It was a one-story, one-garage house, 750 square feet. The outside was a puce color, blotchy and faded.

It wasn't quite noon, but it was already warm, and she could feel trickles of sweat rolling down her back. Hayley took a long drag off her cigarette and waited until she could feel the cold against her throat before she blew a smoke ring, a thick, perfectly formed ring, which glided across the street. Full-bodied tobacco worked best. Menthol worked well too.

The smoke ring slowly disappeared, leaving Hayley to think about what she would see when she entered the house. Inside, there was a wall furnace that didn't work and windows that didn't open. The carpet had been stained so many times it felt brittle if you walked barefoot across the floor. Every room smelled like old shoes and dirty ashtrays. The garage smelled exactly like the city dump.

If Hayley had another place for her mom to live, she'd burn this place down. But she wasn't a pyro and her mom didn't have anywhere else to go, so that was out of the question.

Her mom would never live with her parents. Hayley's grand-parents had moved to Wisconsin years ago, right after her mom threatened to turn her grandfather in for all of the bad things he did when Hayley's mom was a child. He did bad things to Hayley too, but Mom was clueless that way and had no idea. Nobody would believe Hayley if she told them about all the sick family members she had. Most families had one or two black sheep, people they didn't want to talk about, let alone think about. But every member of Hayley's family was a lost cause.

Back when Mom was sober, Hayley and her mom would dream about the good life, talk about how great everything could be someday. Mom was a good storyteller, and Hayley could still remember smelling the ocean and hearing the waves crash against the shore when Mom told her make-believe bedtime stories.

Hayley snubbed out her cigarette and dropped it into the empty film canister she carried around for just that purpose. Jessica, an annoying girl she shared a desk with at work, would be proud since she was all about recycling and saving the earth.

Hayley stood, looked both ways, and then headed across the street. There were no cars in the driveway, so Hayley peeked inside a couple of windows. Nobody appeared to be around.

She tried the front door next. It was unlocked, so she stepped inside. Everything looked and smelled just as she remembered, like one giant armpit after a long, hard run.

"Honey, is that you?"

Excitement coursed through her veins at the sound of her mom's voice. God, how she'd missed her. She hurried to the hallway and stopped when she saw her mom standing there, the light hitting her face just so. Her mom wore an old nightgown. The hem was ripped and the pink satin looked wrinkled and stained. "Hi, Mom."

"Hayley." She opened her arms, and Hayley walked right into them and let her head fall softly against her mom's frail shoulder.

Hayley hadn't been home since the incident that had left her with only four fingers on her right hand. Sadly, her time spent with a serial killer was nothing compared to her time spent right here in this house. Her mother's boyfriend, Brian, had raped her repeatedly as payment for her mother's drugs.

Hayley did not intend to ever see her mom again, but staying away seemed impossible. She missed her more than she ever imagined. There was no holding back. Built-up tears she didn't know she had been storing inside came pouring out.

"It's OK," her mom said, holding her tighter. "My little girl is home. I love you so much."

Hayley wasn't sure how long she and her mom stood in the hallway huddled together like two lost souls, but it was long enough that Hayley's neck began to kink up. When she finally pulled away, she looked at her mom, loving the way her wrinkles made her look cute, not old. Despite the drug and alcohol abuse, her mother was a beautiful woman. Always would be.

She could smell the booze on her mom's breath and that made her sad. She looked into her mom's eyes. "I was wondering, Mom, if I set it up…if you would go to NA meetings again. I'll go with you this time. I think if we're consistent and do it on a regular basis, you'll stand a chance. What do you think?"

Her mom smiled and patted her shoulder as if she was talking about going to the moon someday.

"Mom, I'm serious. You're only in your forties. You have a lot of life ahead of you. Today could be the beginning of something bigger, better, brighter. Don't you think?"

"You always were a dreamer. Just like your daddy."

Hayley exhaled a frustrated breath. Mom never talked about her father. She was fucked up, but Hayley refused to let that deter her from her mission…the reason she'd come to see her mom in the first place. She wanted to start over. She wanted them both to start over, together.

The sound of a car drew Hayley's attention, and she ran back to the main living area and looked out the window. It was Brian. Her mom had called out "honey," Hayley realized, because she thought Brian had arrived. Despite everything that had happened, she was still seeing Brian. And she called him honey.

Hayley locked the front door and then passed her mom in the hallway and entered her mom's bedroom. "Come on, Mom. Let's get you packed up." She opened her mom's drawers, but most of them were filled with rat shit and nothing else.

Her mom stood in the doorway. "Hayley, I can't go with you."

"So you won't go to NA with me either?"

Her mom's hands were shaking as she rubbed the sides of her face. "I can't do it, Hayley. I'm not strong like you. I'm weak. You know that."

"Mom, you're weak because of that hideous man out there. He has you right where he wants you. It's the drugs and alcohol talking right now. Not you. Drugs make people weak. It's not your fault."

Her mom put her hands over her heart. "Hayley, I love Brian. He asked me to marry him."

"Mom," Hayley said, her hands grasping her mom's shoulders. "I don't know what my dad was like, but this man is a hundred times worse. Brian is the devil. And the devil uses drugs to make people do what he wants them to do. He's not going to marry you, Mom. I've been watching him. I see him going home at night. He doesn't sleep here, does he?"

Her mom looked worried.

"He doesn't sleep here, Mom, because he's with a different girl every single night. He's a child rapist, for God's sake, but you already know that."

Her mom's hand came up fast and swift, slapping Hayley hard across the cheek.

Hayley didn't feel a thing. "Every girl he brings home is twenty years younger than you," Hayley went on as if nothing had happened. "I'm not trying to hurt you, Mom. I'm trying to help you. He's waiting for you to start receiving Social Security, and I'm sure he wants this rat-infested house too. He doesn't love you, Mom, but I do."

There was a knock on the door.

"I better get that."

"If you let him in this house, you're never going to see me again."

Her mother put her hand to Hayley's forehead and pushed her hair gently out of her eyes and away from her face. She gazed deeply into Hayley's eyes, looking at her as if she wanted to remember what she looked like, as if this was truly the last time they would look into each other's eyes.

Hayley didn't feel any anger toward her mother, just a pitiful feeling of dark despair and disappointment. Some people were more susceptible to wanting to drink and do drugs too much. It had to do with genetics as well as family history and life situations. She used to feel hurt, anger, and embarrassment, but not any longer. Only the hopelessness lingered.

Another knock on the door, louder this time.

"Don't make me choose, Hayley."

Hayley leaned forward and kissed her mom softly on the cheek. "You made your choice a long time ago, Mom."

Hayley turned and headed for the back door, determined to escape without running into Brian. She would see him soon enough.

CHAPTER 5

NO DELTA BREEZE

It was another scorching hot summer day in Sacramento. An hour ago, Lizzy had changed into a pair of khaki shorts and a light-colored cami, but her lack of clothing and the fan above her head didn't stop sweat from dripping down her back. She wasn't complaining, though. She would take a blistering summer over a mind-numbing winter any day.

Jessica Pleiss, one of two part-time assistants she couldn't afford but also couldn't manage without, walked in at that moment, bringing a wave of dry heat in with her.

"Oh, good, I'm glad you're here," Lizzy said without looking up.

Jessica laughed. "I'm always here at three o'clock on Wednesdays."

Lizzy glanced at the clock. "You're right. Sorry. I'm a little overwhelmed at the moment."

Jessica walked around Lizzy's desk and glanced at her computer screen. "Who's that?"

"Anthony Melbourne, a fitness guru and motivational speaker. Ever heard of him?"

"No, but just looking at those rockin' abs makes me feel as if I should go run a few laps around the park."

Lizzy smiled. "Yeah, I know what you mean. Sadly, I can't remember the last time I set foot in a gym."

"What's the deal with this guy?"

"Looks like we have another missing person case."

"Anthony Melbourne is missing?"

"No." Lizzy handed Jessica the binder. "Andrea Kramer has hired us to find her sister, Diane. She believes Anthony Melbourne has something to do with Diane's disappearance. I'm not so sure at this point, but that's neither here nor there. She's hiring me to keep an eye on Melbourne."

"I thought you said you were too busy to take on too much more."

"True."

"You're becoming a softy."

"Not me," Lizzy lied. At the age of seventeen, Lizzy had been abducted by Samuel Jones, a madman known as Spiderman. After two months of watching him torture his victims, she'd managed to escape with her life, but at what price? She'd spent over a decade hiding from her own shadow until six months ago when her abductor came back into her life, determined to take care of her once and for all. He killed a local anchorwoman and a young girl who had taken Lizzy's defense class. He had sliced through a window screen and taken her while she lay sleeping; the poor girl hadn't had a chance in hell of getting away.

Samuel Jones was dead now. And everyone, including Lizzy's therapist, seemed to think Lizzy should snap out of it—move forward and forget it ever happened. But it wasn't that easy. She wanted nothing more than to let it go and move on, but the harder she tried, the more difficult it was to do.

Jessica grabbed the mail from the incoming tray and took it to the desk she shared with Hayley, the other part-timer. "Is Hayley coming in today?" Jessica asked.

"I'm not sure. She talked about having to attend lab at school." Hayley Hansen had helped save Lizzy's niece. Hayley had lost her pinky finger in the ordeal, but in return had gained a new lease on life. That's what Hayley had told her, but Lizzy wasn't sure she believed it. There was something different about Hayley. She had always kept to herself, but lately she'd been more standoffish than usual. Lizzy thought it might have something to do with Hayley's mother, a woman who had once used her daughter as payment for drugs and who was no longer a part of Hayley's life. For the past six months, Hayley had been living with Lizzy's sister, Cathy, and her niece, Brittany.

Hayley was a smart girl. She had taken the high school proficiency test, received her GED, and was now taking summer classes at Sierra College.

"These pictures came out great," Jessica said after opening a large cardboard envelope. "Hayley definitely has a knack with a camera."

Jessica crossed the room and handed Lizzy three eight-by-ten photos of a man playing tag football with friends, and then two more pictures of the same man carrying a stack of lumber to his truck. "I don't think Mr. H. D. Palmer is going to be receiving workers' comp for too much longer."

"These are good," Lizzy said. "Do you mind dropping the photos at the prosecuting attorney's office on your way home later?"

"Not a problem." Jessica took the pictures back to her desk. "Are you going to visit the mother of that missing girl today?"

Lizzy looked at the clock on the wall. Damn. "I was supposed to be there five minutes ago."

"Mind if I tag along?"

"What about all the paperwork that needs to be done on Jim Thatcher?"

"Finished it yesterday."

"I don't know, Jessica. Ruth Fullerton is a very sick woman and—"

"I'll sit quietly in the corner. I won't say a word. You don't even have to pay me. I just need to do something other than opening and filing mail."

"Fine." Jessica was right; she had become a softy. "Grab the Fullerton file and let's go."

* * *

Mrs. Fullerton's hands shook as she poured tea. It was way too warm for hot tea, but Lizzy wasn't about to say anything. Ruth Fullerton had lost her hair due to chemo treatment for lung cancer. Her head was covered with a tight-fitting brown head scarf. She was thin and fragile looking; too young to be dying.

"Sugar, cream?"

"No thank you."

"How about you, young lady?"

Jessica lifted a hand in protest. "I'm fine, really. Thanks."

Lizzy opened her notebook, and as soon as Mrs. Fullerton took a seat in the cushioned chair across from her, she didn't waste time getting down to business. "I wasn't able to talk to the lead investigator from your daughter's case since he retired eight years ago," Lizzy told her, "but I did talk to Detective Kent Roth."

"Yes, I remember him. A big man with a couple of extra chins."

Lizzy couldn't confirm that since she'd only talked to the man over the phone, but neither did she care how many chins the man had. "Detective Roth," Lizzy continued, "stated the basics, including the dates and location you already told me about. But he also mentioned that there was some tension between your daughter and her father."

"Did he now?"

Lizzy nodded.

Jessica remained quiet, as promised.

"Doesn't surprise me much," Ruth said, "but it's absolute rot. All the detectives that have ever worked on my daughter's case will say anything at all to take the blame off them. From the beginning they had their minds made up, certain that Frank had something to do with Carol's disappearance."

Ruth Fullerton looked annoyed, but there was something else in her expression that Lizzy couldn't quite put a finger on. What was the woman hiding? And why would she hide anything at all if she was dead set on finding her daughter? "Would it be OK if I spoke with Mr. Fullerton myself?"

"You can try," she said, hesitation in her voice. "He's a workaholic and he's rarely home. If Carol were here now she would say nothing has changed."

Lizzy wondered if that was a good thing or a bad thing, but either way she let it go. "What does Mr. Fullerton do for a living?"

"He works for Supremacy Insurance. He's a salesman." Ruth Fullerton took a sip of tea and then set her cup on its matching saucer before pushing herself to her feet. "I have one of his business cards in the kitchen drawer. I'll be right back."

Lizzy made a few notes before she stood and looked around the room.

Jessica had found a photo album on the bottom shelf of the glass coffee table and was flipping through the pages.

As Lizzy crossed the room to take a look at the pictures on the mantel, she felt as if she'd been jolted back into a seventies time warp. The couch was plaid and the built-in bookcase to her left had been painted a burnt-orange color. A brick fireplace was framed by green walls, while the wall to her right was covered with mirrors from floor to ceiling.

If Mrs. Fullerton's daughter had gone missing twenty-one years ago at the age of sixteen, Carol Fullerton would be thirty-seven years old now. That is, if she was still alive. That would put Mrs. Fullerton at about sixty years old.

The eight-by-ten framed photos lined up neatly on the mantel appeared to be standard school portraits: elbows resting on a table, one hand over the other, back straight, hair combed, chin tilted just so.

Lizzy followed the photographs through Carol's life from kindergarten through eighth grade. Cute kid. Nothing from high school. The last photograph was different than the others: black and white, taken outside, her hip leaning against an old car, a wide smile plastered across her face.

"That was Carol two days before she disappeared," Ruth said as she returned to the living room and handed Lizzy a business card.

Lizzy tucked the card into her back pocket and wondered if that's why Carol wore such a big smile the day the picture was taken. Did Carol know she would be gone in two days? Unfortunately, statistics pointed to another direction altogether. "Is that the car Carol was driving the day she went missing?"

"Yes, it's a 1969 Ford Torino. She bought the car from her friend for two hundred dollars, which was a lot of money back then. At the time, we didn't have that kind of money lying around, so Carol asked her grandparents for a loan."

"You also mentioned her friend when we talked on the phone last week—Ellen Thomas, correct?"

"That's right."

"I couldn't locate her under the name Thomas, so I looked up state marriage records and ascertained that she now goes by the name of Ellen Woodson and resides in Auburn."

Lizzy considered that to be a lucky break, considering Auburn was less than an hour away. "I did finally get in touch with Ellen on the phone, but she didn't want to talk to me. She said too many years had passed and although she sends her sympathies for what you're going through, she refused to say anything else."

"I was afraid of that. You might get much of the same from my husband, but please don't let Ellen or Frank discourage you. My daughter is out there somewhere. I know it. We were very close back then. She told me everything. She was my best friend."

Lizzy sighed. She was hearing a lot of that lately. People believed what they wanted to believe. Sisters were sure they knew everything about one another and nobody knew one's daughter better than a mother…or so they all thought.

"If you two were close," Lizzy said, "why would Carol run away?"

"I don't know. But I can't go on like this. My days are numbered. I have to know what happened to her."

Jessica was still flipping through the picture album when the front door burst open and a man came through the door.

Jessica shut the photo book and slid it back onto the coffee table.

"What's going on?" he asked.

The man had a thick head of jet-black hair that was obviously a wig and looked sort of odd on an older man who was small in weight and height. The man was seventy-five percent hair and twenty-five percent everything else. He held a briefcase in one hand and a suit jacket in the other. Sweat trickled down the side of his neck.

Ruth straightened her spine. "Frank, I'd like you to meet Lizzy Gardner. She's the woman who was abducted all those years ago. You know, the girl who escaped the madman and then helped the FBI find the man who killed so many young girls."

Frank wasn't impressed. Not only did he ignore Lizzy's offered hand, he sneered at her. Lizzy pulled her hand back to her side.

"I told you I didn't want any strangers in my house," Frank said. "We've been through this, Ruth. Over and over again. I'm not going back in time just so I can relive every detail with a female cop wannabe who likes carrying a shiny gun because it makes her feel like a man."

"Frank!"

"It's OK," Lizzy said. She'd dealt with worse than Frank before. Sticks and stones and so on; the man didn't bother her. "We'll let ourselves out."

Jessica was already halfway out the door by the time Frank disappeared down the hallway.

"I'll be away this weekend," Lizzy told Ruth once Frank was out of earshot, "but I have a few ideas. I'll call you Monday."

"I'm sorry about Frank. He's not usually so ornery."

"Just take care of yourself and let me do the worrying for a while."

Ruth squeezed Lizzy's hand and nodded, then stood in the doorway until they drove away.

CHAPTER 6

SAN FRANCISCO, HERE I COME!

It was five o'clock on Friday and Lizzy was driving at a snail's pace on I-80 West heading toward San Francisco, which was better than being stuck in the stop-and-go traffic heading east.

The heat had gone from blistering to extreme, which meant you could fry an egg on asphalt. The air conditioner in her old Toyota, a.k.a. Old Yeller, hadn't worked since the beginning of time.

She rolled down a window; hot air against warm, sticky skin didn't help much. She was beginning to rethink the whole summer versus winter thing. The Sacramento heat was downright stifling. Hopefully San Francisco, surrounded by ocean and bay, would be cool and overcast with billowing white fog.

She eyed the oil light on her console. It flickered on and off. She tended to believe everything was fine as long as the light stayed *off* more than *on*.

A ring sounded, and she clicked on her earpiece and pushed a button on her iPhone. "Lizzy Gardner. How can I help you?"

"I can think of twenty ways, but let's start with where are you?"

It was Jared, her lifelong soul mate, if you believed in that sort of stuff. "I'm on my way to an exercise and eating right seminar in San Francisco. It's supposed to be life altering."

"Turn around and come home. I love you just the way you are. And besides, I picked up fresh salmon and that sappy movie you've been begging me to watch with you."

"You rented *Romancing Rachel*?"

"I did, and now my reputation at the movie rental store has been tainted."

She smiled. "That's sooo sweet and I'm so sorry."

"Does that mean that you also forgot our plans to move your stuff into my place this weekend?"

No, she hadn't forgotten, which, she realized, might very well be another reason she had taken the Diane Kramer case. She cared deeply about Jared, but things were moving a little too fast.

"Still there?"

"I'm here."

"You need more time, is that it?"

"I think so."

He sighed. "Take all the time you need. I'm not going anywhere."

"Thanks."

"So what's with the seminar? Since when do you care how many calories are in a Rice Krispies Treat?"

"I'm being paid at an hourly rate to keep an eye on Anthony Melbourne. It's a long story."

"The fitness guy?"

"That's the one." She should have known Jared would know who Anthony Melbourne was since Jared considered raw broccoli to be a delicious snack, and he woke up when it was still dark just so he could spend an hour a day in the gym, longer when he could spare the time.

"So what's this all about? Did his wife ask you to watch him?"

"No, he's not married. A woman came into my office two days ago concerned about her sister who has been missing for more than six months. As far as the police are concerned, the missing woman was not happy with her life and therefore ran off to start over somewhere else. The woman who hired me is convinced her sister is in trouble. The problem is she's basing her theory on female intuition—nothing more, nothing less."

"What do you think?"

"I told her she was wasting her money. She's been doing her own investigation, and I must say she's thorough. I would hire her if she wasn't already too busy raising three kids and a husband."

"Lucky guy."

She laughed. "I should be back home by noon on Sunday."

"If you play your cards right," he said, "I'll make you dinner, followed by life-altering sex."

"Don't make promises you can't keep."

"Be careful," he said, his tone serious.

"I miss you."

"Miss you too."

CHAPTER 7

PETER PETER PUMPKIN EATER

As far as Hayley Hansen was concerned, drug dealers were all the same—scumbags of the earth. They didn't care or even think about the harm their actions caused. They took one life at a time, destroying everything in their paths, including family members who couldn't do anything to save their loved ones.

She walked the darkened streets, knowing she was putting herself in danger. It was way past midnight, and everyone knew that nothing good happened after the witching hour. She had walked these streets many times before, though, and she wasn't afraid.

There were shadowy movements in the alleyways as she passed by. In a not-so-distant apartment building, she heard a man and a woman shouting at each other back and forth, each trying to outyell the other.

Hayley had been dragged to this area a couple of times by her mom when she was small; whenever Brian stayed away for too long this is where they went. Her mother had never brought her inside the drug dealer's apartment. Instead, Hayley was told to wait outside by the pool.

The Greenhill Apartments building was known for its big rooms and even bigger cockroaches. She had stolen a quick look inside the apartment once and saw that that much was true.

She'd seriously hoped she would never step foot on these grounds again, but here she was in the middle of the night looking for Peter Peter Pumpkin Eater. At least that's what he used to call himself. "Hey there," he'd say when he crept quietly into her room. "It's Peter Peter Pumpkin Eater and I'm hungry."

Parts of South Sacramento could be downright frightening. This particular street smelled like her mom's house after a party: like urine, ashtrays, and trash. Every building on the street had at least a few windows boarded up with plywood. Graffiti—not the cool, artistic kind—covered eighty percent of the warped, weather-beaten fencing around the apartment building. The grass, if you could call it that, looked as if it had never been touched by the blades of a lawn mower. Trash floated in the pool, mostly around the edges.

The funny thing was, as much as she despised Peter, he was a mere squid in a shark-infested sea. Squid or not, he deserved to rot in hell. Peter just happened to be the first one on her list: Peter, Randy, and Brian. After those three were taken care of, maybe she could breathe easier and sleep through the night again. Maybe her mom could get her life back in order.

The first apartment on the ground floor had curtains that had been pushed open. Inside, an old lady sat in her big cushiony chair and watched television, her face inches from the screen.

"Hey, baby," came a voice from the shadowy depths of a tall hedge of poisonous oleander.

She ignored the voice and kept on walking. The apartment she was looking for was at the far end of the complex. Although Lizzy's sister had been nice enough to buy her a new pair of jeans and a few shirts, Hayley had opted to wear the outfit her mother had given her a few years ago, back when Mom had been try-ing so hard to get sober. Her mom had been drug free for a few months, and during that time they had gone shopping.

Best day of Hayley's life. Not because her mom bought her an outfit, but because they had never done anything like that before. The two of them spent the entire day window shopping and then ate Chinese food at the food court. Mother and daughter—just out shopping for the day—an honest-to-goodness fairy tale come true. Neither of them particularly loved sweets, but they stopped at the candy store that day too. Twenty minutes later they exited the sweet shop with a bag of sour gummy worms and black lico-rice shaped like tarantulas. They had laughed about that for days.

Hayley didn't want to hurt anyone, she thought as she con-tinued on through the moonlit night. Causing people pain wasn't her thing. The therapist lady she'd been talking to up until a few weeks ago was nice and patient and she kept telling Hayley that the hatred she felt for most of mankind would subside over time. If that ever happened, that would be great. But for now, Hayley had decided to take matters into her own hands. Contrary to popular belief, she didn't hate everyone—just a few disgusting, narcissistic souls.

Hayley knew she could go out every night for the rest of her life and she wouldn't be able to make a dent in the drug-dealing population. She was smart enough to know that there might even be a few misguided drug dealers out there who really wanted to turn their lives around, and that was all wonderfully great. All those people were safe tonight, at least from her.

But not Peter.

Peter Peter Pumpkin Eater needed to pay for what he'd done.

"Honey sweets. You can't just walk by me without saying hello."

The guy had come out from the shadows and was on her heels. She could practically feel his breath on the back of her neck.

While reaching into her hip pocket, she whipped around fast. She was wearing a wig, and the ends of her long red hair hit her chin. The blade of her knife gleamed in the moonlight as she held the sharp tip to his face.

He took a few steps back and nearly tripped on his own feet.

"Come on back here, baby," she said. "I think we should talk about this."

When he realized she wasn't going to lunge at him with her knife, he straightened the collar of his jacket, then turned and walked off with a big man strut in his step. "Don't be sticking no knife in my face, bitch," he said as he walked off.

She continued on her way, shadow man forgotten.

The moon was bright. It wouldn't surprise her to hear the howl of a wolf. Instead, she heard a door slam shut. There were a lot of angry people living in this shithole.

Her shoes, an old pair of Converses, hardly made any noise against the cement walkway as she moved along. She'd found the shoes at Goodwill for seventy-five cents. They would have cost a lot more if the right shoe didn't have a big-ass hole in it.

There it was…apartment 103B.

Half hidden behind a planter filled with dried dead weeds, she slipped her backpack off her shoulder and then took off her sneaks and her pants. If shadow man was watching, she didn't care. She removed the pills from her pants pocket, then reached into her backpack and pulled out a stretchy miniskirt and a pair of gaudy three-inch heels.

Eleven dollars for the entire outfit, including the wig she was wearing. She'd been royally ripped off.

Dressed appropriately now, she carefully tucked the pills into her bra, inhaled the night air, and looked up at the moon through thick false eyelashes. There was something about the moon that appealed to her like nothing else…something reassuring. Maybe she liked knowing she could look upward on any given night and the moon would always be there, no matter where she was. Maybe it was the face on the moon, always smiling down at her, never annoyed or upset: familiar and nonjudgmental.

She forced herself to look back at the cheap brass-colored numbers: 103B.

Peter lived here. Tonight was just the beginning.

Although she'd been keeping tabs on Peter for a while now, she really had no idea if Peter had a mother, sister, brother, or aunt. She never actually came to his door before. Hell, maybe he was married with kids. If he had kids, she might have to figure out a different way to dish out his punishment.

Hayley shrugged. Whatever. She'd just have to wing it. She knocked on the door and waited.

She didn't have to wait long.

Peter looked the same as always: like shit on a stick. His hair was poking out every which way, as if he'd just rubbed a balloon on his head and the electrons and protons were going crazy.

"Christina," he said, his voice slurred, his breath reeking of alcohol. "Is that you?"

"Yeah." She had no idea who Christina was, but that name was as good as any.

He stuck his head out the door to see if anyone was with her. "Where's your ol' man?"

"Don't know."

"Who brought you?"

"I walked." At least that much was the truth.

His hand rose higher on the door frame as if he was trying to look cool or something, an impossible feat on his best day. He had on a dirty white T-shirt and a pair of pants at least a size too big. Apparently, he slept in his clothes. "You're lookin' good," he told her.

"You think so?"

"I always knew you liked me."

"Are you going to let me in, Peter, or should I go back to the ol' man and tell him you wouldn't let me inside?"

A crooked smile appeared. He moved aside to give her enough room to get by. He smelled like scotch, beer, and road kill all mixed together. Funny how certain smells brought back memories, bad and good. Too bad the recollections running through her mind at the moment were all repulsive.

She stepped inside and held her breath to stop from gagging. The greenish-brown shag carpet looked moldy. A stale plastic milk carton sat on the floor next to the couch. Empty beer bottles decorated the room. Her mother's house looked like the Ritz compared to this apartment.

"Nice place," she said.

"Can I get you a shot of whiskey?"

Before she could answer, he curled a calloused hand around the nape of her neck and pulled her lips against his. She hadn't thought anything he could do would surprise her. She was wrong.

Every part of her filled with rage, popping and sizzling like hot oil in her veins. It took restraint she didn't know she had not to bite off his fucking tongue. She used both hands flat against his bony chest to push him away. "Only if you do a shot with me," she managed.

He didn't have to go far, which was unfortunate. A bottle of whiskey sat on a coffee table in front of the couch. He did have to get a couple of glasses, though.

She wiped her mouth with the back of her hand.

The second he disappeared in the kitchen, she retrieved the pills from her bra and slipped them into the quarter-full bottle of whiskey. She put her thumb into the bottle's opening and shook it. When lover boy walked back into the room, she pretended she'd just taken a sip and even wiped her lips with the back of her hand. Then she set the bottle back on the table with a loud thump.

He looked from the bottle to her face. "You look different."

"Thanks."

"It's the hair. I like it." He poured about a shot's worth into each of two plastic cups and handed her one. He drank his in one gulp.

She took a sip and gagged. "This tastes like shit."

His expression changed, reminding her of how easily he angered. "Why are you here?" he asked.

"Isn't it obvious?"

"No," he said, as if someone had whispered her plans into his ear.

Outside in the moonlight she'd felt as if she could take on an army of hoodlums, but everything had changed the moment she entered Peter's apartment.

She hated him, hated him with every fiber of her being. And that was the problem. Hate was an emotion, and emotions fucked with your mind. She tried not to let him see the anxiety she felt merely by looking at him. "Why don't you take me to your bedroom so I can show you how much I've been looking forward to this?"

41

He realized the front door was still open.

With the bottle clutched in his right hand, he used his left to push straggly hair out of his eyes as he went to shut the door. She heard the click of the lock before he led her to his room down the hallway.

A king-sized mattress on the floor took up most of the bedroom. A dingy maroon-colored coverlet hung off the edge. His bedroom was much darker than the living area. She stood at the end of the bed and noticed that he was still standing beneath the door frame leading into the room.

"What are you waiting for?" she asked.

"I'm trying to figure out the real reason why you're here."

"Curiosity."

He grinned, showing two rows of tobacco-stained teeth. "You think I'm stupid?"

She was counting on it.

He took a long swallow from the bottle. "I always knew you liked me, but I could never get you into my bed. So why now?"

"The ol' man strayed, so I figured I would do the same."

"I could frisk you," he said, "but I think it'll be a lot more fun if you just strip down to nothin' instead. One piece at a time. Go ahead. Take something off."

"Well, maybe I've changed my mind about this whole little tryst."

"*Tryst?* You been reading a dictionary or something?"

"*Merriam-Webster's* Eleventh Edition. It's a best-seller."

"Cute. Now take it off. Take it all off, honey."

He took another long swig from the bottle. She removed her T-shirt and then took her time sliding the miniskirt down over her legs before finally stepping out of it.

While she stripped, he drank.

Wearing nothing but a thong, a skimpy bra, and a cheap pair of high heels, she left her clothes in a heap. "I must say my feelings are hurt. Peter doesn't trust me."

He set the bottle on the floor, then straightened and pulled his shirt over his head. He wobbled slightly.

Thank God.

"Where did you get that scar?" she asked, her lips pouty as if she gave a rat's ass.

His chin dropped to his chest as he took a look. "This," he said, trying to touch the scar but missing by a few inches, "is an old war wound."

Seeing the scar made her want to smile, maybe even throw back her head and laugh, but she didn't. She had made that mark with her teeth years ago and was proud of it. The dumb asshole probably thought *that* was bad.

He hadn't seen anything yet.

Hayley turned slightly, her gaze on her backpack. She wanted to make sure everything she needed was close by.

"What's that on your back…a tattoo?"

Shit.

He stumbled forward and pointed a finger at her. "You're not Christina."

No, she thought as she watched him collapse…finally.

Using the pointy toe of her right shoe, she nudged him in the stomach. He was out cold. "And lucky for you," she said, "you're not Brian."

She grabbed her backpack, kicked off her heels, and then quickly changed back into her comfortable clothes. Years ago, when her mom had first dated Brian, she had thought Brian was different. Trusting her mom's judgment, she had been fooled into believing Brian was an OK guy. But it wasn't long before she saw Brian for what he truly was—a monster.

Peter was what she considered to be practice before the big game. If Peter knew what she had planned for his friend Brian, he would have been kissing her three-inch heels in gratitude before he passed out.

Brian would not be nearly so lucky.

No sirree. She was saving the best for last.

Once her shoes were on, she pulled out an assortment of knives and a soldering iron, everything she would need to make sure Peter Peter Pumpkin Eater never pierced a person with his pickled-peppered prick again.

CHAPTER 8

NEVER TALK TO STRANGERS

California, 1989

Carol wondered how long she'd been walking. She already had a blister on her left foot.

No watch. No water. No idea where she was.

And she didn't really care. For the last ten minutes she'd been watching the sky as she walked, transfixed. The sunset was amazing. It was hard to believe she'd never once watched a sunset from beginning to end. It was single-handedly the most beautiful thing she'd ever seen in her life.

Her parents were strict and they always expected her to be inside the house before the sun went down. That was Rule Number One. She had a love-hate relationship with her mom. Frank was another story altogether. Just thinking about him left a bitter taste in her mouth.

She inhaled a deep breath of warm, pine-scented air, and extended her arms above her head, keeping them slightly forward while maintaining a gently curved line. Fifth position: one of many positions she'd learned during her years of ballet. She gracefully dropped her arms to her sides and continued walking, one foot in front of the other.

Exhilarated. That's what she felt at the moment. Liberty and justice for one, she thought with a smile. As she watched the sun dip closer toward the horizon, the rich hues of pinks and reds signaled freedom. Yes, she was free. Free at last, free at last.

A car pulled to the side of the highway a few feet ahead of her. She stopped, looked, and waited.

A man climbed out of the car. He shut the door and came to stand near the back tire, lazily resting his hip against the trunk. From where she stood, he looked like a young man. Cute. Wavy sandy-colored hair framed a nicely shaped face that was golden brown from a day or two in the sun. He wore flip-flops and light-colored denim pants with a hole in the knee, revealing more golden skin. His shirt was a long-sleeved button-down with hardly any buttons fastened. He waved. "Need a ride?"

Rule Number Two: never talk to strangers. Rule Number Three: choose your friends wisely. Rule Number Four: look both ways before crossing the street. She exhaled and continued walking while thinking about what she should do once she was next to him.

"Cat got your tongue?" he asked as she approached.

"What?" she asked even though she'd heard him.

"Want a ride?"

She didn't think she did. And she wasn't sure if she was nervous because he was a stranger or because he was cute. "Do you know how far we are from the national park?" she asked.

"Meeting someone?"

"No."

"It's a good ten minutes from here," he told her. "I could take you there if you want."

She was close enough now to see that he hadn't shaved in a while. He didn't have a beard or anything, but he looked as if he could grow one easily enough if he wanted to. She wondered how old he was…twenty-two, twenty-three?

He smiled, revealing beautiful white teeth.

Butterfly wings flittered about deep inside her belly. Never talk to strangers. Never EVER get into a stranger's car. She looked ahead at the long stretch of lonely highway and wondered why no one ever told her to lock her bedroom door at night. Now that little tidbit of information might have come in handy. If she ever had kids, that would be Rule Number One, Two, Three, and Four.

The car he drove was an old dusty Buick with a missing taillight. The windows were rolled down. The backseat was strewn with clothes, a half-eaten bag of pretzels, and an empty Coke can or two.

He came around to where she stood on the side of the road and opened the passenger door. He made a grand gesture of bowing as if allowing the princess to enter his carriage. It was such a crazy thing for him to do that she found it oddly romantic.

Don't drink and drive. The thought came out of nowhere. Well, that wasn't exactly true. A crumpled can of Coors was sticking out from under one of the seats.

Carol took a good look at the guy stooped over before her. His hair was a little long and stringy, but clean. She could even smell some kind of cologne, something citrusy like lemons and limes combined.

Tired of the fanfare, he straightened and said, "I hate to leave a damsel in distress, especially on this godforsaken deserted highway, but I have places to go and people to see. I saw your car a few miles back, at least I figured it was your car since it wasn't there this morning when I passed by. Anyhow, my name's Dean." He held out his hand.

She shook his hand. His fingers were long and lean and warm enough to send shivers up her arm. "Carol," she replied.

"Don't mean to be rude, darling, but if you need a ride, it's now or never."

Never, never, never take a ride from a stranger. That was probably the rule Frank repeated the most. That thought alone was the decision maker, the deal breaker, the thing that allowed her to push any and all concern aside and get into Dean's car—a stranger's car—an act that could and would be life altering.

The springs under the worn leather sank beneath her as she took the offered seat. Dean shut the door. She looked to the west to watch the sun flash its last brilliant rays and light up the sky in deep purples and ripe oranges, taking her breath away.

Dean climbed in behind the wheel, and she smiled at him as she thought of her favorite quote by Robert Frost: "Freedom lies in being bold."

CHAPTER 9
PRACTICE, DISCIPLINE, AND SACRIFICE

August 2010

"Behind every story of inspiration is a story of training, practice, discipline, and sacrifice. You must be willing to pay the price," Anthony Melbourne shouted from the stage. Every once in a while he jogged from one end of the stage to the other, sort of like Mick Jagger but without the sexy swagger.

"Maybe that means waking up before the break of dawn," he bellowed.

Lizzy imagined Jim Jones might have sounded a lot like Melbourne when he spoke to his followers.

"Maybe it means giving up *Monday Night Football* or *American Idol* each week. You can always find time to exercise. Where there's a will, there's a way."

Many in the audience clapped but none more than the woman standing in the back of the room holding an armload of brochures. The woman with her tight bun and dark suit was downright zealous.

Melbourne had been talking nonstop for two and a half hours. Lizzy had brought a number two pencil and a notebook, not only to add authenticity to her being here but because she had hoped she might learn something…maybe a trick that would help curb her cravings for Rice Krispies Treats and peanut M&M's. But her notebook was blank because the man had said nothing that a million other people hadn't said a zillion times before. Just do it! Where there's a will, there's a way. Motivation is what gets you started; habit is what keeps you going. People do not lack strength; they lack will. It is fatal to enter any war without the will to win it.

What the hell was she doing here?

She could have been curled up in Jared's arms, watching Allie and Noah meet at a carnival and make love in an old dilapidated house.

It was only three o'clock…two more tortuous hours to go. Her eyelids felt like five-pound weights hanging over her eyeballs. She leaned over and reached into her purse, pretending to shuffle through her things while she closed her eyes. Ahhh. Much better. Just a couple of minutes of shut-eye and she'd be good to go.

"You!" she heard someone shout.

Her eyes shot open, but she stayed bent over. What was going on? Who was he talking to? Please don't be—

"You, the one hiding in her knapsack."

Lizzy slowly pulled her head out of her backpack and straightened in her seat.

All eyes were on her.

Lizzy looked at Anthony Melbourne on stage and pointed to her chest.

He nodded. "You look like you're in fine shape. What brings you here today?"

She was sitting in the very back of the large hotel banquet room. There were plenty of people sitting front and center eager to participate. Why her? She had to think fast. She scanned the brochure in her lap, the one she'd been handed on the way in.

"I signed up for your seminar this weekend because…umm… because I have no energy."

"So you're here because you want to fight fatigue with exercise."

"Yes, that's right."

He turned the side of his head toward her and cupped his hand around his ear. "We can't hear you."

She wondered if she was on some sort of ridiculous new candid camera reality show. The guy was nuts. "Yes," she said, louder this time, annoyed by the man's gall at calling her out. "I want to learn all I can about fighting fatigue with exercise," she said loud enough for everyone to hear, "because three grande lattes with triple shots of espresso aren't cutting it any longer."

She got a couple of laughs, although that wasn't what she'd been aiming for.

Melbourne returned to his lectern. "Michelangelo once said: 'If people knew how hard I had to work to gain my mastery, it wouldn't seem so wonderful at all.'"

Lizzy wondered what that had to do with fighting fatigue. Was he comparing himself to Michelangelo?

God save me.

* * *

This was one Monday that couldn't have come soon enough. Lizzy's weekend with the health guru had felt like a lifetime instead of a mere forty-eight hours. She'd raced home on Sunday only to learn that Jared had been called out of town. No life-altering sex. No romantic movie while curled in Jared's arms. Worst weekend ever.

Lizzy glanced around the parking lot watching for her sister, who had yet to arrive. When time permitted, which was fairly often since a girl needed to eat, Lizzy met her sister Cathy for lunch. While waiting for Cathy to arrive, Lizzy sat in her car and skimmed through Carol Fullerton's file.

Ruth Fullerton hadn't paid her much to find her daughter, but Lizzy probably would have taken the case for free if she had to.

The poor woman was dying. Her time on earth was severely limited and she needed to know what had happened to her daughter once and for all.

Last week, Detective Kent Roth had allowed Lizzy to look through the Fullerton file and take notes. At the time of Carol's disappearance, authorities had focused on at least two persons of interest. The police thought they'd caught a break when an anonymous caller reported that Edward Bishop, a neighbor of the Fullertons, had once served time in prison for raping and nearly killing a young girl. Investigators who visited Bishop in prison said that their potential suspect maintained his innocence and refused to speak with officials.

Another suspect was a boy who attended the same high school as Carol. According to Carol's friends, the boy had a crush on her. Apparently, Carol had rejected him. Police didn't have enough evidence for an arrest, and that was the end of that.

A timeline of the day Carol went missing was short and sweet. Carol left for school at 7:30 a.m., and that was the last time Ruth Fullerton saw her daughter. A couple of teenagers said they saw Carol after school at a convenience store buying potato chips and ice cream. It was unclear where Carol went next.

Out of the corner of her eye, Lizzy saw her sister's BMW pull into the lot. She shut the file.

Lizzy felt restless and credited that to Jared being called out of town. Jared was a special agent for the FBI, and he was meeting with a source to gather information on a case. She didn't know when he would be back in town. Bummer. She had hoped to talk to him further about her decision not to move into his place right away. She didn't want Jared to get the wrong idea. She cared about him. If she didn't get so hung up on the "L" word every time he said it, she might be able to tell him she loved him too. Her therapist told her she was overanalyzing. As far as Lizzy was concerned, once someone told another person that they love them, there was no going back. They're vulnerable. Sadly, Lizzy was certain that her inability to say those three words had something to do with her childhood. Her parents rarely told her they loved her—one more issue to deal with before she could live a happy and healthy life.

If her parents couldn't say the words to her, how was it possible for Jared to tell her he loved her? Did he really love her? With all of her flaws and shortcomings?

Unconditionally?

Love was not something two people should take lightly. Love was important. And so was moving in with someone. What if she moved in with Jared and then days later realized she couldn't handle seeing his newspapers piled in the bathroom? What then?

Lizzy sighed, exited her car, and pushed away all thoughts of love as she waved to Cathy across the parking lot.

At that same moment, she spotted a black Ford Expedition with tinted windows. That same car had been parked there the entire time she'd been waiting for her sister. The sun had been in her eyes, though, and she hadn't noticed until now that someone was inside the vehicle. Although she couldn't see the driver, she could make out a dark silhouette.

She headed toward the vehicle, trying to make out the license number. "Don't look," she told Cathy, but it was too late. Her sister turned her head in the direction she was looking.

Tires squealed.

Lizzy took off, running toward the Expedition, intent on getting the license number before the vehicle could get away. The Expedition sped into traffic. Cars honked.

Too late. Damn.

"What was that about?" Cathy asked as Lizzy met up with her.

"I have no idea," Lizzy said. "Whoever it was got away before I could get the license plate number."

"Do you think it has something to do with one of the cases you're working on?"

Lizzy didn't want to worry her sister, so she shrugged nonchalantly and said, "I'm sure it was nothing. I'm just a little on edge."

Cathy sighed. "You look tired. Maybe you should take a few days off and relax."

Lizzy shook her head. "I'll be fine. Come on. Let's eat, I'm starved."

She and Cathy entered the restaurant, Mikuni's, a Japanese sushi bar in Roseville. The staff was fun and energetic and they served the best sushi around. "Irasshaimase!" the chefs called out, a traditional Japanese salutation, as Lizzy and Cathy were led to the seating area.

They both knew what they wanted: Lizzy ordered the grilled white tuna seasoned with a spicy barbeque sauce, while Cathy ordered a popular sushi roll called a Train Wreck.

"Tell me about your weekend," Cathy said after the waitress walked off. "Did you get to talk to Anthony Melbourne personally?"

Lizzy pushed the Expedition out of her mind. "You could say that."

"I bought one of his arm-shaping devices a few years ago," Cathy said excitedly. "Who am I kidding? I have every piece of equipment he's ever sold. I think he's incredible, don't you?"

Lizzy forced a smile, glad she didn't have to answer before her sister rambled on again.

"Anthony Melbourne is an inspiration to so many people. His unbridled enthusiasm for exercise and nutrition is contagious. He uses his knowledge and positivity to keep people moving, no matter what their age."

Although Lizzy was listening to her sister with interest, she couldn't help but think that if Melbourne had been as passionate about his work as her sister seemed to think, Lizzy might have been able to keep her eyes open during his talk this past weekend. But then again, Lizzy had never had a relationship with food other than a desire for the occasional sweet or pastry, especially if she caught a whiff of Cinnabon in the airport. Cathy, on the other hand, seemed to understand the message Melbourne was trying to spread. Food was Cathy's drug of choice. Food talked to her sister and consumed a large percentage of her thoughts.

"Have you seen Anthony Melbourne's infomercial?" Cathy asked. "The guy is incredible. Was he as good-looking in person as he is on television?"

Men like Melbourne did not appeal to Lizzy. He looked like a mountain of testosterone, but she hated to burst her sister's bubble so she skirted the subject altogether. "He seemed like a nice guy."

"After all these years," Cathy went on, still animated, "this is the first time I find myself warming to the idea of you being a private eye. I mean, it's not all about guns and danger, is it?"

"Not even close." Lizzy drank from the water glass that the waitress dropped off and thought about all of the paperwork waiting for her at the office. "I signed up for one of Melbourne's personal training classes. One hour five days a week."

"So you already saw him this morning! How was it?"

"It's a private class, and yet there were six other women there this morning. He took it easy on us today, but I'm sore just thinking about it."

"Is there room for one more?"

"I don't know. Why?"

"Look at me. I've gained thirty pounds since Richard left. My weight is getting out of control. If you can do Melbourne's routine, then I know I can do it."

"What do you mean by that?" Lizzy asked.

"You might be thin, but you're in horrible shape," Cathy said without filters. "Every time we take a walk, you're out of breath and red in the face. You've never exercised a day in your life. At least I used to do track and field and run four miles a day."

She had a point. "I'll call his office later and see if I can add you on."

"Great. I'll help keep an eye on him for you."

"I bet you will." They both laughed and then made room on the table for their food. Fast, efficient, delicious—exactly why Lizzy liked to eat at Mikuni's. As soon as the waitress walked away, Lizzy took a bite of her tuna; it melted in her mouth. "Hey, I've got an idea," Lizzy said. "I also signed up for Melbourne's retreat that's being held at the Granlibakken Conference Center in Lake Tahoe. Want to tag along just for fun?"

"What would I do about Brittany?"

"Hayley would be there," Lizzy reminded her, "but if it would make you feel better I could ask Jessica to stay at your house for the weekend too. She doesn't start school for another few weeks and she loves hanging out with Brittany."

Cathy seemed excited at the prospect of getting out of the house and doing something different. Although Lizzy had never cared for Cathy's soon-to-be ex-husband, Richard, it was easy to see that her sister had been lonely since he moved out.

"Let me talk to Brittany," Cathy said, "but yes, I think a little getaway is just what I need."

Lizzy agreed. For the first time in a long while, she felt the gap between her and her sister shrinking. After Lizzy was abducted, their parents had allowed their grief to consume them. Even after Lizzy escaped the madman's clutches and returned home, her parents were unable to come to grips with what had happened, blaming the world, blaming each other, blaming Lizzy.

To get some much-needed attention at the time, Cathy ended up pregnant and eloped with Richard Warner. Lizzy's niece, Brittany, had been the by-product of that union. No regrets.

"Speaking of Hayley," Cathy said between bites, "I've been meaning to talk to you about something."

"What's up?"

"I caught Hayley leaving the house after midnight the other night."

"What did you do?"

"I made a strong pot of coffee and waited for her to return. It was nearly four in the morning by the time she came back to the house. She didn't look right."

"How so?"

"She was wearing an old ragged sweater and stained shirt and pants with holes in the knees, despite the fact that I just bought her some new clothes. Her hair was a mess, and I smelled alcohol the moment she walked through the door."

"Did you ask her what she was doing out that late?"

Cathy nodded. "She told me she was just walking around, thinking about things." Cathy pointed her chopsticks at Lizzy. "I like Hayley, I really do. I'm not sure if Brittany could have gotten through her ordeal without her. Hayley can be tough and hard-hitting, but she's also kind and caring, helping me around the house, offering to run errands for me, things like that." She shook her head. "If this sort of behavior continues, though, I won't be able to let her stay with us."

Lizzy nodded. "I understand. I'll talk to her."

CHAPTER 10

NO MORE CANDY BARS

Sierra Mountains, Day 1
Early summer, 2010

He checked the metal band around her ankle, making sure it wasn't too tight; easier said than done considering she weighed three hundred pounds. She was the second-heaviest woman to ever enter the program—a program that was a well-kept secret.

Many people might look at Vivian Hardy's mountainous folds and find her disgusting, but he thought the endless rolls were mesmerizing.

Females were genetically designed to be rounded with layers of fat, not skin and bones like the typical fashion model. Fat deposits on the breasts, hips, thighs, and buttocks created the body shape that distinguished women from men.

He liked curvy women. What he didn't like was an overweight woman who let her fat control her every thought...and her life. Attitude was everything. But he would never get rich telling overweight people to be happy with their bodies. The breast-loving, hips-hating society was insane, but it also made for an endless goldmine of opportunity for guys like him who had no trouble turning away a warm beignet covered in fresh powdered sugar.

While Vivian Hardy walked around, testing the limits of her new chain, he held up a logbook. "I want you to write down every single thing you put into your mouth during your stay."

She tried to reach the front door, but the chains stopped her at the red line about two feet from the exit. She went to the window next and worked on the latch.

"The window cannot be opened," he told her.

"What about fresh air?"

"Central air will keep this place at a comfortable sixty-eight to seventy degrees at all times."

"What if I get cold?"

He pointed to the treadmill. "Start walking. It'll warm you up in no time."

The kitchen was small, but the entire cabin was perfectly aligned so that his clients could reach the sink, the refrigerator, the dining room table, the bed, and of course, the bathroom. The bathroom door had been cut short so that the chain could fit underneath when the door was closed. She could even lock the door for added privacy. There was a large metal hook on the side of the treadmill for the chain so the heavy links wouldn't get in her way when she walked. Yeah, exercising with a chain around her ankle may take some getting used to, but all in all, it was a minor inconvenience.

"What about television?" she asked.

"No television. It defeats the purpose. You need to learn to occupy your time in other ways."

"I was told I could have a television if I wanted one."

Damn. This wasn't the first time his assistant had promised his client something that went against his principles, not to mention his clearly defined regimen. "I'm sorry she told you that. Television is not part of the treatment. People have been programmed to want sugary soft drinks and fast food."

"You think television made me fat?"

"I'm sure it played a big part. Your application said that you watch at least five hours of television each day. The advertisers are hypnotizing you, motivating you to want nothing but creamy caramel candy bars dipped in rich chocolate and juicy hamburgers served with mounds of greasy fries."

"I could use a mound of greasy fries about now."

His smile was filled with understanding. His clients were always so eager to get started in the beginning, but within twenty-four hours, they were usually ready to throw in the towel. It had taken Vivian only fifteen minutes.

He pointed to a shelf filled with books from every genre. He then gestured toward the pile of pamphlets stacked on the bedside table. "Instead of television, I suggest reading."

"So this is it? This is the place where it all happens?"

He nodded, feeling proud.

"This isn't what I signed up for. I want out."

"This is exactly what you signed up for." And in three months, maybe four, she would be thanking him.

In the end, they always did.

CHAPTER 11

GOING GREEN

August 2010

For the most part, Hayley and Jessica worked opposite days, so there was always someone in the office to help Lizzy. Today, though, Lizzy had asked them to come at the same time so they could have an office meeting.

"Thanks for coming," Lizzy said. "I know you both like to switch days so you're not too crowded, but I have a lot of work right now and I thought it would be good if we went over our schedules. Until you start school, Jessica, I would appreciate it if you could work eight hours a day."

"That's fine," Jessica said.

"Great. Thanks." She looked at Hayley. "Since you're taking a few summer classes, I was hoping you could come in whenever you're not too busy."

Hayley gave her the thumbs-up.

"OK, then," Lizzy continued, "Jessica, what's on your to-do list?"

Jessica's hair was braided, one long braid hanging over each shoulder, making her look fifteen instead of twenty-one.

"I've been working on condensing our files," Jessica told her. "You know, like scanning important documents in hopes that we can go green by the end of the year."

"Go green?" Lizzy asked. "Whose idea was this?"

"Mine," Jessica said. "Don't worry, I'm not putting the hours I spend on going green on my time sheet."

"The carpets could use a good cleaning," Lizzy said as she glanced at the floor.

"I'm not a maid."

Lizzy smiled, figuring it had been worth a shot.

"As I was saying," Jessica continued, "any duplicate or unnecessary papers should be shredded. When you have more time, I'd like to talk to you about making this office environmentally friendly: using recycled paper, stapleless staples, printing on both sides, that sort of thing. We need to start refilling our pens instead of sending them to the landfills. It's getting out of hand around here."

"What's a stapleless staple?" Hayley wanted to know.

Jessica's eyes brightened. "It's a stapler that cuts tiny flaps in the paper and then bends and weaves the flaps together so that the papers stay secure."

Hayley looked as if she was sorry she asked.

Jessica waved passionate hands toward the ceiling. "All these bulbs need to be replaced with CFLs. The list is endless."

"Great," Lizzy said, "now what about work that actually might bring in some income?"

"I did get one of the three workers' compensation cases dealing with fraud off my desk," Jessica said. "I wrote a report and dropped off the pictures of H. D. Palmer at the attorney's office. I still need pictures of Jim Thatcher and Eric Farrell so I can finish those reports and deliver them to the prosecuting attorney. We're getting close to deadline."

Lizzy and Jessica looked at Hayley since she was their unofficial photographer. Lizzy hadn't had a chance to talk to Hayley about wandering the streets of Sacramento in the middle of the night, but that would have to wait until they were alone. Hayley had definitely been quiet lately. Her eyes, shadowed with exhaustion, were cast downward. "Any luck with Thatcher or Farrell?"

Hayley wore cutoffs and a T-shirt. She was leaning on the desk that she and Jessica shared. Her right knee was bruised. Lifting her gaze, she crossed her arms and said, "Farrell has been a no-show at his weekly bowling league for the past two weeks. Weeds are overtaking his front lawn, which tells me he's not mowing it, which means he might actually be legit. Thatcher, on the other hand, is a clever dude. I don't think he's hurt at all."

"Is he still using crutches?" Lizzy asked.

"Yes and no," Hayley said. "I waited for him at the school after Jessica discovered he played basketball with his buddies after church on Sundays. Sure enough, he pulls up in his bright orange Hummer right on time and then proceeds to make a big show of hopping on one leg to get his crutches from the backseat of his car. After he disappeared inside the gym, I waited about ten minutes before I went inside and pretended to look for someone. Not only was Thatcher playing basketball, he was dunking the ball. That's not easy to do. Not too many guys half his age can touch the rim, let alone dunk. It was impressive."

"Did you get pictures?" Jessica asked.

"Are you kidding? I had six gigantic men staring me down before I got halfway across the court. They weren't happy about me being there, and one guy looked like he was going to drag me out by my hair. I had to think fast, so I made up a story about my little brother running off. I told them he was only ten and that my mom was at home getting ready to call the cops. They didn't trust me any more than I trusted them. The mean guy started asking questions like where I lived, things like that. That's when I broke down and cried."

Jessica looked from Lizzy to Hayley. "You cried in front of five big men?"

"Six. There were six big men. And yes, I cried because I didn't have an answer to his question and nothing scares a man like a crying female. They backed off real quick, and I just ran from the gym as if I couldn't handle the thought of losing my little brother."

Lizzy shook her head. "I told you never to approach the people we're watching."

"I'm eighteen now. You're not going to get in trouble for my actions."

"That's not the point," Lizzy said. "You could get hurt. Using a zoom lens from afar and taking a picture is one thing, but putting yourself in danger like that is something else altogether."

"I've handled worse."

"I don't care. Please don't do that again. If you can't get the picture from the safety of your car, then leave it be. We'll find another way."

"OK, will do," Hayley said, using her four-fingered hand to salute.

"Jessica, I think you need to put Project Going Green on the back burner for now. Today I need you to go to High Street Bank in Auburn and talk to Ellen Woodson. She was Carol Fullerton's best friend at the time of Carol's disappearance. I called Ellen at her home. She picked up but refused to talk to me about Carol."

Jessica picked up pen and paper. "What do you need to know?"

"Anything and everything Ellen knows about where Carol was going the day she disappeared. We need to know if Ellen has any idea of what Carol was going through at the time of her disappearance. Why did Carol leave school, go to the store for snacks, and then drive for hours on I-5 before her car broke down? Where was she going and why? According to Carol's mother, who has the school records to prove it, Carol was an above-average student. She got along well with her mother, she kept her room clean, and she followed her parents' rules without complaint. Carol was known as a friendly person at school and everybody seemed to like her. But Ellen was the one person whom Carol chose to hang with twenty-four-seven. At this point, Ellen is all we have. Over twenty years ago, Ellen was too distressed to talk about her friend's disappearance. Two decades later and she still won't talk. Ellen Woodson knows something."

"Didn't you tell me the other day that Carol's car broke down not too far from a national park?"

Lizzy nodded. "Mendocino National Forest."

"Maybe Carol walked there hoping to find help and then met up with a bad crowd."

"Detective Roth said they did a thorough search of the area and her body was never found. But two separate witnesses at the time stated that they saw a young woman stranded on the side of the highway who matched Carol Fullerton's description. One of the witnesses didn't have time to stop, but he called it in as soon as he reached his destination, letting the police know there was a young girl stranded on I-5. Another witness went to the bother of finding a turnaround to see if he could go back and help, but by the time he got back to her car, she was gone. Fifteen minutes later, he says he passed a Buick and swore that the same girl he'd seen on the side of the road was sitting in the passenger seat. The witness, Mr. Theodore Johnson, has a prior record of assaulting a woman he had been dating. Johnson ended up being their number one suspect. To this day he swears he's innocent."

"What about the car Johnson saw her in?"

"Bingo," Lizzy said, pointing a finger at Hayley. "I don't think the police ever took Johnson seriously."

"Why would the guy call the police if he was guilty?" Jessica asked.

"Exactly. That's why I want you and Hayley to make some calls and use your computer expertise to see what you can find out about the car Mr. Johnson saw that day. We have a make and model and the first three digits from the license plate. It's all in the file."

Lizzy used both hands, palms flat on her desk to push herself to her feet before gingerly making her way to the closet that served as the file room. After only two days of exercising, her body felt as if a Mack truck had hit it.

"What's wrong with you?" Jessica asked when Lizzy returned with the Fullerton file clutched to her chest.

"Remember that Melbourne guy with the amazing abs?"

"Yeah."

"He's my new trainer."

Jessica laughed. "Are you kidding me?"

"I wish I was." Lizzy handed the file to Hayley and then bent over and attempted to touch her toes and stretch out sore limbs. It was no use. She couldn't even reach her ankles.

Clearly, Melbourne would be the death of her.

CHAPTER 12

THE HELPING HAND

Stockton Boulevard used to be a major road that extended through South Sacramento from downtown. It was used during the gold-mining era to travel to Stockton and various farming areas, but in the sixties, Highway 99 had replaced much of the boulevard. Businesses were forced to close down, and the area quickly deteriorated. Helicopters still circled the area at night and shootings were common, but now, with new buildings popping up, the boulevard was slowly being revitalized.

Directly off the boulevard was the special needs school, The Helping Hand, where Diane Kramer had worked for years before she disappeared. The school building and surrounding grounds were not a pretty sight.

Lizzy exited her car and followed the yellow brick road. Literally. Someone had filled missing sections of the cracked cement walkway with pieces of canary-yellow bricks. The fence around the property looked like a patchwork quilt made of chain-link, metal bars, and wood slats. A broken window had been duct-taped together. The only color besides the yellow brick pathway was gigantic neon nonsensical scribbling spray painted across the front entrance by vandals.

Lizzy didn't get to South Sacramento often, but when she did, she tended to keep both eyes wide open.

Inside the school building, sitting at the front desk, was a woman with long, shiny black hair. Her center part was a cleanly shaved three-inch-wide strip down the middle of her head like a newly paved street slicing through black tar. The thick frames of her dark-rimmed eyeglasses matched the color of her hair. Her lipstick, on the other hand, was blood red. There were so many shocking elements to the girl that Lizzy didn't know where to look or where not to look. She didn't want to be rude and stare, so she shuffled through her purse instead until she found her notepad. "I have an appointment with Lori Mulcher."

"Th-that would be m-me," the girl said. Her lip twitched and then her left eye did too, but she didn't come to her feet or make any kind of gesture that would prompt Lizzy to head to a meeting room or a quiet place where they could talk.

Lizzy held out her hand. "Nice to meet you, Lori. My name is Lizzy Gardner. I have some questions I'd like to ask you about Diane Kramer."

The girl's right shoulder jolted upward, and Lizzy had to stop herself from jumping back. Clearly Lori had a severe tic. The young woman began to grimace. Both of her eyes twitched. She made a yelping sound right before she stood. Her hand flung out and smacked Lizzy in the chin and nose.

An elderly woman sitting at the desk behind Lori Mulcher gestured for Lizzy to take a seat in one of three plastic chairs by the entrance.

Lizzy took a seat and then found a tissue in her backpack and used it to dab her nose. It was bleeding. Damn. She packed her nose with tissue and bent her head back to stop the bleeding.

She pretended to admire the popcorn ceiling, which was clearly a health hazard.

Lizzy knew she only needed to be patient with Lori. She'd had a friend in high school with Tourette syndrome who had the occasional flailing limb and a mild facial tic. Lizzy had always defended her friend, making sure the girl knew she could relax around her.

It wasn't long before Lori collected herself and led Lizzy to a private office. Lori didn't talk about the bloody nose; there was no reason to, and they both left the incident in the past where it belonged.

"Are you working with the police?" Lori asked, her stutter hardly noticeable.

Lizzy waited for Lori to sit before she filled the lone chair in front of the severely scarred wooden desk. "No," Lizzy said in answer to her question. "Diane's sister hired me to look into the matter. I was told that you and Diane were close. Is that true?"

Lori shrugged. "We saw each other every day, if that counts for something."

"Did you two ever go to dinner or lunch together?"

"Are you asking me if we're lesbians?"

"No," Lizzy said, although the girl now had her wondering just that. "Andrea, Diane's sister, told me that you and Diane were best friends. That's all. Nothing more, nothing less."

Clearly Lori Mulcher was not happy answering questions about Diane, which struck Lizzy as odd. "I don't mean to be rude," Lizzy said, "but I was under the impression that you and Diane were close friends. If that's true, then I would think you would want to help me and her sister find her."

"If Diane was my friend, don't you think she would have called me by n-now?"

So that was it. Lori was angry with Diane for running off. "That's true, Lori, but this is exactly why Andrea is worried about her sister. I know Diane was depressed, but why would she leave her good friend and a job she loved?"

"Who told you sh-she was depressed?"

"That's the story going around, you know, because of her weight."

Lori waved a hand through the air as if that was the most ridiculous thing she'd ever heard. She grimaced too, and Lizzy readied herself for an episode, but nothing happened.

"She didn't care about her weight," Lori said, "not until she joined that stupid online support group."

For some reason Lori Mulcher thought Diane had abandoned her and she was pissed off. "What support group are you talking about?"

"I never thought Diane would leave like this. She really cared for these kids. They need her. I need her."

Lori shook her head, and when she stopped, her monstrous silver hoop earrings kept going. She still hadn't answered Lizzy's question.

"At least a half dozen students," Lori said, "stop by the office every single day to see when she's coming back."

"Was this Diane's office?"

Lori nodded. "Still is."

"Mind if I have a look at her computer?"

"Go ahead; everyone else has." Lori stood and headed for the door. "It's up and running. Ten minutes is all I can give you, though."

"Thanks."

"And one m-more thing…"

Lizzy looked her way. "What's that?"

"Sorry about the nose."

Lizzy smiled. "Not a problem."

The second Lori left the room, Lizzy began to search through the files on Diane's computer. She would love to take the computer with her, but it was obviously school property. She reached into her pocket and pulled out the Oyen Digital 1TB portable hard drive—described by customer reviews as "fast, reliable, and sexy"—and plugged in the USB cable. The software came loaded on the mini hard drive so it could operate automatically, saving the files to the drive while she looked around.

Her ten minutes were up and the lady sitting behind Lori's desk looked through the open door at her.

Lizzy waved. "Almost done."

The woman stood and reached into her drawer, pulling out a bag lunch. She came to the door. "My name's Arlene Ruiz, but most people call me Lena. I overheard part of your conversation with Lori, and I think you should know that Diane was definitely obsessed with losing weight. Like most of us, the harder she tried to lose weight, the more she gained. I tried to help her, even got my friend who owns a gym downtown to allow Diane free access. She would go for a week or two and then that would be it until next time." Lena Ruiz shook her head and said, "Poor girl."

"Do you think Diane was depressed?"

"Only when it came to her weight."

"If it was so important to her, why do you think she couldn't control it?"

"Beats me, but I can tell you this"—Lena looked around to make sure no one was within earshot—"her sister didn't help matters much."

"What do you mean?"

"How can you forget you're fat if someone keeps reminding you that you are?"

"That's a good question. Did Andrea tell her sister she was fat?"

"Not straight out, but yes, in her own little condescending way she did. That woman would come by all the time. Andrea Kramer treated us all as if we were beneath her, always making sure to point out her fancy car and expensive clothes. She thought she was all that. She would come in here three times a week just to see what Diane had brought for lunch. On her way here, Andrea would stop by the gym I just mentioned, and she would already know whether or not Diane had been a no-show that morning."

"Sounds a little controlling."

"A lot controlling. I would have run away too."

"So you think Diane ran away?"

Lena fiddled with the beads on her necklace as she thought about the question. "I did at first. But after a month passed by, and another, and Diane hadn't called to see how her kids were doing, I knew something very bad had happened."

"Do you know anything about the online group Lori talked about?"

She nodded. "Diane talked about the group all of the time... even tried to get me to join." Lena Ruiz turned about and went back to her desk, where she shuffled through her Rolodex. By the time she returned, Lizzy had safely removed the mini hard drive and tucked it inside her purse.

"Here you go," Lena said. "The group was called the Weight Watcher Warriors."

"You look great," Lizzy told her, "but is there any particular reason why you didn't join?"

Lena shrugged. "Not my thing. I design jewelry in my spare time. I also do a lot of hiking to stay in shape. Besides, I wouldn't want anyone knowing my weight and telling me what to eat."

"I hear you." Lizzy smiled and held up the card Lena had given her. "Thanks for the help."

"Not a problem. If you think of more questions or you need any custom-made jewelry, my number's on the card."

CHAPTER 13

BURNING MAN

For too many hours, Hayley and Jessica had been searching the Internet. Hayley sat at Lizzy's desk across the room from Jessica. Hayley typed a few keywords on the computer keypad and watched the computer screen turn black. "This is ass-wipe stupid."

Jessica didn't look away from her computer screen. "Why? What's the problem?"

"Knowing Spiderman is dead has caused Lizzy to lose her edge."

Jessica cocked her head in the same way a dog might angle its head if someone mentioned the word *walk* or *treat*. Hayley wasn't sure how she felt about Jessica. She was a nice enough girl, it seemed, but she could be a little dense at times. Like now.

"The old Lizzy," Hayley explained, "wouldn't have bothered with the fucking Internet to find the info she needed. She would have hit the pavement instead."

"Do you really have to curse so much? And are you serious when you use terms like *hit the pavement*? This isn't a movie or one of those weekly cop shows. Policemen and women, and investigators like Lizzy, don't need to 'hit the pavement' now that so much information is at their fingertips. It's not stupid. It's life in the modern world. Pretty soon they won't need to chase after criminals in high-speed chases either. The police will tag a car with a laser-guided GPS tracking system. Once the transmitter is attached to the fleeing car, the police can track the suspect over a wireless network, then hang back and let the crook believe he's outrun them."

Hayley tried not to roll her eyes. She wanted to remind Jessica of the last time Jessica was in a high-speed chase. Where was the cool little transmitter then? "So how do they catch the guy using the transmitter?"

"Thinking he's lost the police, the crook eventually pulls over and gets out of his car. The officers know exactly where he is and they nab him."

"Technology definitely serves a purpose," Hayley said. "But at some point, somebody needs to get their ass out on the street and use physical force to get the bad guys. That's all I'm sayin'. Let's go."

Once again, Jessica looked at her as if she'd lost all sense.

Hayley was already at the door. "If you don't want to come with me, can you at least lend me your car?"

"You're not thinking about paying Johnson a visit, are you?"

"Oh, good," Hayley said, not bothering to hide her sarcasm. "For a minute there I thought we might be on different pages."

Jessica's shoulders drooped. "So you *are* planning on visiting Johnson," she stated more than asked. "Didn't you hear a word Lizzy said? She asked you very nicely to stay put. If you make trouble, sooner or later somebody is going to sue Lizzy. She could lose everything."

Hayley looked around at the dingy carpet and two pitiful excuses for desks.

"You know what I mean. Lizzy is trying her darndest to move on. She's been through a lot this past year. If she didn't have her work…and this place…she'd be lost."

"OK, fine. I get it. I'll walk."

"You're still going to visit Theodore Johnson?"

"Of course I am. Nobody is going to sue Lizzy if I talk to Johnson. Don't you get it? Ruth Fullerton is dying. This isn't pretend dying. She'll be lucky if she lasts three weeks, let alone three months. For more than two decades she's been wondering what happened to her daughter. Johnson might have seen Carol Fullerton on the day she went missing. The cops never paid any attention to the man because he had a prior record. Do you have any idea how many people out there have prior records? Too many," Hayley said, answering her own question. "There's no way Johnson would have contacted the police if he was involved. I am not going to allow Ruth Fullerton to die without knowing what happened to her daughter."

"You don't even know her."

"I don't have to know her to want to help her. And you," Hayley said with more venom in her voice than intended, "more than anyone, should know how excruciating it is to go on living when you have no idea what happened to a loved one." For years, Jessica hadn't known what happened to her sister until her body was found in Spiderman's backyard, one of many of the serial killer's victims.

Hayley couldn't tell what Jessica was thinking. She wasn't an easy person to read. "I'm going to go talk to Johnson whether you lend me your car or not. Besides, he lives right around the block from Farrell's house."

Jessica didn't respond.

"Farrell," Hayley repeated. "The workers' comp guy who hasn't been mowing his lawn."

"I know who Farrell is. You don't have to get all snooty with me."

Snooty? Let it go, Hayley inwardly scolded. It wasn't Jessica's fault that Hayley was feeling on edge. She hadn't been getting much sleep lately and it wasn't helping her mood. She opened the door and was instantly hit by a wave of stifling August heat. Before the door clicked shut behind her, she smiled when Jessica called out, telling her to wait up.

* * *

With zero traffic, Johnson's house was less than twenty minutes from Lizzy's office. Jessica figured if all went well, they would still have time to get back to the office before Lizzy returned. She made a right on Pine Street. A row of rundown one-story homes with little in the way of landscaping lined both sides of the street.

So far the car ride had been devoid of conversation, which was a good thing since it would have been difficult to talk over the deafening roar of the Mustang's engine. After driving over a divider and ruining the frame and axle of her Volkswagen van last winter, Jessica's eighty-year-old neighbor, Billy Channel, had offered to sell her his 1987 Ford Mustang for five hundred dollars. Although the vehicle had well over a hundred thousand miles when she'd bought it a month ago, the engine had purred like a well-oiled machine when she'd taken it for a spin around the neighborhood. Innocent-looking William Channel, Billy to his so-called friends, might not be as sweet as he looked. She planned to have a talk with him and hopefully get her money back.

Hayley pointed to a one-story house on their left. "That's Eric Farrell's place," she said loudly enough to be heard over the roar of the engine.

The pale blue painted stucco on Farrell's house was chipping and the stained cement walkway leading to the front entry was cracked beyond repair. The house looked abandoned. Curtains were drawn and the garage was shut. Not one car was parked in front of the house.

Jessica's window was down.

If not for the kids playing in the front yard two houses down, she would have thought she was driving through a ghost town.

"Watch out!" Hayley shouted.

Jessica slammed on the brakes. Tires squealed; the engine coughed and then died right there in the middle of the road as a black Labrador ran off with its tail between its legs.

The kids up ahead were quiet now. The oldest boy in the group gathered the smaller kids together. He shook his head at Jessica as if she'd purposely set out to try and kill the dog and ruin their day. "Maybe they should keep their dog on a leash."

Hayley sighed.

"What?"

"I didn't say anything."

"You didn't have to. If you hadn't pointed to Farrell's house, my eyes would have remained on the road in front of me."

"I was just letting you know where Farrell's house was. I didn't know you were going to stare out the window for five minutes."

"What is your problem?" Jessica asked.

"I don't have a problem."

"Fine. Whatever."

"Fine."

Jessica turned the key in the ignition, but nothing happened. "Damn."

"Sounds like the alternator."

"It's happened before. I need to give it a few minutes before I try to start it again."

"Put the car in neutral and I'll push you to the side of the road."

Before Jessica could protest, Hayley jumped out of the car and began to push. Hayley was stronger than she looked.

By the time Jessica put the car in park, the kids were already playing again, oblivious to their car problems. The dog was nowhere to be seen.

Hayley poked her head inside the open passenger window. "Looks like Farrell is home."

Jessica turned toward the pale blue house. Sure enough, somebody was peeking through the curtains. "That's creepy."

"Yeah," Hayley agreed. "I'm going to walk to Johnson's house. It's right around the corner."

Jessica looked back at Farrell's house. "Wait for me." She grabbed a notebook and pen from the backseat and shoved it inside her purse. After rolling up the windows and locking the car, she took brisk strides to catch up to Hayley.

Hayley, she thought, had proven to be one tough chick six months ago when she'd used herself as bait and purposely let Spiderman catch her. Although Hayley had lost her pinky finger in the deal, according to Lizzy, Hayley looked at life a little differently now. Apparently Hayley planned to change her ways and make something of herself.

But there was something about Hayley Hansen that made Jessica nervous. And it had nothing to do with the new snake tattoo she had carved onto the back of her neck: a thick, coiled snake with a skull for a head, complete with long, slithering tongue coming out of its skeletal jaw. No, the tattoo was sort of cool in its own freaky way. It was the dark, empty look in Hayley's eyes that worried Jessica most.

Hayley looked over her shoulder. "Are you coming or not?"

CHAPTER 14

YOU CAN'T HAVE CAKE AND EAT IT TOO

Sierra Mountains, Day 30

Vivian woke, her head spinning as she looked around. It took her a moment to make out the numbers on the clock.

Two thirty. Not a.m., but p.m.

Sunlight filtered in through the tiny space between the curtains.

Had she really slept until two thirty in the afternoon? She couldn't remember ever sleeping that late before. Yesterday she slept in until one in the afternoon. The day before that it was twelve noon before she opened her eyes.

She looked at the calendar.

Today was her thirtieth day in this hellhole.

Thirty days.

What had she gotten herself into?

The first week here she'd been beyond terrified by her predicament. By the end of her second week, she was no longer scared; she was livid. And now, one month after being abandoned in this tiny mountain cabin, not counting one quick visit by Melbourne's assistant, she felt something else entirely. Determination. She wanted two things: answers and freedom.

Where was Melbourne anyhow?

Did anyone besides Melbourne and his assistant know that she was here? The thought caused her heart to beat double time.

And where the hell was Diane? Diane was the reason she was here. She'd met Diane Kramer when she joined the Weight Watcher Warriors online group. She and Diane had an instant connection. They also had the same weakness for cupcakes with sprinkles. Cupcakes were their drug of choice. Although they both cheered on the other warriors in their group, it wasn't long before she and Diane were e-mailing each other on the sly. They both knew in their heart of hearts that the whole losing weight thing was sort of hopeless, yet neither of them had ever straight out said as much.

They both weighed over 250 pounds. Actually Vivian had recently hit three hundred. She had Diane beat by forty-five pounds. They both came from obese families and they both had one skinny family member who liked to rub their extra poundage in their faces. Diane had her sister to deal with while Vivian had her mother watching her every move, at least until Vivian had moved to California to get away from her.

Unlike Vivian, Diane didn't see her sister for what she was: an egotistical, controlling, and judgmental bitch.

Diane honestly believed that her sister cared about her and wanted her to lose weight so she could go on to live a long, healthy life. Baloney. Once she lost one hundred pounds, Diane's sister promised her that life would be grand. Everything around her would start coming up roses.

What a bowl of crap.

Problems didn't melt away with fat.

But Diane could be stubborn, and when it came to her sister, Diane was flat-out blind.

Vivian slid off the bed. As she made her way into the bathroom, she realized her knees weren't bothering her. She lifted a leg, testing it out, surprised that she felt hardly any pain at all.

She washed her face, brushed her teeth, and then glanced at the scale on the bathroom floor. She raised an arm and purposely made her fat jiggle. Then she raised a leg about six inches off the ground and jiggled the extra flesh there too.

Nothing had changed. Melbourne had left enough temptations to keep three people her size well fed for months.

No reason to bother weighing herself.

She shivered as she made her way to the kitchen. It was freezing in here, but there was no way she was getting on that treadmill. Hell would have to freeze over before she would do one sit-up. Melbourne said he'd visit on a regular basis, but in the thirty days she'd been here, she had yet to see his face. His assistant, Jane, had made an unexpected appearance after one week, but the woman had been brainwashed by Melbourne, Vivian figured, because she completely ignored Vivian's pleas to be released. Apparently, she had come to make sure Vivian was eating right.

But the visit had seemed odd.

Jane never once checked her weight or even glanced in her logbook. Jane even tried to get into the bedroom that Melbourne kept locked, but she couldn't find the right key and she'd been clearly frustrated. Jane had left the cabin almost as quickly as she'd come.

The strangest part was that there was something familiar about Jane, but Vivian had yet to figure out where she might have met the woman before.

After taking a seat at the dining room table, Vivian grabbed the serrated knife she'd left sitting there day after day. Once she had her right ankle propped on her left knee she got to work, using the knife to saw back and forth across the metal cuff around her ankle.

It took only fifteen minutes of sawing before her wrist grew tired. She examined her work. She'd been sawing the cuff for weeks and yet hardly a dent had been made. How was she going to get out of here?

She looked from the knife to her ankle and touched the blade to her flesh. Movies had been made about people cutting off limbs to survive. Squeezing her eyes shut, she pressed the blade down and slid the blade toward her. Ouch! She opened her eyes and looked at her ankle. She'd hardly drawn blood.

Maybe tomorrow, she thought as she set the knife on the table.

The milk was long gone and the eggs had probably gone bad. There was powdered milk, but that sounded so gross.

Her sole purpose in signing up for Melbourne's secret torture chamber had been to find Diane. But she had yet to find a single clue as to whether Diane had ever been here.

Where are you, Diane?

Vivian had called the police a few weeks after Diane went missing. The police argued that she and Diane hadn't known each other long enough. Nobody, the sergeant said, could truly know what was going through Diane's head when she decided to run away, certainly not her new online friend.

Feeling defeated, Vivian stood and walked to the kitchen sink. Outside the window, she saw a momma deer and its fawn. Peaceful. Happy. Not a scene she could relate to. Her childhood had been one long and crazy fighting match. And her adult life had been a lonely food fest.

In a weird way, food had become her best friend.

She didn't like when people blamed others for their problems…or for their weight. But way down deep, she blamed her mother for everything, absolutely everything.

Leaving the deer to their happy, peaceful lives, Vivian began to open the kitchen drawers, one at a time. Opening the drawers had become her morning, or should she say afternoon, ritual.

The first drawer was filled with silverware. After pulling every fork, spoon, and knife from the plastic container, she examined each utensil closely. When that was done, she peered into the dark recesses of the space where the drawer belonged. Reaching her hand deep inside, she brushed her fingertips over the wood structure, hoping beyond hope that if Diane had been here, she'd left a note.

But there was nothing.

It took Vivian over an hour to go through every drawer in the same manner only to come up empty-handed.

Depressed and severely hungry, she made her way to the pantry where all the goodies were kept. Boxes and boxes of cookie and cake mixes. Melbourne said he left fattening foods here because in real life there were always endless temptations.

No shit. Tell me something I don't know, asshole.

She didn't know whether to make blueberry muffins today or gingerbread cookies. She grabbed both boxes and then made her way back to the kitchen. The bowl she'd used the other day to make an angel food cake was still in the sink. So were the mixing utensils.

Outside the window, the female deer seemed frantic, pacing around the fawn. What was wrong? What had happened to happy and peaceful?

Vivian's heart dropped to her stomach when she saw the cause of the female deer's frustration. The fawn had managed to get its head caught between two fallen trees that had left just enough room for the fawn to stick its head in and trap itself. The more the fawn struggled, the more obvious it became that the poor thing might break its neck.

Vivian reached toward the windowpane but stopped herself from knocking. Doing so would only scare the fawn further. The female deer stopped pacing and began to lick the fawn instead. The young deer relaxed enough to pull its head free.

Thank goodness!

Vivian watched mother and baby run off and disappear through ponderosa pine and Douglas fir.

Her heart was beating triple time again. What if she injured herself or had a heart attack? What would she do then? She had been so focused on finding Diane that nothing else mattered. She'd put down a huge deposit of five thousand dollars to come here. She worked for herself doing random editing jobs from her apartment, she was a saver, but there was no way she was going to pay the remainder of the money she owed. Melbourne wanted fifteen thousand dollars. He was crazy.

Hoping to calm herself, Vivian read the back of the cake box. Ingredients needed: one-quarter cup of oil and three-quarters cup of water.

She found herself gazing out the window again, focusing on the tiny space between the trees where the fawn's head had gotten stuck. Her gaze dropped to the metal cuff around her ankle.

An idea struck her.

The cuff wasn't as tight as it used to be.

That was the answer to her problems.

This morning she had noticed that the fur-lined metal cuff hadn't felt as tight around her ankle. She'd also noticed it while she was sawing with the knife. She had definitely lost weight.

But how? And if so, how much?

She'd been eating cakes and cookies nearly every day, ignoring the stockpile of frozen fruits and vegetables in the freezer. She dropped the muffin mix into the sink and ran to the bathroom, the chain clanking against the wood floor as she went. She jumped on the scale and watched the numbers go up and down, playing with her psyche, before finally holding steady at 263 pounds.

No way. She stepped off the scale and then back on.

There it was again. Two hundred sixty-three pounds. Minus the ten pounds for the metal chain, bringing her weight to 253 pounds.

She had lost forty-seven pounds.

No frickin' way.

She'd been on every diet in the world and hadn't lost that much weight.

Jiggling her arm again, she had a tough time believing she'd lost that much weight. She'd been eating cookies, but she hadn't been eating as much food as she usually did. At home she ate lots of homemade bread, candy, and popcorn drenched in butter. She'd also been sleeping…a lot.

Exiting the bathroom, she took a seat on the edge of the bed and stuck two fingers between her ankle and the cuff. She used to be able to fit only one finger. She tried to pull her foot from the cuff. There was no way. Not even close. She needed to lose at least another finger in width, which meant another fifty pounds, at least.

She wanted out of here. And as far as she could tell, there was only one way out. Before she put too much thought into her plan and changed her mind, she moved quickly to the pantry and grabbed as many boxes of muffin and cakes mixes as she could carry.

Hurrying to the kitchen sink, she dropped the boxes on the counter and then turned the faucet full blast. She ripped open the first box and dumped its contents down the drain. With robotic motions, she repeated the process. Rip box open, dump contents. Rip box open, dump contents.

It wasn't long before she was down to the last box of cookie mix. She thought about saving it, just in case, but then she looked out the window to the spot where she'd seen the fawn escape.

She needed to stay calm. She needed to use her head.

For the first time in her life, she wanted something more than cookies and cupcakes.

She wanted freedom.

CHAPTER 15

THE ONLY WITNESS

"So," Hayley asked Theodore Johnson again, "you're absolutely certain that the girl you saw on the side of the road over twenty years ago was Carol Fullerton?"

He rubbed the back of his neck and said, "I'd bet my life on it."

"Who was the guy she drove off with?"

"No idea."

Jessica stood by the door, her arms crossed. She didn't want to be inside Theodore Johnson's house any more than she would want to be talking to her deadbeat father who had run off when his family needed him most.

But Hayley looked perfectly comfortable talking to a man who had done jail time for beating his girlfriend to a pulp. Johnson lived with his eighty-year-old mother, who sat in the corner of the living area watching a game show. The volume was turned full blast, bells and whistles piercing Jessica's eardrums every time a contestant answered correctly.

Jessica zeroed in on Hayley's face, hoping Hayley would look her way so she could give her the let's-get-out-of-here look.

No such luck.

Hayley was concentrating on Johnson's every word. Hayley had a knack for this interviewing business. For starters, she had no fear. Johnson could just as well be an escaped convict; it wouldn't make any difference to Hayley.

In the past, Lizzy had hinted to Jessica about the repulsive things Hayley had been forced to endure throughout her young life. Lizzy liked to talk about how strong a person like Hayley would have to be to survive such unspeakable happenings and go on to live a normal life.

But Jessica was pretty sure nobody had ever taken a good, long look at Hayley. If they watched her as she'd been watching Hayley for months now, they would see that she was far from well adjusted. As far as Jessica was concerned, Hayley was a timed fuse grenade just waiting to explode.

Johnson, Jessica noticed, was beginning to look sort of bug-eyed, as if he needed his next fix before he got out of control. In the past thirty seconds, his hands had become fidgety and a thick sheen of sweat had gathered on his forehead.

"Come on, Mr. Johnson," Hayley prodded. "I'm not a cop or a detective. Hell, I'm lucky if the lady I work for even pays me."

Jessica inwardly smiled. Wasn't that the truth?

"But I'm here today," Hayley explained, "because Carol's mother, Ruth Fullerton, is dying. Mrs. Fullerton needs to know what happened to her daughter. Do you get that?"

Hayley raised her arms in frustration and said, "Does anybody in this fucking world have compassion anymore?"

Johnson's mom looked away from her television set to see what the raised voice was about, but the bells and whistles quickly drew her attention back to the screen.

"I don't have any money, Mr. Johnson, but Jessica does. She's one of those goody-two-shoes types who save every penny and do everything right. She's going to give you…How much money do you have, Jessica?"

"Are you serious?"

"I'll pay you back next week. How much money do you have on you?"

"I don't know. Twenty dollars. That's all I have."

"Twenty dollars, Mr. Johnson. We'll give you twenty dollars if you just tell us something…anything."

He raked his hands through his thinning grayish hair. "Do you have any idea what it's like to be suspected of a crime you didn't do?"

"No, I can't say that I have any ideas about that," Hayley answered. "I also have no idea how it would feel to be dying and not know what happened to my only child. It sucks, Mr. Johnson. I would have to guess that it would suck to have family and friends look at you, wondering if there might be the tiniest possibility that you killed a young girl and stashed her body somewhere along Interstate 5. I don't think I would like that at all. In fact, I hate when people can't stop for ten goddamn seconds and put themselves in someone else's shoes. How hard is it to close your fucking eyes and imagine being that person? Of being accused of doing something you didn't? No, I wouldn't like it one bit." Hayley let out a long sigh as she turned toward the door, ready to give up.

Thank God, Jessica thought.

"Burning Man," he said under his breath.

Hayley turned back to face the man. "What did you say?"

Jessica uncrossed her arms and stared at him too, wondering if he could possibly have anything new to share about the Fullerton case.

"I saw a broken-down car," he said. "But I didn't see anybody there. Might have been ten or fifteen minutes later when I glanced in my rearview mirror and saw a girl sitting on the edge of the highway. By the time I found a turnaround and came back, she drove right by me. She was sitting in the passenger seat of an old Buick."

Jessica was holding her breath, waiting to see if he had more to add.

Hayley hadn't moved either.

Thankfully they didn't have to wait long before he said, "I recognized the man driving the Buick."

Jessica's jaw dropped.

Hayley took a step back toward the man. "No shit."

"No shit," he repeated. "It was one of the men who organized Burning Man that year."

"You've got to be kidding me! Do you have a name?"

He shook his head. "Once I became a prime suspect for trying to be a good citizen, I didn't care about what I'd seen any longer. I didn't tell them shit. The assholes had it all figured out before I could utter two words."

"I'm sorry."

"Yeah, me too."

Hayley looked at Jessica. "Can you give him the twenty bucks now?"

Theodore swatted his hand through the air. "Keep your money. I'm getting too old for handouts."

* * *

Lizzy sat in front of her computer in her bedroom and plugged in the mini portable hard drive. Right click. Explore. Copy and paste from external drive. Done.

The entire transfer took less than fifteen minutes. Many of the files from Diane Kramer's computer appeared to be form documents, PowerPoints used in the classroom, and an endless array of worksheets and student directories that included names, addresses, and telephone numbers of the children Diane had taught over the years.

A few clicks of the keyboard brought Lizzy to report cards and saved e-mails from parents voicing concern and/or praise for Diane.

She read the Word document files titled Books to Get, Miscellaneous, and Medical. The next file she found looked a little more interesting. It was titled Things To Do. It was a short list: Dentist Appt. 2 p.m. Friday, pick up prescription, join Weight Watchers, movie with Lori, work on progress reports, go to the gym.

The problem, Lizzy realized, was that the list had been created two years ago. She moved on, clicking file after file, skimming for now. She looked at the clock. It was almost seven thirty. Time flew when she was not having fun.

She had told Jessica she would be back at the office before dark. Jessica was a responsible person. She would lock up and take Hayley home if Hayley needed a ride. Jessica had done as much before.

Lizzy glanced at her iPhone. No missed calls.

After she looked over a file, she deleted it. All of the files were still on the portable hard drive, so nothing would be permanently deleted. She had no desire to look at each file more than once. This simple yet time-consuming process of elimination could take weeks if she didn't stay focused.

At the sound of her doorbell, she wondered who it could be since she wasn't expecting anyone. She pushed herself to her feet and limped to the door.

Linda Gates, her therapist, wanted Lizzy to get used to checking the door without getting her gun first.

Spiderman was dead, she reminded herself.

But some habits never died. She opened the top drawer of the Pembroke table near the front entrance. Her gun was right there. Her palms itched to pick it up, but she didn't. Instead, she stared at it for a moment longer before forcing herself to look out the peephole.

She smiled.

Jared wore jeans and a dark T-shirt that showed off his nicely worked arms and toned body. That's what happened when you went to the gym on a regular basis. Despite the great body, what really grabbed her attention was the picnic basket he was carrying.

Lizzy was down to two locks on her door, which was a far cry from the six deadbolts she used to have. She opened the door and smiled. "When did you get back into town?"

She leaned forward and tried to lift the lid of the picnic basket, but Jared stopped her. "Not so fast. It's a surprise."

Meww.

She laughed. "What's in there?"

"My new roommate," he said. "Are you going to let us inside?"

Moving aside she let him in and then locked the door behind her before joining him in the living room.

Jared set the basket in the middle of her living room floor and flipped open one side of the basket. The cutest little black-and-white kitten stared up at Lizzy with big, adorable blue eyes.

Lizzy dropped down to the floor and sat cross-legged next to the basket, forgetting all about her sore muscles as she drew the kitten into her arms. "Aren't you the cutest thing in the whole world," she purred into the kitten's soft fur.

"And what am I, chopped liver?"

"What's her name?" she asked in a voice reserved for babies and kittens.

"After much deliberation I had the kitten's name narrowed down to Rumpelstiltskin or Harriett, so"—he leaned over and reached deep inside the basket and pulled out a tiny book—"I got you this...a book of names."

Holding the kitty close, she came to her feet and stood on tippy-toes so she could brush her lips against Jared's stubbled jaw. "Where did you find her?"

"After arriving home less than three hours ago, I took a shower and then ran to the store for milk. I was almost to the entrance when I overheard a mother telling her child that five out of six wasn't bad. But apparently the woman had to work for a living and they had been there all day already and couldn't afford to take the kitten home. Their next stop was the pound."

Lizzy made a sad face.

"I kept walking, reminding myself I didn't have time for this. Then the kid started crying, and when I looked over my shoulder, I saw Rumpelstiltskin's head peek out of the box." Jared shook his head. "She was looking right at me with those big blue eyes. I inwardly cursed the kid, the cat, and the heartless mother, reminding myself of all the reasons why I should keep on walking just like everyone else sauntering by the sad little trio without consequence."

Lizzy laughed.

"It's not funny. A man in a suit mouthed the word *sucker* as he dashed past me and disappeared inside the store."

"That's horrible."

"I thought so."

"But you are the sweetest, most adorable man in the world," Lizzy told him.

"That's more like it."

Jared was a sucker for poor, helpless creatures, which was just one of the many reasons why she cared about him so much. "Is she mine?"

"It's complicated," Jared said.

She kissed the kitten's belly before setting it on the floor. Together they watched Rumpelstiltskin wander around on wobbly legs.

Lizzy wrapped her arms around Jared's waist and looked into his eyes. "Complicated in what way?"

Jared pulled Lizzy tight against him and kissed her good and long. "I've missed you," he said after pulling away. "But on the ride over here, me and Rumpelstiltskin formed a special bond. And besides, I already promised Stiltskin that she could come home with me. But you, Lizzy Gardner, get to give her a proper name, and when you're ready to move in, me and Rumpel will be waiting with open arms."

She dropped her arms to her hips. "Are you blackmailing me, Jared Michael Shayne?"

"I would never do such a thing."

He kissed the side of her neck.

She reached a hand beneath the hem of his shirt and reveled in the feel of his hard, warm torso against her palm.

That's all it took. Jared picked her up and carried her down the hall and into the bedroom.

She pulled his shirt over his head. Then he pulled off her shirt too. She had a difficult time with his belt, so he took over from there. He stood naked at the end of the bed before she could slide the sandals off her feet.

He smiled and slid one sandal off at a time. The man made everything he did look sexy. Her jeans and red panties came next. Then he climbed onto the bed, hovering over her before he slid his hand behind her back and unhooked her bra with one quick flick of his wrist.

"Impressive."

He smiled. "You haven't seen anything yet."

Reaching for him, she stroked the length of him, enjoying the look of blissful satisfaction on his face. "If that's true," she said, "I'm in *big* trouble."

He let out a growl and then proceeded to make a meal out of her, starting with her neck and nibbling his way over her collarbone and lower until she was rendered speechless.

CHAPTER 16

DON'T JUDGE A BOOK BY ITS COVER

Jessica climbed behind the wheel and turned the key in the ignition. Nothing happened.

Hayley climbed in on the passenger side and took a seat.

"The car still won't start. I'm going to call a tow truck."

"That would cost a fortune," Hayley said. "Put your foot heavy and flat on the accelerator before you turn the key next time."

"That doesn't work. I just need to give it a minute before I try again."

"Let's knock on Farrell's door," Hayley said, "and see what he's up to."

"No way, Jose."

Hayley thought only ten-year-olds said shit like that, but like most things that came out of Jessica's mouth, she let it go. "I thought you wanted to be a criminologist?" Hayley asked instead.

"What does that have to do with anything?"

"How are you going to figure people out if you're too afraid to talk to strangers?"

"I'm not afraid to talk to strangers."

"Well, what was your problem with talking to Johnson then?"

"He's a criminal and a full-blown druggy."

"You don't know that."

"Give me a break. His hands were shaking. He was experiencing shortness of breath and was sweating profusely."

"I guess you didn't see the stack of vitamins and prescriptions on the coffee table, did you?"

"I figured those were for his elderly mother."

"Wow, you don't stereotype, do you?"

"OK, then what were the pills for?"

"He wasn't shaking; those were tremors. Theodore Johnson has full-blown Parkinson's. The prescription was for L-dopa."

Jessica took in a long, deep breath. "OK, I admit I was too quick to judge. Happy?"

"No. Not happy, but satisfied. So which one of us is going to knock on Farrell's door?"

"I have a perfectly good cell phone if we want to call a taxi. Why would you want to bother Farrell?"

"He's on our watch list and his house is right across the street staring back at me."

Jessica dropped her foot on the gas pedal and turned the key. The engine had no choice but to sputter to life.

"Don't go anywhere," Hayley said, her tone firm. She tipped her chin toward Farrell's house, prompting Jessica to look over her shoulder. They both watched Farrell's garage door open. A white minivan backed out onto the street.

"Let's follow him."

"Why?"

Hayley reached under her seat and grabbed the digital camera Lizzy had lent her for just these types of instances.

"It's going to be getting dark soon and we still haven't checked in with Lizzy."

Hayley waved her comment off. "Lizzy would have called if she needed us. Come on, let's go. We're going to lose him."

Hayley was surprised when Jessica didn't argue further. Jessica made a quick three-point turn. It didn't take long to catch up to the minivan. There was a driver, but no passenger inside the van. It was definitely Farrell behind the wheel. His crew cut and big ears made him easy to spot.

After removing the lens cap, Hayley made a few adjustments for exposure so she could get a decent picture if they caught Farrell getting out of the car without assistance. According to his file, a fall at work had aggravated his knees. He was supposed to be wheelchair-bound for another six weeks. The fall had supposedly taken away his ability to get around and therefore he was suing for loss of wages.

"He's getting onto the freeway."

"Don't lose him."

Jessica stepped hard on the gas. The engine noise went from tolerable to deafening as Jessica did her best to stay a few cars behind the van.

"I wonder where he's going."

They didn't have to wonder for long. The minivan took a right off the Harbor Boulevard exit. They took a left on Harbor and a right on Industrial. A few minutes later, they followed the van into a deserted parking lot.

Farrell parked in front of a rundown auto mechanics building complete with a row of abandoned cars that had been picked apart. Across the street was a gas station with a mini-mart.

"I don't like this," Jessica said, revving the engine to keep it from puttering out and dying on them. "I think we should go."

"Just stay calm." Hayley examined the camera in her lap. "Let's wait a few minutes to see if he gets out of the car."

"We shouldn't be here. I never should have listened to you."

"Why does everything I do piss you off?" Hayley asked.

"You really want to know?"

"I wouldn't ask if I didn't."

Jessica pointed a finger at Hayley and said, "For starters, you're selfish. You come into work whenever you feel like it. You don't care about anybody but yourself. You're not the only one in the world who was dealt a crappy dysfunctional childhood."

"Really? You mean I'm not the only fourteen-year-old to get fucked day after day, week after week, by her mother's boyfriend and all of his friends? Well, thank you, Jessica. I feel better already. And here I thought I was the only one. Wow."

Hayley screwed the lens cap back onto the camera, put the strap over her shoulder, and opened the car door.

"What are you doing?"

"See that market across the street?"

Jessica nodded.

"I'm going to go inside and get something to drink. Then I'm going to sit on the sidewalk over there and wait and see what Farrell does next. In the meantime, you can drive on home before it gets dark."

"I'm not leaving you here in the middle of nowhere. Lizzy would kill me."

"Have it your way," Hayley said before shutting the door and heading for the market.

Jessica's shoulders slumped forward as she watched Hayley walk off. Once again, Hayley had managed to make her feel like crap. Twice in one hour. Johnson was not a druggy; the man had Parkinson's. And poor Hayley had been forced to endure multiple rapes at a young age, for how many years, she wasn't sure.

Jessica thought about calling out to Hayley and apologizing, but she'd already disappeared inside the store.

A bad feeling settled in the pit of Jessica's stomach. She looked at her cell phone and thought about dialing Lizzy's number. Lizzy would tell her what to do. But that would only serve to get Hayley into trouble and then Hayley would hate her more than she already did.

Jessica placed her phone on the console at the same moment a big hand reached inside her window and opened her car door. Before she could process what was happening, Farrell unlatched her seat belt and pulled her from the car, his beefy hands clamped around her upper arms, his knuckles white as he shook her.

"Let go of me!"

"Somebody's got to teach you two not to meddle in other people's business," Farrell growled.

"You better let me go or I'm going to call the police."

"I'll be the one calling the police. You and your friend might just end up spending a night in jail for trespassing. There isn't a neighbor within a block of my house who didn't see you two speeding through the neighborhood, almost killing our kids before deciding to trespass."

"I wasn't speeding. And it was a dog I almost ran over, not a kid. That dog ran into the street without warning. And we didn't trespass. We had a legitimate reason for being in your neighborhood and it had nothing to do with you. Now get your hands off me."

"I've had enough of you two following me and getting in my way." He shook her so hard, spittle flew out of Jessica's mouth.

Jessica was about to scream when she saw Hayley run up from behind the man and put him in a chokehold.

Everything happened fast after that.

Farrell let go of Jessica, and he might have taken Hayley out with one quick jab of his elbow if it weren't for the three-inch blade she held against his throat.

A drop of blood hit the cement.

It took Jessica a moment to grasp what she was seeing. "Hayley, no!"

CHAPTER 17

WHAT'S LOVE GOT TO DO WITH IT?

Thoroughly satisfied, Lizzy's hand rested on Jared's naked chest.

She had fed Rumpelstiltskin an hour ago, and the kitten was curled up on the chair in the corner of her room. She'd slept like a baby last night. No nightmares. No waking up in a cold sweat. She turned on her side and nibbled on Jared's ear. "I think that might have been the best night of sex we've ever had."

"Good, because I need you to keep that thought for the next two weeks."

She propped herself up on an elbow so she could see his face. "You're leaving again?"

"Not until Saturday morning." He kissed her forehead. "We have the rest of the week before I leave. And besides, I'll be back before you have time to miss me."

"Not true. I miss you already."

"I'll set you up on Skype so we can get some face time."

"I don't like Skype."

"You don't know that until you try it."

She flopped backward until her head hit the pillow. "What about kitty?"

"It's all taken care of. My neighbor agreed to watch Pinoc-
chio."

"You mean Rumpelstiltskin?"

"Yes, that's what I meant." It was Jared's turn to swivel to his
side so that he was hovering over Lizzy. He played with a strand
of blonde hair near her ear.

"You knew you were going to be leaving. Why did you wait
so long to tell me?"

"I knew you would be sad, and I didn't want to ruin our one
night together with one big tear-fest."

She smiled. "Ridiculous."

"That's right—ridiculously in love with you. That's what I
am."

Lizzy didn't respond. She never responded when he used the
L word. Although they had dated back in high school, they had
only been reunited six months. Even if the fluttering of butterfly
wings she felt every time he looked at her were the stirrings of
love, it was too soon. Way too soon.

His eyes glistened, making her feel adored as he gazed at her
before he brushed his lips across her forehead. He pushed himself
from the bed and looked around for his clothes, giving Lizzy a
chance to admire his naked form in all its glory. He had a killer
ass and a well-toned physique that made it difficult to possess a
single coherent thought.

She should have already moved in with him.

What kind of an idiot was she? Hell, she should have asked
him to marry her, for God's sake, but she couldn't…or wouldn't…
and instead she said absolutely nothing.

"What are you thinking about?" he asked after he was dressed
from the waist down.

"My missing person case…Diane Kramer," she lied.

"The one whose disappearance might be connected to Anthony Melbourne?"

Lizzy nodded. "I managed to get Diane's hard drive from her computer at work downloaded onto a portable disc. I was going through the files when you rang the bell last night."

"Find anything?"

She nodded. "A couple of interesting to-do lists and lots of e-mails to the parents of her kids."

"Kids? I thought she was single?"

"She is. She's a special needs teacher. And she must have made quite an impression on these kids because it's obvious they looked up to her. It seems she's made a difference in many of their lives." Lizzy sighed. "From what I've read and heard so far, I agree with Diane's friends who don't believe she would have left the school and her kids."

Jared sat on the edge of the bed and slipped on his socks and shoes. "Any suspects?"

"A few. I'm beginning to understand why her sister Andrea is having me follow Melbourne. Something tells me Diane's disappearance has everything to do with her weight."

"How so?"

"According to friends and family, that's all she talked about. She was over two hundred pounds and she might have been depressed. She tried every diet known to mankind. Pills, gimmicky equipment, some kind of weird cotton ball diet, you name it. I recently learned from one of Diane's coworkers that she joined an online group called the Weight Watcher Warriors."

"Can you join the group?"

"I don't know. I didn't think of that."

"You might want to join and see what you can find out as a new member."

"That's brilliant. I'll join the group and see if anyone mentions Diane." Excited about the prospect of finding a lead, Lizzy pulled on her shorts and T-shirt.

After Jared put on his shirt, she wrapped her arms around his waist. She might not be ready to live with him, but she couldn't fathom the idea of living without him. "I don't want you to leave," she told him. "There are so many things I need to talk to you about."

He held her tight and kissed the top of her head. "Maybe this is exactly what you need. A few weeks without me will give you a chance to think things through."

Her cheek was pressed against his chest. She wanted so badly to tell him she loved him…but she was afraid, she realized. Just the thought of saying the words to him caused her heart to beat faster.

She was afraid of being vulnerable and needy.

What if she grew to love him *so* much that she would no longer be able to stand on her own two feet? What then?

Telling him she loved him would be synonymous with saying, "Here I am…here's all of me, the bad and the good. What you see, is what you get."

Was she afraid he would judge her or reject her?

She sighed. Her apprehension had nothing to do with Jared and everything to do with her. She was afraid of being honest with *herself*.

Love sucked.

CHAPTER 18

NOBODY'S PERFECT

Always aware of her surroundings, Lizzy kept her eyes on the cars parked nearby as she climbed out of her car. Her gaze swept over the buildings and the street as she headed for her office. Up ahead, people walked in and out of the coffee shop. Summer or winter, it didn't matter; everybody needed their caffeine. No unusual shadows; nobody watching from afar. Her shoulders relaxed as she entered her office, bringing inside a surge of dry Sacramento heat.

"How's it going?" Jessica asked from her desk at the back of the room.

"Not too bad for a Wednesday." She walked around the front of her desk and put her purse away. "Sorry I haven't been around much. Jared will be heading off on business for a few weeks and I wanted to spend some time with him before he leaves."

"How about your workouts? How was that this morning?"

Lizzy felt heat rise to her face. Her best workout had been last night in bed with Jared. A treadmill and a few lunges didn't compare. But she wasn't the type to kiss and tell. She glanced at her watch. "My workouts are later on Wednesdays. I'm supposed to meet Cathy at the gym in forty-five minutes for another session of torture."

Lizzy sat at her desk and began to sort through the mail stacked in her in-box.

"So what do you think about Melbourne?" Jessica asked. "Is he hiding something?"

"The only things that man is hiding are his flaws. Nobody could possibly be that perfect."

"Are you still sore?"

"No, it only hurts when I blink."

Jessica laughed.

"Did you and Hayley have any luck yesterday with the Fullerton case?"

Jessica grabbed a file from her desk and walked it over, placing it in front of her. Lizzy saw the bruise on Jessica's upper arm, prompting Jessica to yank on the sleeve of her shirt to cover the fingerprints.

"What happened to your arm? Who grabbed you?"

Jessica went back to her desk and sat down. "It's nothing."

"It's obviously a handprint. I'm not your mother, Jessica. I'm not going to lecture you about the guys you hang out with, but I also refuse to—"

Jessica whipped around fast. "You think my boyfriend did this to me?"

"Whoa, there. I didn't even know you had a boyfriend."

"I don't…not really," Jessica muttered. "But none of that matters because Casey had nothing to do with the handprints."

"Handprints? You have more than one of those?"

Jessica huffed at her obvious misstep and then gently rolled up both sleeves so Lizzy could get a good look at her bruises.

Lizzy had never seen anything like it. Whoever had done this to Jessica had left indents on both of her arms.

"I wasn't supposed to tell you," Jessica said, "but yesterday, after you left, and at your request, Hayley and I did a search on the Internet for information on Theodore Johnson."

Lizzy had to bite her tongue to keep from interrupting. Instead, she grabbed a pencil and began chewing.

Jessica walked back toward Lizzy and took a seat in the cushioned chair reserved for clients. "As it turned out, Johnson lives with his mother in a house about fifteen miles from here…right around the corner from Eric Farrell, the guy trying to collect workers' comp."

Please don't let those bruises have anything to do with Farrell, Lizzy thought. She pulled the pencil from her mouth. "Please tell me that you two did *not* visit Mr. Johnson at his home."

"You promised you would hear me out first."

Lizzy began chewing again.

"I hate to put all the blame on Hayley, but I want you to know that I tried to talk her out of it. She wouldn't listen. She's the most stubborn person I've ever met in my life."

After a calming breath, Jessica continued. "Yes, we went to Johnson's home. But you'll be happy to know, thanks to Hayley's determined questioning, he gave us a lead." Jessica gestured with her chin toward the file on Lizzy's desk. "It's all in the file."

At the moment, Lizzy couldn't care less about the file. "But Theodore Johnson didn't cause the bruising on your arms, did he?"

Jessica shook her head. "I know you have to go soon, so I won't bore you with the details, but long story short—after Hayley and I finished talking to Johnson, we saw Farrell leave his house. He was driving a white minivan. He's supposed to be wheelchair-bound, remember? Hayley happened to have her camera ready to go, so we followed him."

"I've told you both never to get out of the car to take a picture."

"We didn't. Well, I didn't. We followed him approximately ten miles from his house to an abandoned auto shop. Hayley went across the street to get something to drink at a mini-mart, and the next thing you know Farrell shoved his arm through my window, opened my door, and dragged me out of my car. He shook me so hard I thought my neck was going to break."

Lizzy tossed the pencil into the jar and grabbed her phone. "I'm calling the police. That asshole is going to pay."

"Put your phone away, Lizzy. Please. If you don't, Hayley will be the one who pays, not Farrell."

Lizzy's adrenaline had skyrocketed. "What are you talking about?"

"Hayley must have been watching from the mini-mart because before I knew what was happening, she had the man in a chokehold. That's how fast everything happened. It was crazy."

"Hayley had Farrell in a chokehold?"

"She did."

"Impossible. That man is built like a machine."

Jessica rubbed the back of her neck. "Farrell is all muscle, but he's also short, which is why Hayley was able to get her arm around his neck in the first place."

"Please tell me Hayley is all right."

"Hayley is fine. At least for now. If anyone tries to press charges against Farrell, though, he's threatened to press charges of his own."

"On what grounds?"

"Same as mine—aggravated assault."

"How so? There's no way she could've hurt—"

"She held a knife to Farrell's throat," Jessica interrupted. "He peed in his pants too, and to tell you the truth, Farrell wasn't the only one who thought his days on earth were limited."

"How bad?"

Jessica wrinkled her nose. "Just a nick, I guess, but if that man had made one wrong move, he would be in the hospital right now or maybe even in the morgue."

"You really think Hayley is OK?"

"Physically, yeah, she's fine." Jessica stood and returned to her desk.

Lizzy wondered what Jessica meant. Physically Hayley was OK, but not mentally? She looked at the clock. Damn. She was already going to be late. She was being paid to watch Melbourne. She'd have to deal with this later. Hayley and Jessica were not the best of friends. There was some obvious animosity between them...and that could not be good for business. But carrying knives?

Lizzy and Hayley needed to have a serious talk.

* * *

Although the gym was big enough to fit a hundred people, only six ladies were in attendance for Melbourne's "private" class.

Lizzy couldn't help but wonder if Andrea Kramer had any clue as to what she was spending her hard-earned money on. Or maybe it wasn't *her* hard-earned money she was spending. Bottom line, somebody's money, hard-earned or not, was going to waste.

If Lizzy ever decided to continue working out after she was done following Melbourne, she figured she didn't need a trainer to torture herself. The treadmill was doing a good job all on its own.

Melbourne headed their way. He wore a tight-fitting T-shirt that hugged his massive biceps, along with black gym shorts and brand new shoes with thick soles to absorb maximum impact, no doubt. He stood at about six feet five. He had a nice symmetrical face with everything in the right spots: chin more square than round; mouth not too wide; good, strong nose; blue eyes; and his head appeared to be bald by choice, not because of male pattern baldness based on genetics.

"You probably shouldn't stare at him," Cathy said. "It's way too obvious."

"What's too obvious?"

"That you've been bitten by the Melbourne bug."

The Melbourne bug? "I'm only trying to figure out what thousands of women see in him. He doesn't even have any hair."

"He's hot. Not all men can get away with the look. He's got a nice-shaped head, and together with his perfectly maintained five o'clock shadow, he's got it going on."

Lizzy tried to imagine Jared without hair, and although the idea of it didn't compute, she knew without a doubt that Jared would look sexy with or without a full head of hair.

"Ladies, if you can talk, you aren't working out hard enough."

Lizzy tried not to roll her eyes.

"OK, ladies," Melbourne said, clapping his hands together to get their full attention. "Today we're all going to become acquainted with the elliptical machines. You'll be able to work your arms and your legs with less stress on your knees, hips, and backs. I want all of you to start at a resistance level of eight or above. I expect you to push yourselves."

The other women got up from their mats and headed for the elliptical machines. A woman from the Jane Fonda era, complete with leotard and tights, sprinted to the other side of the room and jumped on the first elliptical.

Lizzy couldn't help but wonder if the woman was a "secret client," a consumer hired to evaluate staff or inspire other consumers. No, she decided. Ridiculous. Those secret consumers were paid to be discreet. Jane Fonda's clone was anything but.

Lizzy's sister wasn't much better. There was an energetic aura hovering over Cathy today. Lizzy felt as if she needed a water break every five minutes, but Cathy, despite the sweat dripping from her chin, had yet to stop and rest. Lizzy couldn't remember the last time she'd seen her sister look so…so animated.

Before Lizzy could join the others on the elliptical, Melbourne grasped her shoulder and squeezed.

Her instinct was to brush his hand off, but she refrained. She wanted to befriend the man, not distance herself from him. "Hello," she said, confused.

He snapped his fingers and that's when she realized he recognized her from the retreat in San Francisco.

"I remember," he said, smiling. "The seminar—" He wagged a finger at her. "You were the one sleeping with your head in the knapsack."

She strained her neck to look into his eyes. "How did you know I was sleeping?"

"Let's just say I've been doing this long enough to know what's going on around me."

His blue eyes sparkled. She looked deep into his eyes, hoping to see what was really going on inside that head of his. Was he responsible for Diane Kramer's disappearance? It was no use. He had a naive, ingenuous look to him. He looked like a young, taller, bald Jack LaLanne, a man who happened to be exceptionally passionate about his work.

"You weren't the only one nodding off," he added. "I needed to get everyone's attention."

"So you used me."

"Absolutely."

She smiled. The man might actually be a little bit charming, which seemed appalling to her. He had too many muscles to be charming. Before she could continue the casual conversation, Cathy popped into the middle of things, her unbridled enthusiasm putting the Jane Fonda woman to shame.

"Hi," Cathy said, offering a friendly hand to Melbourne. "I'm Cathy Warner, Lizzy's sister. I'm sure Lizzy already told you that I've been one of your biggest fans since forever. There isn't a thigh or arm contraption, book, or T-shirt of yours that I don't own."

"But do you use those contraptions?" he asked.

Cathy laughed as if he'd meant it as a joke, which he hadn't. Then Cathy tapped a finger against his muscular shoulder, obviously copping a feel.

Lizzy might have been embarrassed if it weren't so damn funny.

"Did Lizzy also tell you that we're all signed up for your retreat in Lake Tahoe?"

"What retreat?" another woman asked, running back to join their ever-growing circle. Within seconds, most of the women were gathered around Melbourne, everyone gawking at the man as if Brad Pitt or George Clooney were the one standing there. This Melbourne guy tortured women daily with his get-skinny-quick schemes and thigh devices. And yet each and every one of these women looked possessed by some invisible force, each overcome with desire.

What was she missing?

As the women flirted and laughed at his every word, Lizzy watched him closely. She would love to ask him about Diane Kramer and see what he had to say. But it was too early yet. She needed to be patient and stick to Andrea's plan since that's what she was getting paid to do. She would keep an eye on the man and see what Melbourne was hiding, if anything.

CHAPTER 19

RANDY TUCKER'S TURN

Taking care of Randy Tucker, number two on Hayley's list of scumbag rapists, was proving to be much tougher than she'd first imagined. Peter had been child's play in comparison.

She had been watching Randy Tucker for a month now, but the problem with Randy was that he had no schedule. Every day of the week was a new day spent with new people in new places.

At least Peter had a schedule. He walked to Shotgun's Bar & Grill and drank beer every morning for breakfast, sold drugs during the day, and then he either raped and pillaged or chugged beers at the Scorpion. After his worthless day was over, he went home and most likely drank himself into a stupor.

Randy, though, was a horse of a different color. He preferred pills over alcohol, but of course he indulged in both. Hayley had seen him grab a bite to eat at a diner once. Some mornings Randy woke in a park or a ditch at the side of the road. Some nights he didn't sleep at all, just wandered around in the dark looking like a zombie.

He had a few ladies he visited, but mostly he wandered.

The only thing Randy Tucker did on a semiregular basis was hang out in front of Bill's Liquor Store. Usually a car with tinted windows or a hooded figure on a bike would show up. An exchange of money for dope would be made before Randy wandered off again.

And there he was now.

Figuring she'd have at least an hour to wait before he collected his goods, Hayley was surprised when the exchange took place less than five minutes after he appeared.

A black car with tinted windows drove up to Randy. He leaned low, his head disappearing inside the car for a few seconds. The sedan disappeared into the night, and Randy headed for the empty field behind the liquor store.

Hayley waited in the shadows of tall oleander. Cathy's car was parked around the corner, but she wanted to give Randy time to swallow a few pills before she approached him.

Hoping he would head east toward the abandoned warehouse, she wasn't surprised to see Randy tromp his way through the weeds and head west instead.

Shit. She'd have to go with Plan B.

She ran back to the car, grabbed her backpack from the backseat, and slung the thick strap over her shoulder. She locked the car and then checked her hair in the side mirror, making sure the wig wasn't lopsided before she ran to catch up to him.

Out of breath, she saw him round the corner, making a right on Second Street. Once he was out of sight, she walked as fast as she could in her new three-inch pin heels. She wasn't sure which was worse, the heels or the wig.

Looking down, focusing on not breaking an ankle in her heels as they clicked against pavement, she took the same right on Second. Her head snapped up at the sound of voices.

DEAD WEIGHT

She stopped walking. In fact, she could've heard a pin drop or, in this particular case, a needle.

Stupid. Stupid. Stupid.

"Hey there, Suga' Nips."

Three guys. One girl. The odds were not good.

Slowly, keeping her gaze directed on their faces, she slid the backpack off her shoulder and reached inside, thinking about her options with every breath she took. The rings she wore on her fingers were as good as, if not better than, wearing brass knuckles. But that wouldn't be enough to take care of the six-foot-three monstrosity standing front and center.

She should turn around and walk away. But if she did that, she wouldn't know how many of them were coming after her. She needed to be proactive and take out the biggest guy first: the guy with the big grin, four silver teeth, and red, white, and blue stars tattooed around both eyes. The stars were sort of cool, and under different circumstances she might have commented.

"Lookin' for someone?" Randy asked.

"As a matter of fact, I was. But"—she looked up at the road sign—"looks like I took a wrong turn." She could feel the twelve-inch baton as she wrapped four fingers around the handle. With a push of the button, it would extend to a little over twenty inches. She also had a knife strapped around each thigh. A Stubby knife with a birch handle and a three-and-a-quarter-inch blade, and her SOG, a small but lethal knife: all in preparation for Randy—not Randy and friends.

She took a step back, rethinking her original proactive stance.

Be smart, she thought, as she turned to walk away.

"Whatcha got in the bag there?"

She turned the corner, pin heels clicking as she went. The big guy was on her ass. Fuck.

119

She walked just past the bus stop bench and then dropped her bag and turned toward him, holding her baton in front of her.

He stopped where he was, his grin bigger than ever.

"Why don't you just turn around, go back to your buddies, and leave me alone," she said. "I don't want any trouble."

"Is that right? A girl dressed like that"—his eyes roamed over her—"walking around town in the dead of night is not only looking for trouble, she's asking for it." He shook his big head. "No," he added with a chuckle, "let me rephrase that, sweetie. She's not asking for trouble, she's *begging* for it." He laughed.

"Wrong again. Why don't you listen with your fucking ears instead of your dumbass pea-sized brain? If I was desperate for a moron like you, why would I turn around and walk away?"

He pointed a finger at her. "I was gonna play nice, but now you've gone and hurt my feelings. I don't let bitches talk to me like that."

He walked forward, coming around the back of the bus stop. When he was close enough, Hayley pushed the button on her baton, extending it long enough for him to grab it, sending a shock through his body. "What the fuck?"

He stumbled backward and she took full advantage.

She went after him like a cheetah goes after its prey: without hesitation, touching his beefy arm with the prongs and holding it to his flesh, dumping energy into his muscles at a high-pulse frequency. She'd practiced enough times that it felt like second nature. Just lunge and hold.

He was confused, but it took another five seconds before his knees finally buckled and he went to the ground. Luck was on her side when he hit his head on the back of the bench on his way down.

Hayley ran to her backpack, grabbed the handcuffs she'd brought for Randy, and cuffed the big guy's left wrist to the closest bench leg. No sooner had she begun to walk off when someone called out and she heard hurried footsteps close behind. Shit.

Hopefully, it was Randy. Because she hadn't gotten a clear view of the third loser, she had no idea what she would be dealing with. She looked over her shoulder. Not Randy. Tonight the only luck she had was bad luck.

She waited until she could feel the asshole breathing down her neck, then whipped around and held the baton in front of her. His right foot came up quick and her baton rolled into the street. *Clink. Clink. Clink.*

That pissed her off. The baton had cost her two paychecks. Picking up her foot, she stamped down hard, sending her three-inch pin heel right through his foot. He howled, and for the first time ever she was grateful for stilettos.

Before he finished screaming, she slammed her knee into his balls, and then came up fast with her palm to his nose, breaking it on the first try. All of those defense classes had actually come in handy. Who knew?

While he rolled around in pain, Hayley stepped into the street, straightening her skirt as she went, and picked up her baton. Returning to his side, she held the prongs on her baton to his neck, holding it there until the juice nearly ran out.

With him in a trance, like a fucked-up, rageaholic zombie, she didn't bother heading for the car. As she passed by her backpack, she picked it up with one swipe of her hand and headed for Randy.

It was Randy Tucker's turn.

CHAPTER 20

FEEDERISM

Lizzy had been sitting in her car outside Michael Denton's house on Cedar Street in Rocklin for over an hour. Other than Melbourne, it seemed Michael Denton was the only other man in Diane Kramer's life.

Lizzy had hoped to stop back at the office and check in with Hayley and Jessica before heading home, but once again, that probably wasn't going to happen. She needed to talk to Michael Denton today, not tomorrow.

It was past five o'clock, and yet the heat was not letting up. Lizzy's legs were sticking to the car seat. Not pretty.

When Andrea Kramer had hired her, she'd said that ninety-five percent of her billable hours were to be focused on Anthony Melbourne. The other five percent could be spent how Lizzy saw fit.

Other than the people at Diane Kramer's work and the Weight Watcher Warriors group she had joined this morning, Michael Denton was the only other person Diane might have been in contact with before she disappeared.

Lizzy checked her cell phone. No messages. A few minutes later, she saw the man she'd been waiting for pull his silver Honda

Civic into the driveway. She waited for him to lock his car and head for the front door before she made her move and followed after him. The moment he turned the key and opened the door to his house, she called out to him. "Michael Denton?"

He turned toward her. "Can I help you?"

Michael Denton was five foot ten, maybe five eleven. He was twenty-nine years old, but he looked much older. His hair was curly and wiry and the same brown color as his eyes. He looked apprehensive.

"Hello," Lizzy said. "My name is Lizzy Gardner. I'm a private investigator, and I was hoping you wouldn't mind answering a few questions about Diane Kramer."

"I've already talked to the police. I answered all of their questions…on more than one occasion, I might add."

"I know. I've seen the files, but Diane's sister, Andrea, is not happy with the results."

"That woman is never happy."

Lizzy angled her head. Michael Denton was the second person this week to put Andrea in a negative light.

"Sorry," he said with a shrug. "That was out of line. I don't even know the woman."

Lizzy tried to put him at ease and keep him talking. "Don't worry. You're not the first person to speak about Andrea negatively. Sounds like Andrea might have been overly concerned for her sister."

"I don't know if I would call it concern. The woman seemed obsessed with her little sister. She never left Diane alone. There were times when Andrea would call Diane every five minutes. Excessive, don't you think?" He shook his head. "I don't think Diane cared, but it drove me crazy."

"Were you and Diane dating?"

He pointed to his chest. "Me and Diane?"

Lizzy nodded. "Yes. Were the two of you in a relationship?"

"No. It was nothing like that." He looked at the keys in the door. "Do you want to come in?"

"I would love to."

By the time Michael Denton made himself comfortable and got them both a glass of ice water, nearly ten minutes had gone by, giving Lizzy plenty of time to take a look around his living area, which was quaint and homey. Two end tables and the recliner were decorated with large handmade doilies. The walls were covered with pictures she assumed were family and friends, every frame a different color and size. At closer view, she noticed that nearly every woman in every picture was eating: pizza, cake, donuts, and cupcakes...odd.

"I'm sure you've heard and now you can see," Michael said, gesturing toward the wall of pictures as he entered the room, "that I have a fat fetish."

Lizzy blushed.

"It's not a big deal," he told her. "In fact, I have a girlfriend."

Lizzy raised a curious brow. She pointed to the wall covered with pictures. "Which one is she?"

"She won't let me hang her picture. In fact, she won't let me feed her either."

Lizzy tried to get it all straight in her mind, but too many pieces were missing. "All the women in these pictures allow you to feed them, but that's the *only* thing going on between you and them?"

"That's correct."

"So simply feeding them cupcakes, or whatever, turns you on?"

"Yes," he said matter-of-factly. "There are many forms of fat fetishism, but I'm what most would refer to as a fat admirer. Not only do I like feeding overweight women, I prefer to date women who are clinically overweight."

"You mean obese."

"Sure. Call it whatever you want. I've already got the Fat Acceptance Movement group coming around, giving me grief."

"Why is that?"

"They argue that feeders like me take pleasure in seeing fat women immobilized and helpless."

"Is that true?"

"Not at all. In fact, I encourage the women I feed to exercise regularly."

"Really?"

"Really."

"What do these women get out of it?"

"Most of them like my cooking." He smiled. "My plan is to open a bakery and call it The Sweet Life."

She smiled back at him. "Cute. You said 'most of them' like your cooking. What about the women who don't come here for the cooking?"

"The others come to me because they too have a fetish. It turns them on to have someone cook for them and feed them, knowing the turn-on is mutual."

"So everyone gets turned on and then they run home to their significant other for the happy ending."

"Exactly. In the end," he said, arms extended wide, "everybody's happy."

"But your girlfriend does not get any sort of sexual gratification from being fed by you."

He laughed. "That's putting it mildly."

"But she goes along with this," Lizzy said, gesturing at the wall, "because it makes you happy."

He nodded. "And she trusts me, of course."

"Of course."

"So do you think Diane Kramer had a fetish?"

"Definitely."

The answer surprised Lizzy. "But Diane had nobody at home waiting for her."

Michael scratched his chin. "Are you sure?"

"From what I've gathered, she had few friends, but you were the only man in her life."

"Well, that's not true. Diane had a major crush on Anthony Melbourne."

"Did she tell you as much?"

He laughed. "Are you kidding me? He's all she talked about."

Lizzy looked at the wall of pictures again.

"There was another woman I used to feed who had a crazy thing for Melbourne too," Michael said. "Her name was Debra Taphorn."

"Do you still see her?"

He shook his head. "Debra was one of the first women I ever fed. She was a regular too. But then, out of the blue, she told me that Melbourne had invited her to enroll in a program of his. A program that only a select few were invited to join. She wouldn't say anything more than that, and I never saw her again."

"Did you tell the police the same thing?"

"I can't recall," he said, "but it's more than a possibility."

Lizzy pulled out a notepad and pen and wrote down the woman's name. "Do you have an address?"

"No. Most of the women I feed don't want me to have phone numbers or addresses, especially if they're married or living with

someone. I'm pretty sure some of them give me fake names too."
He shrugged. "As long as I get to feed them, I don't mind."

"Do you ever turn anyone away?"

"Oh, sure." He snapped his fingers, giving Lizzy a start. "I just
remembered something. I used to have a picture of Debra, but I
took it down recently."

Michael headed for the kitchen and Lizzy followed him. She
watched him open the first of many drawers and shuffle through
papers. He leafed through dozens of old pictures before he pulled
one out and said, "Here she is, Debra Taphorn."

Lizzy took the picture. Debra was blonde with green eyes.
Her face was round and her eyes appeared to be smiling into the
camera as she sunk her teeth into a lemon-filled donut.

Lizzy's stomach growled.

"Somebody's hungry. Want me to make you something? It
won't take me but a minute to find something tasty for you to eat."

Lizzy smiled. "Oh no you don't."

He laughed, a laid-back sort of laugh that made it easy for
Lizzy to see why a woman might let Michael Denton feed her…if
she was into that sort of thing.

"Can I keep this picture?" She held up the picture of Debra
Taphorn.

"Sure, why not."

CHAPTER 21

100 POUNDS TO GO

Sierra Mountains, Day 40

Vivian woke to the sound of a key turning in the door.

She sat up just as Anthony Melbourne entered the cabin. He smiled brightly as if they were the best of friends.

Not being a violent person, Vivian was surprised to find that she wanted nothing more than to pick up the chain attached to her leg and wrap it around Melbourne's neck. And then she wanted to squeeze as hard as she could until his tongue turned purple and his eyes bulged from their sockets.

He set a cardboard box and two plastic bags next to the door. "How are you doing?" he asked.

She knew she looked like hell. She hadn't taken a shower in five days. "Are you serious?"

His smile grew wider, literally ear to ear, making his face look like one big blob of silly putty.

"Feeling a little cranky?"

"You cannot be for real, you fucking asshole."

He shook his head at her as if she were five. "You haven't read the pamphlets I left for you, have you?" He didn't wait for her to answer. "If you don't eat at least five small well-balanced meals with plenty of protein and healthy fats, your hormones will get out of whack, and one of the symptoms is crankiness."

"Fuck you."

He went to the kitchen.

She could hear cupboards being opened and closed. She could already smell Lysol. The man was cleaning the kitchen.

She couldn't believe he expected her to pay him fifteen thousand dollars to be restrained, deprived, and tortured. Unlike others who might think this a grand plan, she had come to terms with her weight long ago. All she wanted to do was lose a few pounds. She had put down five thousand dollars as a deposit, promising to pay the rest upon reaching her goal weight. She had only spent the money in hopes of finding Diane. Sure, it was a lot of money, but she knew that Diane would have done the same for her had the situation been reversed.

She slid off the bed and went to stand just outside the kitchen.

He was on his hands and knees scrubbing the floor just like her mother used to do. "I want out," she said. "I will sign anything you want me to, declaring to all of your lawyers and the world that the decision was mine. I don't want a refund. I don't want anything from you. I just want you to unlock me and let me go."

He kept scrubbing, didn't even bother to look at her when he answered. "Sorry. Can't do."

"Why not?"

"What you're experiencing right now is just part of the process. Everybody goes through it. You just happened to get to stage three faster than most. In fact, you skipped stages one and two altogether."

Vivian didn't care about stage one or two, or even three. She only cared about getting out of here. "You've done your job. I've lost over sixty pounds. I want to go home."

That got his attention and he looked at her, his eyes narrowing as he scanned her body from head to toes.

She hated him—hated him more than she'd ever hated anyone in her life.

"I'm impressed."

"Great. So can you unlock this cuff around my ankle?"

"No. Sorry."

"Why not?"

He stood, put the rag and bottle of cleanser under the sink, and then walked past her. In the top drawer of her bedside table, he pulled out a ledger and held it up for her to see. "You were the one who wrote your goal weight right here on the dotted line. You still have another one hundred pounds to go before our work here is finished."

"*Our* work here? I haven't seen you do anything besides wax the floors."

He smiled and put the ledger back where he'd found it.

"You haven't done jack shit for me." She pointed to the pantry. "You left enough cake and cookie mixes to feed an army."

"Nothing you won't see when you're back in the real world."

"I threw all of the mixes away." She raised her arms in the air. "I've conquered my cravings. I can do the rest on my own at home." She didn't like the desperation she heard in her voice. Nor did she appreciate the way he was shaking his head at her as if nothing she could possibly say or do would make him change his mind. He was a busy man with a mission. He had yet to stop and listen. He had picked up his box and bags and was now in the pantry unloading cans of soup and other assorted food items.

"What did you do to Diane?"

He sighed, turned toward her, and said, "I don't know what you're talking about. I never met anyone named Diane."

He did. She could see it in his eyes. When she'd said Diane's name, he'd flinched. A mere twitch of his body, but still, it was something. "Diane Kramer attended your workshops and retreats. She's your number one fan. She bought every single T-shirt and worthless piece of exercise equipment you ever sold. She's been missing for months, and I know you're involved somehow. She came here. I know it. And now she's missing. Where is she? What did you do with Diane?"

CHAPTER 22

THE GIRL NEXT DOOR

It was Friday morning and Lizzy could not believe how quickly the days flew by when she had to exercise every morning. Five minutes on the treadmill felt like two hours, whereas the twenty-three hours between workouts felt like five minutes. It wasn't fair.

Lizzy was in her car, headed for Jared's house. She hadn't had time to change out of her gym clothes, but she felt as if she needed—make that wanted—to see him before he left for two weeks.

What did it mean that she was going out of her way to see a man when she had absolutely no time to spare? If she didn't solve a case or make a few insurance fraud clients happy, she was going to be out of work before she knew it.

She was falling hard and fast for Jared Shayne, and the sick feeling she felt inside was almost enough to cause her to make an illegal U-turn and head back to work.

Almost.

She and Jared had talked on the phone a few times since their last night together. They had planned to meet up Wednesday night, but he ended up having a late meeting. She hadn't asked him what it was about, but now she wished she had. Crap. This is exactly why she didn't like to date. After exercise class this morning, she'd had three missed calls from Jared, but he wasn't picking up and he hadn't left a message.

She sighed. She'd been in a semi-crappy mood ever since she'd told Jared she wasn't ready to move in with him. A part of her hadn't liked the fact that he took it all so well.

What was he supposed to do? Beg until she moved in out of pity for the poor guy?

She gripped the wheel tighter.

In the rearview mirror, she noticed a dark SUV. Shivers coursed over her when she realized it was a Ford Expedition, the same car she'd seen when she met her sister for lunch. She sped up. The Expedition sped up too.

The next exit was about a half mile up ahead.

Lizzy took the exit and pulled over to the side of the road and waited. Concentrate on breathing, she reminded herself. Stay calm. The Expedition took the same exit and passed her, but she couldn't see the driver through the tinted windows. She put her foot on the gas and sped through a yellow light to keep up. The Expedition stopped at a red light less than a block ahead of her. As she approached, she noticed that the license plate had been removed. Lizzy put her car in park and opened her door. The Expedition sped off, running the red light, swerving to miss a pedestrian on the crosswalk.

Damn it! Lizzy got back in her car and waited until the light turned green. A block ahead, she made the same right turn as the Expedition. The street was empty. At a speed of about twenty-five mph, she checked parking lots and alleyways, but it was no use. The Expedition was gone. And her nerves were shot. She needed to talk to her therapist. Linda Gates always made her feel a little better, a little calmer. Shifting her thoughts to other things, like her plans for the weekend, was a technique Lizzy used to distract herself when she became paranoid, a lingering effect from her time spent with a madman.

But it was no use. Somebody was keeping tabs on her. Melbourne, perhaps? Frank Fullerton? One of her workers' comp cases?

Suddenly she felt very unpopular.

It wasn't long before she exited the highway again. She made a right on San Rafael and then a quick left. Recently Jared had moved from San Francisco to Davis. She'd been to his new house only a couple of times, since they spent most of their time together at her place. Pulling up to the curb in front of his house, she climbed out and shut the door. The scent of jasmine wafted around her as she headed up the walkway.

Somebody called her name.

Turning about, she was surprised to see a pretty blonde with flawless long legs coming her way. Wonderful. Jared was living next to Barbie.

"Hi," the woman said, "are you Lizzy?"

Lizzy nodded. "And you are?"

"I'm Charleen Sydney Bingaman, but everybody calls me Charlee." She gestured at the newly painted two-story house across the street. "I just moved in three weeks ago."

Lizzy didn't know what to say, so she pointed to Jared's house and said, "I'm sort of in a hurry. I need to talk to my boyfriend." Inwardly Lizzy rolled her eyes. Her boyfriend? Oh, brother.

Charlee followed her up the walkway. "I thought you were his sister."

"Nope."

"I guess I was just sort of hoping…"

Lizzy stopped right there and looked up into big gorgeous eyes. "Excuse me?"

The woman's shoulders fell. "I'm sorry. That was rude of me. It's just that Jared has been helping me move in, and he's so charming. And when he brought me the lasagna he'd made and asked me to take care of little Hannah for a few weeks, I just sort of thought—hoped—"

"That he was available," Lizzy finished for her.

"Exactly." Cameron Diaz's look-alike shrugged her shoulders and did this cute little thing with her mouth that worried Lizzy to no end.

"So you're not married?" Lizzy asked.

"No."

"No kids?"

Charlee laughed, which Lizzy took as a definite no.

"I don't mean to pry," Lizzy said, "but how can anyone afford to live in this neighborhood unless—"

"I'm a doctor."

"Of course." Embarrassed, Lizzy continued to Jared's door and knocked. "Well, it's been nice chatting with you, Charlee, but I really do need to talk to Jared."

"I guess he didn't tell you then."

The woman was becoming a nuisance. "Tell me what?"

"He was called away earlier than planned."

"Really?"

Charlee nodded and held up a key. "I was just about to feed Hannah when I saw you drive up. Do you need help getting inside?"

At a loss for words, Lizzy gathered the courage to look into Charlee's eyes and speak without sounding like a jealous bitch. "I have a key," she lied. "But it's in the car and I'm in a hurry, so if you could let me in, I would appreciate it very much. And who is Hannah?"

"That's the name of Jared's new kitten. Jared told me she didn't have a name and she's so precious that I thought she needed an adorable name…thus the name Hannah."

Lizzy shrugged. "Sorry. Hannah already has a name and it's Rumpelstiltskin. Now if you could just let me in, I'll grab Rumpel and we'll be on our way."

Charlee Theron or Bingaman or whatever the hell her name was seemed to be thinking about whether or not to let her inside Jared's house, which annoyed Lizzy further. She didn't have time to take care of the cat, but hell would have to freeze over before she'd leave Rumpelstiltskin with this woman. There had to be a kind, elderly lady in the neighborhood who Jared could have asked for help. What was he thinking?

The woman opened the door before Lizzy could build herself into a frenzy. Lizzy stepped inside and realized she couldn't remember the last time she'd spent the night at Jared's place, if ever. She went to the kitchen on the pretense of looking for Rumpelstiltskin. She grabbed a Rice Krispies Treat from the covered Tupperware on the counter and took a big bite.

"I made those."

"Delicious," Lizzy said with her mouth full.

"Hannah…I mean"—she wrinkled her nose—"Rumpelstiltskin is asleep in her bed."

Lizzy didn't pretend to know where the bed was. Instead, she followed Charlee-Long-Legs into Jared's guestroom. Lizzy could only pray she didn't see any bras and panties lying around.

Thank God. Nothing but a nicely made bed and the smell of kitty litter. She really wasn't in the mood for a full-out cat fight.

Lizzy picked up the kitty, kissed her on the head, and made a beeline for the exit.

"Don't you want her things?"

"No, that's OK. I've got it. It was really nice meeting you, Charlee. I guess I'll be seeing you around."

"Guess so," Charlee said with obvious regret.

* * *

Lizzy sat at her desk in her office downtown, stared at her iPhone, and thought about Jared. Rumpelstiltskin was curled under her desk on top of a sweatshirt she'd found in the file room.

Jessica had been sitting quietly at her desk looking at the computer screen for the past thirty minutes when she said, "Lizzy, you've got to look at this."

When Lizzy failed to respond, Jessica hit the pause button. "Are you OK?"

"I'm fine."

"Jared's new neighbor is really getting to you, huh?"

Lizzy swatted that ridiculous statement away with her hand. "No. I just have a lot on my mind. What's going on?"

"Come over here. You have to see this crazy video."

Lizzy made her way to Jessica's desk and hovered over her so she could see the screen.

Jessica hit replay and started the video over. "Now watch this. Somebody took this entire video that you're about to see using their iPhone. I'm guessing whoever took the video must live three or four stories above the crime scene."

Together Jessica and Lizzy watched three men standing on a dark corner. They were making an exchange—most likely money for drugs. Suddenly a silhouette of a girl with long hair came around the street corner and abruptly stopped when she spotted the three men.

Although the film was fuzzy and a little dark, it was clear that the girl was backing away. She was also reaching into her backpack. She finally turned to leave.

"Run," Lizzy whispered.

"Just wait."

"What's happening? Where is she?" Lizzy wanted to know. "Where did she go?"

"That's exactly what two hundred thousand viewers were wondering when they watched this," Jessica said.

Lizzy watched the biggest guy out of the bunch follow after the girl. The video focused on the two remaining men who continued with their business.

After a few minutes, the second guy disappeared.

"Oh, that's not good," Lizzy said. "Two against one. It's bad enough that the first guy was the size of a gorilla."

"I know. I know."

Lizzy felt sickened to know she was completely helpless. There was nothing she or anyone else could do to help the girl. Why was Jessica showing her this? Why did two hundred thousand sick people watch this thing? Probably the same reason she couldn't look away. The whole world was sick.

Lizzy gasped when she saw the girl return. She appeared to be OK. Thank goodness!

The only man left put his hand out like a traffic cop, obviously trying to stop the girl from whatever it was she was about to do. The girl held something in her hand. It looked like a big stick. Much smaller than a bat. "What is she holding?"

"It looks like one of those batons that police use during riots. Don't you think?"

Hovering closer, Lizzy tried to make out all the fuzzy, blurry parts of the video. The girl poked the guy with the baton, but nothing happened.

The door to the office came open and Hayley walked inside. Jessica hit the pause button and waited while Hayley handed Lizzy a package. "Here are your tickets for the Melbourne retreat you asked me to get."

"Thanks for going out of your way. I was there this morning and completely forgot about the tickets."

"Melbourne is a strange one," Hayley said.

"What do you mean?"

"Here's this guy who's supposed to be promoting exercise and eating right, and yet apparently he hasn't done his homework."

Jessica and Lizzy both waited for Hayley to explain.

"While I was picking up the tickets from his secretary lady, he brought her in a late lunch or an early dinner, whatever you want to call it. Guess what he brought her?"

They both shrugged.

"A big ol' cheeseburger and french fries. No salad. One tiny slice of tomato. That was the only vegetable. Or are tomatoes fruit? I always forget."

"That is weird," Jessica agreed.

"Yeah, and not only that, but in the thirty seconds that I watched their exchange, I swear to you that girl is in love with her boss."

"Are you talking about Jane? Five foot three, round face, red hair in a tight bun, Jane?"

Hayley nodded. "That's the one."

"I met her at the retreat in San Francisco," Lizzy said. "She was overzealous but maybe she's just passionate about

Melbourne's work. From what I've seen and heard, women go crazy over that guy. Personally, I don't get it."

"I don't know," Hayley said, "the whole thing was just weird. The way she looked at him, the way he looked at her. She would blush and then look away and then stare at him as he walked away. And I was standing right there waiting for her to hand me your tickets. It was flat-out weird." Finished, Hayley looked at Jessica's computer screen. "What's going on?"

Jessica turned back to her computer and hit the play button.

The shadow of the girl in the video, Lizzy noticed, quickly forgetting the whole Jane/Melbourne drama, was holding what looked like a fisted hand to the man's face.

The man was about five foot ten and thin. Whatever the girl had held to his face caused him to drop to the ground. He rolled around, using his shirt to rub at his eyes.

"She must have used mace," Lizzy said.

"Yeah," Jessica agreed.

"Or pepper spray," Hayley added. "It's much more painful."

Lizzy looked at Hayley.

Hayley lifted her hands in question. "What?"

"What do you think she's doing now?" Jessica asked, still staring at the screen.

"Who knows? It's probably a fake," Hayley said. "Kids cut school and spend their days making this kind of shit. Everybody wants their two minutes of fame on the Internet."

Lizzy watched Hayley head for the file room. She tried not to worry. She didn't want to mother the girl, but Hayley didn't look right—she looked tired and maybe even angry.

"This isn't a fake," Jessica called out. "You have to watch the whole thing. Lizzy, what do you think the girl is doing to that man?"

"I don't know," Lizzy said, "but why hasn't the video person put down his or her iPhone and called the cops?"

Lizzy didn't like what she was seeing. The girl in the video was now sitting on top of the man. She was straddling him, holding him to the ground. The girl jerked up the man's shirt and pulled an object, possibly a knife, from beneath her skirt. Using her knees to keep his arms pinned to the ground, she proceeded to mark him or cut him or maybe even write something on his chest. It was hard to tell.

The guy was obviously crying out for help, but he appeared to be too wasted to get away. None of it made sense. "We need to call the police."

"No need," Jessica told her. "According to the comments, this video has already been all over the news. The police were called. In fact, they received several calls last night, but the girl and this guy were both gone by the time the police arrived."

"The police must have taken their sweet time," Lizzy said, frustrated. "I mean come on, look at that guy. If I had to guess, the way she's straddling him and the way he's trying to get free, I'd say she was carving a pumpkin."

Disgusted, Lizzy headed back for her desk. "Any word on the other two men?"

"The bigger man was handcuffed to the bus stop bench. He had ecstasy on him and was arrested on drug charges. The other guy, the second one to disappear in the video, hasn't been identified or found. No witnesses have come forward other than the person who posted the video to the Internet."

"Very sad," Lizzy said before calling Hayley back into the room for a quick meeting.

The video was done. Jessica swiveled in her chair so she was facing Lizzy.

Hayley took her usual position on the edge of the desk she shared with Jessica.

Meow.

Lizzy bent down and picked up the kitten. "First, I'd like you both to meet Rumpelstiltskin."

Jessica made a face. "Are you serious? Is that the poor thing's name?"

Lizzy kissed the kitty and held her closer to her chest. "What's wrong with Rumpelstiltskin?"

"Have you read the fairy tale?" Jessica asked. "It's about a selfish, horrid little man who wants to take the queen's daughter from her. You can't name that cute kitty Rumpelstiltskin."

"It's just a fairy tale," Hayley pointed out.

Jessica turned on her. "Would you want to be named Rumpelstiltskin?"

"I'm not a kitten," Hayley said. "But sure, call me Rumpelstiltskin if you'd like. I've been called worse."

"No bickering in the office," Lizzy said. "First I need to know what's going on with the lead you got from Theodore Johnson."

"I talked to a woman who is on the committee for Burning Man," Hayley said. "The woman told me that from 1986 to 1989 the event was more of a bonfire ritual. She said she'd try to find a list of people in charge and then get back to me."

"Great. Let me know when she calls."

Hayley nodded.

"I need to talk to you both about babysitting this weekend," Lizzy went on. "You both agreed to watch Brittany, but I wanted to double-check and make sure you would both be there. I have to pick up Cathy in an hour. We'll leave all of our contact info at Cathy's house, but I need your assurance that you'll both stay at the house with Brittany."

"It's not a problem," Jessica said. "I'm happy to do it."

"I have a few things I need to do," Hayley said, "but I'll be there for the most part."

"What is it exactly that you have to do?" Jessica asked, trying to keep her annoyance to a minimum.

"I don't think that's any of your business."

"Well, I just—"

"Girls," Lizzy said, interrupting Jessica and stopping either one from saying anything more. "Hayley, can you please stay in for one weekend? It would make me feel better about things if you could do that."

"Fine. I'll stay in."

Lizzy set the kitten on the ground. "I also need you guys to watch Rumpelstiltskin."

"I'm allergic to cats," Hayley said.

"Figures," Jessica muttered.

Hayley turned and headed for the file room.

"Hayley, one more thing."

Hayley swiveled around until she was facing Lizzy again.

"This Monday night you and I are scheduled to teach a defense class to young women at Oakmont High School. Are you still available?"

"I'll be there," she said before she continued to the file room.

"How do you work with that girl?" Jessica asked Lizzy, her voice low. "She's temperamental and stubborn. She refuses to work as a team."

"She's a hard worker," Lizzy said. "Not only does she complete every job I give her, she does everything with passion. She goes above and beyond. Not unlike someone else I know."

Jessica shrugged. "It's your investigative company."

Lizzy hid a smile as she set the kitten on the ground and watched her wobble around until she found the rubber band she'd given her earlier to play with. She rolled onto her back, swatting the rubber band, lost in her own little world. If only life could be so simple and carefree.

CHAPTER 23

REMEMBERING SPIDERMAN

Hayley had plans tonight. And they didn't include babysitting. Lizzy had put the pressure on her to keep an eye on Brittany as a favor for all Cathy had done for her, but Hayley knew that Brittany wasn't the only one Lizzy wanted her to watch over. Jessica might be in her twenties, but she possessed the naïveté of someone much younger.

"OK," Jessica said in an overly cheerful voice as she rubbed her hands together. "What should we do? Make cupcakes?"

Brittany spoke first. "I'm trying to lose a few pounds—"

"Gotcha," Jessica said, cutting her off. "Then how about a game of Trivial Pursuit or Scrabble?"

One glance from Brittany told Hayley that it was time to step in. Hayley had been living with Brittany long enough to know that the look meant: *save me.*

"I can't remember the last time I had a cupcake," Hayley told Jessica. "Do you really know how to make them?"

Jessica looked skeptical until Brittany jumped on the bandwagon. "I guess I am sort of hungry. Do you know how to make bran muffins or some sort of healthy cupcake?"

Jessica snapped her fingers. "I know just the thing. Do you guys mind if I run to the store? I'll only be a minute."

"It's OK with me," Brittany said before she turned back to whatever show she was watching on television.

It took Hayley a minute to realize Jessica's gaze was focused on her, as if Hayley would care if she disappeared for the rest of the night. Although Hayley was eager to take off, despite telling Lizzy she would stay in, she shrugged and said, "Knock yourself out."

After Jessica was gone and the house was quiet again, Hayley sat on the other end of the couch from Brittany and stared blankly at the television screen. She had too much on her mind right now to focus on what show was on or what the actors were saying. Judging by the fake audience laughter it was a comedy. But then why, she wondered, did Brittany look so sad?

Although she'd never been the touchy-feely-talk-about-your-problems sort of person, Hayley found herself saying, "Everything OK at school?"

A few seconds passed before Brittany glanced her way. "Yeah, why?"

"You've been quiet lately. And now that jabbermouth is gone, I thought maybe we could talk."

Brittany picked at a thumbnail. "I wish you didn't move out."

"I didn't want to," Hayley said. Lizzy didn't know she was living on the streets. Cathy thought she'd moved in with her aunt, a well-thought-out fabrication on Hayley's part.

"Mom said you've been up to no good."

Silence.

"Is that true? Are you up to no good?"

Hayley refused to lie to Brittany. They had been through too much. "I don't sleep well. And when I can't sleep, I need to get outside and breathe in fresh air. I almost always end up walking too far. Before I know it, it's three in the morning and I'm still out wandering the streets." That much was true.

"I can't sleep either."

Hayley turned all the way toward Brittany, her right foot tucked under her left leg. "Maybe it will help if you talk about it." Hayley didn't believe that, not for a minute, but that's what Linda Gates, the therapist, always said. Besides, talking about things probably couldn't make matters worse.

"I climb into bed," Brittany said, "shut my eyes, and most nights I see blood. Lots of blood. Your blood."

Brittany wasn't looking at her, and Hayley had to strain to hear every word. She wasn't sure if Brittany was finished, and she didn't want to stop her from getting it all out, so Hayley waited.

"Do you remember when Spider—I mean *he* was going to slice off your middle finger?" Brittany asked, glancing at Hayley to see if she was listening.

Hayley nodded. She knew Brittany didn't like to say or hear the name Spiderman because Cathy had told Lizzy, who then told Hayley. Hayley liked Cathy Warner. She had a good heart, and she meant well, but Cathy wasn't a say-it-like-it-is kind of person like Lizzy. That was Hayley's favorite thing about Lizzy. She never held back. She said what was on her mind, didn't make everyone guess what she was thinking or feeling. If Lizzy didn't like something, you knew it. If she was proud of you for a job well done, she told you.

"When he put the knife to your finger," Brittany went on, her voice a little louder than before, "I screamed as loud as I could. I remember squeezing my eyes shut as tight as possible. I didn't want to see him hurt you just to get to me. I thought he'd done it, too. I thought he'd cut off your other finger."

He *had* cut Hayley's middle finger, but not clean through, only enough to make it bleed like a motherfucker. The doctors had been able to save her middle finger, so now she was missing only her pinky.

"And that's what I see," Brittany said, "every single night after I shut my eyes."

"You see the blood?" Hayley asked.

"No, I see your bloodied, sliced-off finger lying on the floor. That's all I see. Just a bloodied finger."

"My finger has healed incredibly well. You'll be glad to know that it's in perfect working condition and I've gotten a lot of use out of it in the past few months." Hayley held up her hand and flipped Brittany the bird. "It's not pretty, but it does the job."

Brittany gave her a tight, slightly forced smile. Not the laugh Hayley had been going for.

"I'm not trying to make fun of your nightmares, Brittany, but I think you need to understand that *we*—me and you," she said, waving a finger between them, "are the lucky ones. Spiderman was evil. And now Spiderman is dead. I'm not going to tell you to just 'let it go' because that's too fucking easy to say and too fucking hard to actually do. But just between *me* and *you* and nobody else, I'm telling you to forget about him. That asshole could have taken all five of my fingers and I'd still be sitting here telling you the same thing. Every single time you shut your eyes and see my bloodied digit, I want you to think about your aunt Lizzy. For months, she watched that asshole torture innocent people. Those girls weren't lucky like us. Don't you see? It's up to us to live for them. Otherwise we might as well be dead too. Life is too fucking short, the biggest cliché in the book of clichés, but it's the one I tell myself every time the bad thoughts start floating to the top of my brain. Eight fingers, nine fingers, it doesn't matter. Don't let Spiderman take anything away from you. Absofuckinglutely nothing."

A few moments of silence passed between them before Hayley said, "I didn't plan on having this talk with you tonight, but I did find something a few weeks ago that I've been meaning to give you."

Hayley went to where her backpack lay near the door. She shuffled through the contents and pulled out a picture she'd cut out of a magazine. She walked back to the couch, handed the two-inch-by-two-inch picture to Brittany and waited for a response.

Hayley had expected to see a confused look, maybe even a hurt look, but she never expected to see the smile that she got in return when Brittany finally looked up at her.

"I heard that that was your favorite movie before all of the shit hit the fan around here."

Brittany nodded, her gaze once again pinned on the Spider-man picture—the real Spider-man with Tobey Maguire hanging in the middle of nowhere right before the famous kiss scene.

"The next time you think of Spiderman," Hayley said, "I want you to think of that picture. Don't let the asshole take anything away from you. Those memories you have of Peter and Mary and that stupid upside-down kiss, no matter how lame, are yours to keep. We're smart people, Brittany."

Brittany looked at her again.

Hayley smiled. "So let's be smart."

* * *

"I didn't know we were going to hike," Lizzy complained.

Cathy chuckled. "I sort of figured it out when I saw hiking boots on the list of what we were supposed to bring."

"Well, I guess that explains why you've always been called the smart one in the family."

Cathy looked over her shoulder at Lizzy. "Good thing that woman hired you to look for her missing sister. Otherwise, you'd still be sitting in your office sucking down pastries and Rice Krispies Treats. It's a wonder you never gain any weight."

Lizzy's attention fell on Melbourne as he waited for them to catch up to the group. He was in his element today, Lizzy thought. "Your body is a temple," he was saying as they approached. "This hike today will determine if you have the drive to succeed in life."

"Is he serious?" Cathy whispered.

Lizzy nodded.

Standing ramrod-straight, Melbourne wore a pair of lightweight nylon cargo shorts with lots of pockets and a dark polyester T-shirt that fully outlined every hard-earned muscle on his body. He didn't have an ounce of fat on him.

A bandanna circled his large neck, and on his head, he wore a beige hat with an upturned brim and chinstrap that made him look much too serious to be leading a beginner's group.

"Everybody has their water?" Without giving anyone a chance to answer, he waved his hand onward. "Come on, people, it's time to go. I hike at my pace, so try to keep up if you can."

A woman raised a hand. "This is my first hike. If I lose sight of you, how will I know which way to go?"

Good question, Lizzy thought.

"Follow the markers," he said matter-of-factly, "and watch out for rattlesnakes."

Cathy's eyes widened.

Another woman began to run to keep up with their fearless leader.

It wasn't long before Lizzy and Cathy were trailing behind. With every thigh-burning step up the mountain, Lizzy could feel her resolve melt away like snow on the faraway mountaintops. She was out of breath. "Can you believe that guy?"

Cathy shook her head. "He expects way too much out of people. He's lost half the group already and I don't think he cares."

"It's a good thing Andrea Kramer is paying me big bucks to get in shape," Lizzy said, "since I'm obviously not going to get a chance to talk to the man today. What a joke."

Cathy waited for Lizzy to catch up. "There isn't one person you've talked to that has any clue where her sister might be?"

Lizzy paused to catch her breath. "Nope. It seems Diane hardly has any friends. Nobody knows where she might have gone. How sad is that?"

"It's horrible, and it makes me think of Hayley. Good thing Hayley has people like you and her aunt who care about her."

Lizzy drank some water. "What are you talking about?"

"Hayley said she talked to you about moving in with her aunt."

Lizzy shook her head. "I have no clue what you're talking about. Hayley isn't living with you?"

"She moved out on Wednesday. She said she was going to stay with her aunt for a while. She made the decision less than twenty-four hours after I told her I had a problem with her disappearing in the wee hours of the night."

"She doesn't have an aunt. What were you thinking?"

Cathy arched a brow. "Don't even think about putting this on me. I took Hayley in because she helped Brittany. I am pinching pennies right now, but I lent her my car and I bought her clothes and food. I still lend her my car whenever I'm not using it. I rarely asked her to help out around the house, other than unloading and loading the dishwasher every once in a while. That's it. And then I talk to her about her wandering the streets in the middle of the night and she tells me a day later she's moving out. I asked her if she talked to you and she said she had. I asked her to leave me her aunt's name, address, and telephone number too."

"Did she give you an address?"

Cathy nodded. "It's at home in the kitchen drawer where I keep my address book."

"Crap."

"What is going on? I thought you were going to talk to her."

Lizzy sighed. "I was, but things have gotten out of hand lately. Between Jared letting the neighbor name our kitten and exercising every day and having too much to do, I'm feeling overwhelmed. And now Hayley. And this," she said, plopping to the ground and waving her hands toward the hills. "I have piles of paperwork at the office, and yet here I am."

"Look around you," Cathy said. "It's beautiful. We should have done this a long time ago."

Lizzy looked out at the wilderness. They had spent the morning hiking through lush forests and now they were on a ridgeline overlooking a lake and meadows covered with wildflowers. "You're right. It's beautiful. But I'm not here to enjoy the beauty around me or breathe in the fresh air or to find myself. I'm here because there is a young woman missing. She's out there right now, possibly wondering if anyone is looking for her. Her sister is up to her elbows in kids and a husband. Right now it seems I'm all Diane has. How fucked up is that?"

Cathy wore a large brim hat, long-sleeved shirt, and heavy backpack. Her stance was that of a true hiker as she looked out over the mountain ridge. She inhaled deeply and then gave a subtle nod of her head. "It's not fucked up at all," she said matter-of-factly. "I'm the one who has my priorities all messed up. You have a purpose in life, a calling. And you're good at it. You're the most caring person I know. You care about everyone you've ever met. You see the good in everybody. I'll never understand you, but don't ever stop caring, Lizzy. If I was the one missing, I'd feel pretty darn safe knowing you were out there looking for me."

Her speech was followed by a long pause. It wasn't often that Cathy complimented or praised Lizzy.

"Come on," Cathy said with a wave of her hiking stick. "Let's do this. Let's get to the top of Mount Tallac and find out what Melbourne knows about Diane Kramer."

CHAPTER 24

BABYSITTERS SUCK

Brittany Warner decided that having two babysitters was even worse than being stuck at home under the watchful eye of her own mother. "Did my mom give either of you the password to my computer?" Brittany asked her babysitters.

Both Hayley and Jessica shook their heads.

Hayley was staring at the television, but Brittany was pretty sure she wasn't watching whatever was on. She thought of Hayley as a big sister, but Hayley lived in her own little world for the most part. She was smart; so smart, Brittany figured, that she was a genius, the sort of genius that was borderline insane. "Can one of you drop me off at my friend Kristin Kilarski's house?"

Hayley didn't bother responding this time.

Jessica held her cell phone to her ear, shook her head again, and mouthed the word *no* for good measure.

"I thought you two were cool. Well, at least I thought Hayley was cool," Brittany amended.

Jessica scowled and put her phone against her chest so whomever she was talking to couldn't hear. "I'm cooler than her."

"Then prove it by dropping me off at Kristin's house."

Jessica told the caller she would call back. Then she crossed her arms over her chest. "You're a tricky one, Brittany Warner, but it's not going to work. I'm not going to lose my job just so you can hang out with your friends. For one weekend, Hayley and I are the best friends you've ever had, so grab a bran muffin and have a seat."

"Can I borrow your phone at least?"

"No way."

Hayley held her cell phone out for Brittany to use. "No long distance calls, OK?"

"Thanks!" Brittany grabbed the phone and disappeared in the other room.

"You shouldn't baby her so much."

"Lending her my phone is babying her?"

"Didn't you read the note that Cathy left? Brittany is grounded. She went to a movie after school without telling anyone. Can you imagine what Mrs. Warner must have been thinking while she was looking for her daughter?"

Jessica didn't give Hayley a chance to respond. She just kept talking. "Six months ago Brittany was kidnapped by a madman."

"I know. I was there."

"You really are a bitch."

"Why? Because I was there?"

"You know that's not why. It's because you go out of your way to take sides against me whenever you can."

Hayley smiled.

"Why is that funny?"

"Because you think everything is about you."

"I do not."

"You do, Jessica. I have never once formed an opinion based solely on disagreeing with you. You're the one who has a problem with me. Not the other way around."

"Then why do you roll your eyes every time I come up with an idea?" Jessica wanted to know.

"Because most of your ideas are lame."

"Like what? Name one idea I've had that's lame."

"The Going Green Project for Lizzy's office."

"It bothers you that I care about the earth?"

"It's the way you go about doing things…trying to force your ideas down everyone else's throats."

"Wow. OK. I'll remember that. Anything else?"

"You really want to know?"

"I'm asking, aren't I?"

"That's true, you are asking for this," Hayley said. "Stop talking to Lizzy about me behind my back."

Jessica's face flushed. "Are you spying on us?"

"Yeah, I'm spying on you, JessicASS, because everything you say is so fucking riveting."

"What did you just call me?"

"Jessica. Isn't that your name?"

Jessica's eyes were tiny slits now. "What else?"

"I don't think you can handle the truth."

"Very funny," Jessica said since they were just now getting to the end of *A Few Good Men*.

"You try so hard to be Miss Goody Two-Shoes," Hayley went on. "It's fucking annoying."

"Well, you swear too much, trying so hard to be such a bad ass."

Hayley sighed. "The difference between me and you," Hayley said, "is that I didn't ask you what you thought about me because I don't care what you think."

Brittany stepped in the room just then, her eyes big and round, her face pale.

Hayley came to her feet. "What's wrong?"

"Somebody is crawling around outside Mom's room."

"Stay here with Jessica."

"You can't go out there," Jessica said when she saw Hayley move toward the sliding glass door and unlock the bottom latch.

"I'll be right back."

Jessica and Brittany stood huddled by the door, peering out through the glass into the dark, listening and waiting.

* * *

The lodge where Cathy and Lizzy were staying was average on all counts: food, entertainment, décor. A pair of snowshoes decorated the wall. There was a table with two chairs, a television, all the standard things you would find in a hotel room, but the best part was the view: tall pines and blue skies.

The two sisters were already tucked into separate and equally uncomfortable twin beds. The lights were out, yet neither of them had fallen asleep.

"Did you see how innocent Melbourne looked when I asked him about Diane Kramer?"

"He looked innocent because he is innocent," Cathy answered. "He said he knew her and that he'd talked to the police and that he was worried about her whereabouts. He wasn't trying to hide anything."

"Wow, love really is blind."

Cathy chuckled in the dark. "To tell you the truth, I didn't like the way he wouldn't allow anyone to rest during the hike. He pushes people too hard. Everyone is at different levels, and this was supposed to be a beginner's retreat. That was a tough mountain. I don't know how you did it."

"I didn't even make it three-quarters of the way up. Sorry I stopped you from seeing the view from the top."

"Don't be silly. But that's exactly what I'm talking about. Half the people on the trail today didn't make it to the top, but did that stop Mr. Perfect from heading onward and upward without looking back? I appreciate his passion, but he's a workhorse and he expects too much out of people. Despite all of that, I still think he's innocent."

"I don't know. When I asked him about Diane, just for an instant I saw a flash of anger pass through his eyes. It was subtle, but it was there."

"How would you feel if the police had talked to you, the girl's sister talked to you, and now your brand new client and number one fan are talking to you about Diane? Personally I would be a little perturbed."

Damn. She had a point. "Do you mind if we leave a little earlier than planned tomorrow?"

"No, not at all. I wasn't going to tell you, but I'm meeting with Richard tomorrow night. He's taking Brittany and me out to dinner."

Lizzy couldn't believe what she was hearing. "You're not letting your ex-husband back into your life after everything he did to you, are you?"

"No, of course not."

"I understand if you're lonely, Cathy, but do not go to dinner with Richard. Sign up for Match.com or Fish in the Sea or whatever it's called…something, anything but Richard."

"He made a mistake. People make mistakes, remember?"

"Yes, I know people make mistakes. Sometimes they make them over and over and over again. But he was never right for you. You married him for all the wrong reasons. You said so yourself. So why in the world would you even go to dinner with him? I bet you a million bucks his new girlfriend saw right through his narcissistic shit and dumped him like a hot potato!" Lizzy was glad her sister couldn't see her face in the dark.

"For starters," Cathy said matter-of-factly, "he's the father of my daughter. We've been through a lot together. And there was a time when I did love him."

"When? Why? How?"

"Cut me a break, Lizzy. The divorce will be final in a few weeks. I'm not going to do anything crazy, OK?"

"OK."

"I'm tired. I'm going to sleep."

"Good night," Lizzy said. "I love you."

"Love you too."

* * *

"Oh my God! Let him go!" Jessica shouted from the door. She left Brittany's side and ran outside to where Hayley was using her knee to hold a man to the ground. "Is that a knife in your hand? Do you carry that thing around wherever you go?"

"You know this loser?" Hayley asked.

"His name is Casey. Let him go. Now!"

Hayley took her knee out of his stomach and slid her knife back into the leather sheath fastened under her pant leg.

"What is that thing wrapped around your leg?" Jessica asked.

"It's nothing." Hayley took a good, long look at the guy. He didn't look like Jessica's type. In fact, the idea of Jessica dating at all didn't compute. She took a whiff of the man. "Have you been drinking?"

"Leave him alone." Jessica bent down next to Casey. "Are you all right?"

He sat up.

He was fine. "Why don't you ask your dipshit friend why he's lurking around Cathy Warner's backyard? I think that's the question we need answered."

"I think you need to mind your own business," Jessica told her.

"The side gate was open, and I could have sworn I saw somebody," Casey said as he put a hand to his throat. "Maybe I should leave."

"I think that's the best idea I've heard all night," Hayley agreed.

Jessica pointed at the house while she looked at Hayley. "Go away," she said. "You've done enough."

"He's been drinking," Hayley said. "I don't want him coming inside." Hayley headed for the house where she could see Brittany standing at the door.

* * *

Jessica and Casey came to their feet. "That's the girl I've been telling you about."

"I guess you left out the part about her being crazy."

"She's not crazy," Jessica said in Hayley's defense, but even as she said the words, she wasn't so sure. "And you never told me you were coming over."

He shrugged. "I swear I saw someone back here. I thought maybe it was you and your friend." He looked toward the tall, dark trees in the corner of the yard. "I didn't know your friend kept watch and carried knives."

"She's not my friend."

Casey raked a hand through his long, tangled hair. Her brother had introduced her to him a few months ago. Casey was twenty-five years old, and he had a full-time job at a grocery outlet. The few times they talked, he'd made her laugh. He did smell like beer, she thought, but she hadn't known him for very long and she didn't want to scare him off too soon by mentioning it. Jessica rubbed her arms. "If she tells Mrs. Warner and Lizzy that you were here, I could lose my job."

"I wouldn't worry about it," he said. "If she's smart, she won't say a word. Not unless she wants everyone to know she carries knives in weird Rambo-like homemade sheaths. That's one crazy chick," he muttered under his breath.

Jessica sighed. "You better go. I need to get back inside."

He didn't waste any time taking off, heading back the same way he'd come. "I'll give you a call sometime."

She watched him leave, figuring another one bit the dust.

CHAPTER 25

STARVING TO DEATH

Sierra Mountains, Day 61

Vivian stood and waited for the dizziness to pass before making her way to the kitchen. She knew she needed to eat, but she was no longer hungry.

For anything.

Even the thought of eating pumpkin spice cupcakes with cream cheese frosting made her want to puke.

Three weeks had passed since Melbourne's last visit. The moment he left the cabin, she'd allowed herself liquids only, which included chicken broth. She also spent three to four hours a day on the treadmill.

Melbourne seriously seemed to think he was doing her a favor. According to Melbourne, the contract she signed had some sort of no-backing-out clause. She didn't recall reading anything of the sort, but that was water under the bridge. There was nothing she could do about any of that now.

Unless she could escape, she might just be another missing person on a milk carton. Her only hope would be if somebody talked to her mother. Although she and her mother rarely talked, she had called her mom before she left to come here. In case something really bad had happened to Diane, she wanted at least one other person to know where she was. She even mentioned Anthony Melbourne's name. Her mother was her only hope.

For many years now, Vivian had done everything she could to make sure people stayed away from her, including paying her rent in advance. Her landlord knew better than to bother her; the few times he had tried, she'd given him a piece of her mind.

Karma, Vivian thought, karma had come back to bite her in the ass.

As they often did, her thoughts drifted back to Diane. Had Diane been here?

Vivian had spent hours every day looking for clues, but so far she'd come up empty-handed. It was hard to tell if anyone had ever stayed here before.

Melbourne was definitely a neat freak. If he touched something, he wiped it clean afterward, and then squeezed hand sanitizer onto his palms and rubbed his hands together for way too long. Melbourne had cleaned the insides of the appliances and the top of the cupboards when he was here last. He was a busy man. Why didn't he have people do that for him? Unless nobody but Jane, his minion, knew about this cabin and what went on here.

Melbourne had seemed a little too excited when he took her measurements. Not excited in a perverted way, though. Obsessed would be the word she would use to describe his actions: obsessed with cleanliness and obsessed with her measurements and weight.

Although he'd seemed excited about her weight loss, he didn't look at her with longing or desire. But that didn't mean he wasn't strange. He was an odd duck all right. She figured he might suffer from some form of OCD since he obviously had an unhealthy fear of germs.

Vivian set the can of chicken broth on the counter. When she turned to get the can opener, something happened. She looked down at her foot and saw that it had nearly come out of the cuff. She let out a whoop of joy and then grabbed the chain and walked quickly back into the main room.

Sitting on the edge of the pull-out bed, she propped her ankle on her knee and began to work the cuff, pushing and twisting.

Afraid she might break her foot, she let up some and gently tugged at the cuff. She was so close.

Butter, she thought. She needed butter!

Recalling the bottle of vegetable oil, she went to the pantry, unscrewed the lid, and poured half the bottle in and around the cuff.

The thought that today might actually be the day she would escape made her try harder. Holding tight to the cuff around her ankle, she pushed as hard as she could.

It slid right off! She was free!

For the next thirty seconds, she stood inside the pantry, dumbfounded. Seconds passed before she finally took a few steps. Walking felt strange without a chain attached to her foot. She went to the kitchen and used a towel to wipe the oil from her foot.

At the realization that she was truly free, she walked back to the bed and hopped onto the lumpy mattress. She jumped up and down, making the hinges creak in protest. Next, she ran to the treadmill, set it on seven, and ran for the first time ever.

Finished with the treadmill, she looked around, a madwoman let loose. It took another minute or two before she could finally sit down and calm herself.

Think, Vivian, think.

What would she need to bring with her? The extra-long T-shirt she was wearing was all she had.

Giddy with joy and insanely lightheaded, she hurried to the wall that was covered with fabric; a wall she'd never been able to reach with the chain around her ankle. She yanked at the corner of the fabric and the sheet fell to a heap on the floor, leaving Vivian to stare at her reflection in the floor-to-ceiling mirror.

She stepped closer.

The billions of neurons in her brain were unable to register that the person looking back at her was Vivian Hardy, the same girl she'd been looking at for thirty years.

There were no other mirrors in the cabin. Not even in the bathroom. This was the first time she was seeing herself in a long while, maybe the first time ever, since she couldn't remember the last time she'd taken a good, long look at herself.

She raised a hand to her face and brushed her fingertips over her chin and neck. The long T-shirt she wore ended at her knees. Her calves looked small. Every few years she ordered a new pair of boots, but she always had to send them back because she could never get them zipped over her calves.

She lifted the T-shirt as high as she could without taking it off, unable to believe what she was seeing. Her stomach looked so much flatter. She was no Cindy Crawford, but as far as Vivian was concerned, she was close.

Moving to the bathroom, she looked at the scale as if it was a fiery dragon she'd come to conquer. She stepped on it and watched the numbers flicker up and down.

Tears trickled down her face as she looked at her feet and remembered the day she'd considered sawing off her foot in order to escape. She hadn't been able to go through with it, of course. Thank God.

The numbers on the scale stopped moving. She weighed 197 pounds. Under 200 pounds. Impossible. That would mean she had lost 103 pounds.

No way.

In a daze, she left the bathroom.

She walked into the main room and looked around before heading for the bedside table. She picked up her journal and held it close to her chest.

It would be hot outside. She had a dingy pair of slippers but no shoes. She went to the pantry and filled a plastic bag with bottled waters. As she collected what she needed for her hike down the mountain, a rattling sound caught her attention.

She stopped what she was doing and listened closely.

Someone was at the door.

It couldn't be Melbourne. She had another week before he was due to show up.

Setting the bag on the pantry floor, she ran back to the bed, grabbed the cuff and chain and covered the bottom half of her body with blankets. She feigned a look of boredom as the door came open.

* * *

Hayley stood front and center inside the gym at Oakmont High. The big, round clock on the wall told her it was a few minutes past 7:00 p.m. There were at least twenty girls in attendance. Not bad for a Monday night.

Lizzy sat in a chair at the side of the room. She was the finisher, the one who would teach the girls a few classic moves.

"If somebody comes up from behind and grabs you," Hayley told the class, "do not hesitate to turn and knee him in the groin. You want to scream out too. The faster you react, the better chance you have of catching your assailant off guard."

Hayley pointed to the girl in the front who was raising her hand.

"What if I'm so scared that I freeze up and I can't move?"

"That's why you want to practice at home as often as you can. I know it's scary and that no amount of training or practice is going to take the fear out of the situation if it happens to you, but if you are always aware, nobody can catch you completely off guard, and that's half the battle. Knowing what you're going to do will give you an extra few seconds. And those few seconds will allow you to be proactive."

Hayley heard the door to the gym open. She wouldn't have paid the sound any mind at all if all of the girls in attendance weren't staring that way—some giggling, a few looking shyly toward the floor.

"Girls," Lizzy said with a clap of her hands. "I'd like you all to meet our surprise guest for the night, Tommy Ellis."

What was the big deal? Hayley wondered. He was a preppy boy, a preppy boy with dark hair and bangs that swept across his forehead. He was about five foot eleven and slender. Overall, he looked like a dork.

Lizzy led him to the front of the gym where Hayley was forced to shake his hand.

Slender fingers for a boy. Clammy to the touch. Dork.

He smiled. She didn't.

He didn't waste any time stealing the limelight. Turning toward the girls in the gym, he clasped his hands together and smiled brightly. "At the Self-Defense Institute," he began, "we want you to feel empowered by the time you leave our first class. That doesn't mean we want you to feel overconfident. It means you leave our classes knowing something about *awareness* and *prevention*. The more prepared you are, the less likely you'll need to be prepared. It's like buying life insurance. Once you buy it, you no longer need it."

He laughed, but the kids in the class were too young to have ever thought about buying life insurance. Hayley shook her head. Dork.

"Criminals," he continued, "have a built-in motivation to go after you. It's called desire. Once they're on the prowl, all they need to do is find a target. Do you think a criminal is going to go after the girl with her head down, a girl who is texting her friend? Or will he go after the girl whose head is up, alert, keys in hand?"

"Girl who is texting," many said at once.

"That's right. And don't get me wrong. We're not trying to *scare* you; we're trying to *prepare* you. The most important thing you need to remember is that you don't ever want to be caught off guard."

Said that already, Hayley thought, but kept it to herself. His little talk was getting redundant.

"Keep your head up," Tommy added. "Walk with intent. Know where you're headed. If you drive and you have a set of keys, keep your keys grasped between your fingers, ready to poke out an eye if you need to. Got it?"

Most of the girls nodded. A few looked bored—no one more than Hayley. And that's when Dorky Boy turned to face her as if he could read her mind. "Hayley, right?"

"That's right."

"Could you come here?" He pointed to the space in front of him.

Hayley obliged by coming forward.

"If you're walking in an unlit and secluded area, are your chances better or worse as far as being approached by a stranger?"

"Worse."

"That's right. *Risk*," he said to the girls. "Don't put yourself in situations where the risk is too great. If you find yourself in that situation, be—" He pointed at Hayley and waited for her to fill in the blank.

Not only was he a dork, he was a very annoying dork. "Be aware," she finished with as much enthusiasm as she could muster for Lizzy's sake.

"That's right," he said excitedly as if these girls were five instead of fifteen. "It's not about winning. It's about staying alive. If a criminal takes your purse, let them have it and run the other way. If, for some reason, you are forced to fight back, then remember that there are *no* rules. Use your fingers to poke eyes, bite anything you can get your teeth around, and pull hair. Best thing to do?"

He pointed to a girl raising her hand in the back.

"Kick him in the nuts," she said, which was automatically followed by laughter.

"That's right, except for one thing. Hayley, do you mind?"

Hayley raised a skeptical brow. "You want me to kick you in the nuts?"

More laughter.

"Go for it," he said.

And Hayley did without hesitation. She went for it. He was annoying and she couldn't wait to put him in his place. Instead of going for his groin, though, she went for his leg, wrapping her leg around his. She had him to the ground in three seconds flat.

"Impressive," he said as he looked up at her, his voice low enough so he couldn't be heard. "I guess I should have used one of the girls from the audience."

"Might have been a good idea." She held out her hand and helped pull him to his feet.

"OK," he said, laying on the charm as he turned to the younger girls. "What just happened was all part of my plan."

A few giggles erupted. Most of the girls weren't sure whether he was joking, which he was.

"Those moves that Hayley just used on me are for the more advanced. With lots of practice," he said, giving Hayley a funny look, "that's what you'll all be shooting for."

"So who wants to be my next guinea pig? I need a volunteer, somebody who's never had the chance to kick a guy in the groin."

Fifty percent of the hands in the room shot up. A couple of girls jumped up and down, hoping to be picked.

"You," he said, pointing to the youngest girl in attendance.

"She's probably ten years old," Hayley whispered behind him.

"Thanks, but I'm not taking any chances this time."

Hayley smiled, despite herself.

* * *

Class was over and Lizzy needed to take off, but first she needed to talk to Hayley, so she called her over. Lizzy smiled as Hayley approached. "Thanks for coming tonight. You did great as always, and I want you to know that I really appreciate the way you worked with Tommy."

"Not a problem."

"I think he likes you."

"Who?"

"Tommy Ellis."

"You're shittin' me, right?"

Lizzy let the curse word go. Hayley had improved tenfold since Lizzy had met her less than a year ago. "I'm serious," Lizzy said. "Look at him."

They both glanced his way. Tommy smiled at them before returning his attention to what he was doing. He was sitting at a table they had set up, and kids were introducing him to their parents and trying to get them to sign up for his weekly classes.

"He's a great guy," Lizzy went on. "He's only twenty years old and already part owner of the Self-Defense Institute in Roseville."

"That's great. Are you trying to marry me off or something?"

Lizzy laughed. "Never mind. Forget I said anything."

"Will do."

Lizzy shook her head. The girl was as stubborn as a mule. "There is one more thing I need to talk to you about before I go."

Hayley was getting twitchy, her foot tapping. Patience was not one of Hayley's virtues.

"Cathy mentioned that you moved out to live with your aunt. As far as I know you don't have an aunt."

"True that."

"Then why did you lie to my sister?"

"Because I didn't want her to worry."

"Did Cathy ask you to move out?"

"Not in so many words, but it was obvious she didn't like me going out at night."

"Yeah, about that, what are you doing out walking around the streets of Sacramento so late at night? You know better than most that sooner rather than later you're bound to find trouble being out that late."

"Lizzy, I've been on my own for a long time now. I care about you and your sister, and I really do appreciate everything you've both done for me, but I can't keep living my life the way Cathy and you want me to live it. I'm not anything like either one of you. Your sister is great, but I was beginning to feel like a dog that's kept in one of those horrible crates. Just thinking about it gives me shivers. I don't ever want to feel trapped again. I'm sorry."

"So where are you living?"

"Nowhere in particular; here and there. Cathy still lends me her car three days a week so I can get to school and to work. Jessica has lent me her car too. I pay for my own gas. I sleep in the car if it gets chilly."

Lizzy's head dropped, her chin nearly hitting her chest.

"I'm used to it. It's really not that bad."

Lizzy lifted her head and placed a hand on Hayley's shoulder. "Move in with me."

"I thought you were moving in with Jared."

"Long story, but that's all been postponed for now. We'll talk about that later. I'm begging you, Hayley. Move in with me starting tonight."

"Oh, I don't know. I have plans tonight."

"I have an extra key in my purse," Lizzy told her. "I'll give you the key and you come in at any hour. No questions asked."

"I don't think it would work."

"Why not?"

"Because I already know that I'll come home late."

"Yeah? So?"

"You get freaked out as it is. You wouldn't be able to lock all of your dead bolts on your front door. And we both know that no matter how quiet I try to be, you'll wake up."

"OK, so?"

"You'll start making me hot chocolate or something stupid like that and I'll feel guilty that I woke you up and then you'll stagger back to your bedroom, unable to sleep for the rest of the night."

Lizzy laughed. Mostly because Hayley was absolutely right. "There's something you missed," Lizzy said.

Hayley arched a questioning brow.

"If you refuse to come live with me or you don't come to my place at all and there is no door being opened in the middle of the night, I'll be up all night worrying about you. I'm not going to sleep anyhow, so you might as well say yes and make me semi-happy."

"I can't afford to pay you rent."

"You can help me take care of Rumpelstiltskin."

"I'm allergic to cats, but either way, that's not her name any longer."

Lizzy frowned. "Who says?"

"Brittany, Jessica, and I changed her name over the weekend."

"What's my cat's name then?"

"Hannah."

"You can't be serious? My cat's name is Hannah?" That was the same name Jared's perky neighbor picked out. What were the odds?

Hayley nodded.

"Whose idea was that?"

"That lame Hannah Montana show was on, and we all went with it. All three of us agreed. Personally I don't care what you call the cat, but we took a vote."

"OK, well then, your rent will be paid by helping me take care of Hannah. You said you were allergic to cats, so you don't have to pet her. Just feed her once a day and help me change Hannah's litter box every once in a while." God, she really didn't like that name.

"OK, it's a deal," Hayley agreed. "But I can't make any promises about how long this little arrangement is going to work."

"One day at a time."

"Perfect. One day at a time."

CHAPTER 26

FRIENDS ARE FOREVER

The Mexican restaurant was crowded, which made it easy for Jessica to remain anonymous. She sat on one side of the restaurant and pretended to read a book and sip her iced mocha while she waited for Ellen Woodson to get her lunch.

After Ellen was handed an empty cup, it took her about twenty seconds to fill it with soda and exit the restaurant.

When Ellen left, Jessica followed. She had followed Ellen from the bank where Ellen worked about a mile away from the mall where they were now. Ellen usually took about an hour for lunch. Trying to get the woman alone was proving nearly impossible.

Until now.

The moment Ellen entered Macy's department store, Jessica made her move. "Hi, my name is Jessica Pleiss and I need to talk to you about Carol Fullerton."

Ellen turned on her with a wild look in her eye. "Are you kidding me? You've been following me, haven't you? I thought I saw you ten minutes ago. You're following me into a department store and asking me about my best friend? A girl who died years ago?"

"Who said she was dead?"

Ellen tried to collect herself.

Bingo. Lizzy was right. Ellen Woodson knew something about her friend's disappearance.

"I assumed," Ellen said tartly. "It's been a long time since I saw Carol. She was a very happy person. She never would have run away. Of course I assumed she was dead."

"How long?" Jessica asked.

"What?"

"How long has it been exactly since you saw your best friend?"

Flustered, Ellen started walking again and said over her shoulder, "Fifteen, maybe twenty years. I have no idea. I have things to do. I need to run."

Jessica stayed at her side. "Most people would know exactly how many years it had been since they saw their best friend."

"What do you want from me?"

Jessica was still pissed off about Hayley telling her she was afraid to interview people. And yet, Jessica realized that she was more afraid of the possibility that Hayley might be right. If Jessica wanted to be a criminologist, she was going to need to open up, be bold, fire hard questions at the right people at the right time. And sometimes, like now, she was going to have to lie if it meant cutting to the chase and getting to the bottom of things. "We have reason to believe that Carol Fullerton is alive," Jessica lied, hoping to get a reaction.

Ellen stopped walking. "What are you talking about?"

"I work for Lizzy Gardner—"

Exasperated, Ellen rolled her eyes. "I told Ms. Gardner I didn't want to get involved. It has been way too long. I don't want to open old wounds."

"What old wounds exactly?"

Ellen was on the move again. "I sold my car to Carol. I didn't fill the car up with gas. According to the investigator, she ran out of gas. How do you think that makes me feel?"

"I don't know; tell me." Another lie, Jessica realized. She'd read the file and she knew the car Carol Fullerton was driving did not run out of gas. The woman just assumed Jessica didn't do her homework.

"I won't do this," Ellen said through gritted teeth. "My life is complete shit. I refuse to make it worse by dredging up bad memories."

"Bad memories?"

Ellen Woodson was walking faster now.

Jessica had to hurry to keep up. "Why won't you talk to us?"

"Open your ears and read my lips. It happened a long time ago."

"That's why it's called a cold case, Ellen. Until this case is solved, people are going to want to talk about it."

"Leave me alone."

"Do you have children?"

"That's none of your business."

"I know that you and Carol did a lot of fun things together. You were best friends. Really, you were Carol's only friend. Why would talking about her be dredging up bad memories?"

"That's not what I meant. I feel guilty for not having gas in the car. The bad memories I have are from the moment she disappeared."

Jessica ignored her answer and stayed on her heels. "If you and Carol were so close, why would you not want to help a dying mother find her only child?"

Ellen whipped around so fast, Jessica nearly bumped into her. "Because her mother doesn't deserve to find her!"

Jessica stood speechless for exactly three seconds. "She is alive and you know where she is!"

Ellen's face flushed with color and she jogged to the nearest cash register.

Jessica ran after her. "Where can I find Carol?"

"Could you call security?" Ellen asked the salesclerk. "This woman is harassing me."

The salesclerk looked at Jessica.

Jessica held up both hands, fingers splayed. "I'm sorry. I was just asking her a few questions. No need to call security. I'm leaving."

After one last probing look into Ellen's eyes, Jessica walked away with a smile on her face. She had done it. What a thrill. And the strangest part was that she had the urge to call Hayley and tell her.

Instead, she called Lizzy.

The moment she heard Lizzy's voice on the other end of the line, Jessica said, "You're never going to believe what just happened. We definitely need to keep a close eye on Ellen Woodson. I am one hundred percent sure she knows where Carol has been hiding out."

* * *

The woman who worked the front desk at Supremacy Insurance brought Lizzy and Jessica straight into Frank's office and offered them each a glass of water that they both politely declined.

Frank Fullerton stood until they were seated.

He looked exactly as he had the first time Lizzy met him, when she and Jessica had gone to the house to speak to his wife.

If Lizzy didn't know better, she'd swear he was wearing the same wrinkled suit.

Immediately after the woman shut the door to his office, leaving the three of them alone, Frank's expression changed. His eyes went cold; his lip turned into a snarl. "You better have a damn good reason for coming to my workplace and taking up my valuable time."

"We have reason to believe your daughter is alive," Lizzy blurted.

He shook his head as he sunk even lower into the chair behind his desk. "You sound like my wife."

"She believes Carol is alive?" Lizzy asked.

He actually chuckled. "If she didn't, would she have hired you?"

"Yes, I believe she would have. Before she dies, your wife wants to know what happened to her daughter. She wants closure. I would think you would want the same thing."

"Not at the expense of spending every day for the rest of my life looking for her."

"I see."

"You don't see anything," he said.

"The truth is, Frank, you've been lying to Detective Roth since the day your daughter disappeared."

"Ridiculous."

"You told Detective Roth you walk the highway where your daughter vanished every weekend during the summer."

"That's the truth."

"But you just told me that you don't want to spend the rest of your life looking for your daughter."

"I said I don't want to spend *every single day* looking for my daughter."

"Family, friends, and volunteers," Lizzy continued, "used to help you look in the mountains near the spot where Carol went missing, looking for clues as to what happened to her."

"What about it?"

"I've talked to the volunteers, including family and friends, and they all say the same thing: that you went searching for your daughter *one* time." Lizzy leaned forward and held up one finger. "A girl is missing and her father tells the detective working the case that he walks the highway where her car was abandoned. Not once a year, not once a month, but every single weekend during every summer since she disappeared. But that's not even close to the truth. Why would you lie about that, Frank?"

"I didn't lie. There were plenty of people to look for my daughter back then. One more person wasn't going to help matters. For the past five years, I've gone out there on the weekends."

"So for the past five to ten weekends you've gone out there to look for clues, just in case something was missed?"

He nodded.

Lizzy shook her head. He'd obviously been lying about it for so long, he believed it himself. "Detective Roth has been keeping tabs on you for a few years now. He goes so far as to put a camera on the highway near the area where Carol's car was abandoned. He does that just to be sure he doesn't miss your car, should you pass by. I could understand you missing a weekend or two, but you have *never* walked the highway where your daughter disappeared. Never. Not once. And yet you're sitting here now lying to me and my assistant, trying to make us believe you're a grieving father who still looks for his daughter even after all these years. Never mind that you just told me you don't want to spend the rest of your life looking for your daughter. So which is it?"

"I think it's time for you to leave."

"Her car was abandoned," Lizzy said, ignoring him. "When the police found her car, they found some of Carol's belongings: school books, a hairbrush, and snack foods. According to friends of Carol's, she was in good spirits and had no reason to run away from her life."

"That's right. She was happy and smart and she didn't have a care in the world."

"Investigators initially operated under the theory that Carol was troubled and decided to escape from the demands of her life for a while. As a result they didn't immediately begin to look for her, but your wife was adamant about that not being the case, which is why friends and family began to search on weekends."

"Sounds about right," Frank said with a sigh.

"The official search did not begin until five days after her car was found. When the search finally got underway, helicopters, search dogs, and ground teams covered the area. The dogs picked up her scent on the highway where her car had been abandoned and lost the trail before the first exit to the national park."

"No footprints were found," Frank added. "Why are you telling me all of this? You might as well read me the entire file."

"Either Carol was picked up by someone driving on the road or she walked to the closest house to ask for help."

He raked his hands through his fake hair. "Tell me something I don't know."

"Police say they did not treat Carol's case as an abduction because they saw no signs of a struggle at the scene."

He nodded.

"Your daughter e-mailed one of her teachers and told them she'd be absent for a few days because of a death in the family. But again, family and friends—your family and friends, Frank, not mine—said no one in the family had died."

"That's right." He picked up the phone. "You've got one minute to get out of my office."

"Why did your daughter run away, Frank?"

"That's the million-dollar question."

"What did you do to her?"

Frank hung up the phone, stood, and walked out of the office.

"He's guiltier than sin," Lizzy said.

Jessica nodded. "One hundred percent."

"But why hasn't anyone else figured that out?"

"It sounds like Detective Roth knows he's lying," Jessica said.

"Roth has always been suspicious of Frank," Lizzy told her, "and has spent many weekends watching and waiting for Frank to appear near the spot where Carol's car was abandoned, but he has never used a surveillance camera."

Jessica smiled. "You're so good you're bad."

Lizzy smiled too.

"If only we could find Carol and ask her."

"Thanks to your great work today we're going to find her," Lizzy said. "If Frank won't tell us why Carol ran away, we'll just have to find Carol and ask her ourselves."

"Obviously Carol has no interest in being found," Jessica said.

"That's just too frickin' bad, isn't it?"

CHAPTER 27

PEOPLE CHANGE

The Rocklin Apartments were long and sprawling stucco buildings located near the Roseville Galleria Mall.

Lizzy knocked on apartment number 33 and waited for the occupant to open the door.

The woman who answered was definitely Debra Taphorn, the same girl in the photograph Michael Denton, the feeder, had given her. If not for the big green eyes and dimples, though, Lizzy never would have recognized her. Judging by her thin, heart-shaped face, she was literally half the person she used to be.

"Hi, I'm Lizzy Gardner, private investigator."

Debra's eyes widened. "You're the one who was abducted by that lunatic."

"Yep, that's me," Lizzy said. "I need to talk to you. Can I come in?"

Debra frowned. "I don't know. I really don't have much time. What did you say this was about?"

"I didn't, but the truth is, I need your help." Lizzy shifted her weight from one foot to the other. "It's about Diane Kramer."

"I've never heard of her."

Lizzy reached into her purse and pulled out the picture that Michael had given her of Debra when she was at his house.

Debra stared at the picture for a long moment. All color left her face. "Talk about having your past come back to haunt you. Where did you get that?"

"From Michael Denton. Can I come inside?"

"Sure." Debra moved to the side so Lizzy could enter.

Debra Taphorn's apartment was spacious and immaculately clean. The large windows provided for a lot of natural light. The walls and the furniture were shades of cream and white. Lizzy took off her shoes but realized it probably wasn't necessary since Debra was wearing heels inside. Better to play it safe and get on the woman's good side.

"Michael told me that the two of you used to be close," Lizzy said when the silence quickly became awkward.

"How well do you know Michael?" Debra asked.

"I know he's into feederism and that he used to enjoy feeding you."

"You don't beat around the bush, do you?"

"You said you didn't have much time."

"You got me there," Debra said as she gestured toward the kitchen. "Can I get you anything?"

"No thanks. I just have a few questions and then I'll leave you alone."

"Is it about Michael?" Debra asked. "Because if he said I had anything to do with him other than the food thing he's lying. I never—"

"He never insinuated that you two were an item."

Debra sighed. "Mind if I sit down?"

"Not at all."

Debra's shoulders relaxed as she moved into the main living area and took a seat on the edge of a cream-colored ottoman. "OK, why don't you tell me exactly why you're here?"

Standing near the kitchen, Lizzy stayed right where she was. "Like I said, I'm a private investigator. I've been hired to investigate a missing person. Her name is Diane Kramer."

"Never heard of her," Debra repeated, putting her hands up for emphasis. "I swear."

"I believe you, but the thing is I keep running into nothing but dead ends. That is, until I talked to Michael Denton. There is one common thread between you and Diane...Anthony Melbourne."

"Is that so?"

Lizzy nodded. Although she hated to lie, something she'd been doing a lot lately, the sudden nervous *tap tap tap* of Debra's left foot told Lizzy that she might be on to something. "My sister and I attended Anthony Melbourne's retreat at Lake Tahoe recently. I asked him about you specifically and he mentioned that you were his star pupil."

"He said that? He said my name?"

Lizzy nodded. "He was very excited about all the weight you lost. I know he helped you, Debra. I know that he's very good at what he does, but I also know he's hiding something."

"I'm not supposed to talk about it and you really shouldn't be here." Debra stood and went to the door, Lizzy's hint that it was time to leave.

Lizzy didn't move. "How did you lose the weight so fast? Michael said you lost over one hundred pounds in less than four months. Is that true?"

"I can't say."

"You won't say."

"OK, I won't say. I signed a confidentiality agreement. If I say too much, I could be sued and lose everything I've worked so hard for."

Lizzy stared the girl down. "Diane Kramer was two hundred fifty-five pounds the last time her sister saw her. Diane was obsessed with her weight and with Anthony Melbourne. If something happens to her and it has anything at all to do with Melbourne, I'll be sending the FBI to your door, Debra. The feds do not take kindly to secrets, especially secrets that could ultimately cause harm to others."

The stare down continued.

Neither of them blinked.

One thing was clear. Debra Taphorn knew something. Just spit it out, she wanted to say to the woman, but she held her tongue.

"Look," Debra finally said. "I'm sorry about the missing girl, Diane, or whatever her name is. Anthony Melbourne's program changed my life. Two nights ago my boyfriend asked me to marry him." She held up her ring finger for Lizzy to see.

Two carats, maybe three. Impressive. Lizzy had never gone diamond shopping in her life. If she couldn't even move in with Jared, it was a big possibility that diamonds were not in her future. "Congratulations," Lizzy said.

"Listen, I've got to get to work."

Lizzy slipped on her shoes, and then reached into her purse and pulled out her business card. "If you change your mind, give me a call."

Debra nodded and continued to hold the door open.

Lizzy left the apartment building feeling deflated. She was batting zero on all accounts: two missing girls and only a handful of clues. And then there was Hayley, sneaking out at night. What was she up to?

And what about her sister? Cathy was so lonely that she was actually entertaining the idea of dating her loser of an ex-husband. Why couldn't Cathy take a break from men altogether? Just a year, not forever.

Feeling momentarily overwhelmed by life, Lizzy walked across the parking lot. She opened the door to her Toyota and slipped in behind the wheel. The fabric on the passenger seat was curling at the edges. It really was time to get a new car, but she couldn't stand the idea of letting Old Yeller go.

With a sigh, she inserted the key into the ignition, looked up, and saw four words written in big red letters across her windshield. Was it written in blood?

Lizzy climbed out. At closer inspection, she realized the message had been written in lipstick, CoverGirl's Cherry Bomb, if she had to guess. MIND YOUR OWN BUSINESS!

* * *

Anthony Melbourne guzzled another eight-ounce glass of water as he looked around his office, his gaze settling on the nicely framed picture of him shaking hands with George W. Bush, the forty-third president of the United States.

Although fitness buffs like Arnold Schwarzenegger and Lou Ferrigno had always intrigued him, Anthony could relate much more to Richard Simmons.

Like Simmons, Anthony had been obese throughout his adolescence. Simmons weighed over 250 pounds when he graduated from high school. Anthony had weighed over 275 when he graduated.

He used to blame his weight on his parents. They were both obese. After graduating, he decided to do the opposite of what his parents had done. He refused to waste time in front of the television. He refused to put anything into his mouth that wasn't made from natural foods. His parents were slobs; he became a clean freak. They binged; he ate healthy portions throughout the day. They never exercised; he opened a gym and spent most of his day there.

So many parents around the world, he thought, had no idea how their hearts, minds, and bodies affected their kids' everyday lives. Parents were selfish when they failed to realize the fundamentals of parenting. Children imitated those in charge.

His gaze fell on another, more recent picture Jane had hung on his wall. Jane had taken the picture at the top of Horse Tail Falls the last time they hiked to the top. Jane was a big girl, but she was healthy and strong. Not only was she the best assistant he'd ever had, she was funny too. If she ever quit her job and left him, he wasn't sure what he would do.

The idea of not being able to look out his door and see her sitting at her desk made him feel sick to his stomach. Although Jane didn't know it, because he'd never told her, he'd stopped traveling around the world because of her. Why travel around the world when everything he wanted was right here in Sacramento? Right here in his office, in fact.

Jane Andrews—the love of his life.

He felt the urge to walk out there right this minute and tell her how he felt once and for all. Surely she could see that he felt more for her than simple friendship?

His phone rang and he picked it up. "Hello?"

Nothing but heavy breathing coming through the line. "Who is this?" he asked, although he already knew. The hang-up calls used to be sporadic, but lately the calls came every hour on the hour. He thought about calling the police, but they were already watching him like a hawk. The police thought he might have something to do with Diane Kramer's disappearance.

That bothered him to no end.

He provided a service for overweight and obese women who couldn't help themselves. He would never purposely hurt anyone. His programs had worked on thousands of women all over the world. He received hundreds of e-mails daily, praising him for the work he did.

The heavy breather was still on the line. Unusual considering the caller usually hung up after five seconds. "Andrea, is that you?"

No answer.

"Why don't you tell me what you want so I can help you?"

More breathing.

He already knew what she wanted. They had grown especially close during Andrea's time spent at his mountain cabin. With his help, she'd lost half of her body weight. In the beginning, he'd been attracted to Andrea. But she was a needy, possessive woman and he'd quickly lost interest. But she wouldn't take no for an answer. She'd become obsessed with him, bringing him gifts and popping in to visit him at all hours of the day. It wasn't long before his assistant and Andrea were butting heads right here at his gym in front of his clients. That's when he'd asked Andrea to stay away. Enough was enough. Although Andrea wouldn't admit it, he was sure she was the one who had told the police he had something to do with her sister's disappearance. And now she'd hired a private investigator to keep an eye on him. It was all too much. In fact, it was time to take care of Andrea Kramer once and for all.

"I've had enough of this nonsense."

More silence.

Anthony hung up the phone. He went to the door and opened it, disappointed to see that Jane had already left for the day. Adrenaline pumping through his veins, he grabbed his keys and left the gym.

* * *

After stopping by Ruth Fullerton's house and being told by the nurse that she was sleeping, Lizzy ran to the store to pick up some more kitten food along with a few unnecessary toys for Hannah.

She was home now.

Judging by the bowl and the silverware in the sink, Hayley had been home at some point, but now she was gone again. That girl did not sit still.

Last night, their first night as roommates, Lizzy hadn't slept a wink, just as Hayley had predicted. It would take time for them both to get used to having each other around.

As Lizzy sat at her desk in the corner of her bedroom, Hannah played under her feet while she waited for her computer to kick on. After a few minutes, she was surprised to see her in-box already flooded with new e-mails from the Weight Watcher Warriors group. She had been accepted into the group and everyone was welcoming and friendly. That was a good sign.

There was a private message from Heather Champion, the woman in charge. Although the tone of Heather's e-mail was friendly, Heather was firm about having all the information she needed about Lizzy. How long had she been trying to lose weight? What were her goals? What diets had she tried in the past?

Lizzy wrote Heather back and told her she had tried every diet known to mankind. She tossed in a few diets that Andrea

Kramer had mentioned, like the disgusting chewing-your-food-forever diet.

Next Lizzy wrote an introduction e-mail to the entire group, thanking everyone for being so welcoming. Recalling what her sister, Cathy, had said about trying to lose weight, Lizzy talked about feeling hopeless about the whole weight issue. Lizzy closed her message by mentioning that Diane Kramer was the one who told her about the group and had anyone heard from her lately?

Lizzy clicked send.

Tiny teeth gnawed at Lizzy's ankle. She bent over, picked up Hannah, and carried her to the bed. Lying on the mattress, she held Hannah in the air and said, "What am I going to do with you?"

A *ding ding* sounded on the computer, telling Lizzy she had a message. Figuring it was another WWW introduction, she set Hannah on the floor and sat in front of her computer.

Someone from WWW had already e-mailed her back about Diane. It was a private message from "Petunia." Apparently, Petunia and a few other women were concerned about Diane and had been wondering about her leaving the WWW group without saying good-bye. What was particularly concerning to Petunia was that Diane had befriended another WWW group member by the name of Vivian Hardy. In Petunia's words, Vivian had been discouraged about her weight.

More interesting, though, Petunia wrote that Vivian had also disappeared from the group a few months ago. No good-bye. Not a word to the group. She had suddenly disappeared off the face of the earth just like Diane Kramer.

Lizzy's pulse was racing by the time she read the last line: Vivian Hardy lived in Sacramento, California. Lizzy sent a quick e-mail thanking Petunia. It only took her five minutes to find

Vivian Hardy's address: a scary thing these days, having such easy access to a person's whereabouts. The apartment building where Vivian lived was less than fifteen miles away. She printed off directions and said, "Come on, Hannah. I need to pay Vivian Hardy a visit."

She placed Hannah in the section of the kitchen that had been gated off. Everything Hannah could possibly need was there, including a scratching post and a soft bed filled with goose feathers. Hannah was getting spoiled.

* * *

"Fuck."

Lizzy pulled over to the side of the road, both hands squeezing the steering wheel. She was lost. Why did she have to go flying out of the house right that very minute? Not only was it getting dark, she'd hardly slept in the past forty-eight hours. She wasn't thinking straight.

Her cell phone rang. She picked it up before it rang a second time. "Hello?"

"There you are. I've been trying to get a hold of you all day."

"Oh, Jared. I miss you. Come home."

"What's wrong?"

"Everything."

"That bad, huh?"

"Yes. For starters, let's talk about Charlee." She couldn't believe that was the first thing that came out of her mouth. All day she'd been telling herself that if Jared called she wouldn't bother talking about Charlee at all.

"Charlee?" he repeated.

"Yes, Charlee. Don't play dumb with me. I'm parked on the side of the road in the middle of nowhere and I have a pounding headache."

"Lizzy, why are you parked on the side of the road? It's getting late."

"It's not even eight thirty," she said. "Does it usually get dark this early?"

"It's way past your bedtime."

She couldn't stop herself from smiling if she tried. "Am I really that boring?"

"You really are, but that's what I love about you."

That word again. She hated that word, and yet it was so damn comforting to hear. Maybe she didn't really hate the word after all. "Charlee isn't boring," she said, then rolled her eyes at how ridiculous she must sound.

"Lizzy, you're worrying me. What are you talking about? Spit it out. Who's Charlee?"

"Your cute, perky, big-breasted Barbie doll neighbor."

"Her name is Charlee?"

Lizzy let her head fall to the steering wheel. "I guess that does make sense that you wouldn't know her name. After meeting her, I'm surprised I remember her name. She's Cameron Diaz, Jennifer Lopez, and Uma Thurman all mixed into one ridiculously beautiful woman."

"Wow. How did I miss all of that?"

"What? You didn't meet her?"

"Yes, I'm sorry to say that I did meet her, but I didn't remember her name. And somehow I failed to see what you saw and I'm not trying to downplay anything. She must not have been my type."

"Dingy-brown-haired, flat-chested, boring girls are your type. That makes me feel better. I'm so glad you called."

He laughed. "Do you want to call me back later when you're feeling better?"

"Would you mind?"

"Not at all."

"I do miss you," she said.

"I miss you too."

Lizzy hung up, and for the first time in a very long time, she felt like crying. What was wrong with her? She was too young to be going through menopause. She wasn't pregnant. It wasn't even close to being that time of the month. She was a wreck. "You just need sleep," she said aloud.

As she gazed out her window, she noticed something stuck under her windshield wiper. Probably an advertisement, she thought, as she climbed out of her car. Only the corner of the paper was showing since most of it had disappeared under the hood of her car. She pinched the corner of the paper and then lifted the wiper. It was a picture of a girl. Her pulse raced. She recognized the woman. It looked like a younger version of Andrea Kramer. It had to be Diane. From the looks of it, she'd lost a lot of weight—too much weight.

Lizzy looked around at the empty streets and then quickly got back in the car. Under the light, she saw that the picture was smeared with something that looked a lot like blood. The photo appeared to be one of those instant pictures taken with a Polaroid camera. She wondered how long the picture had been stuck beneath her windshield wiper. Careful not to touch the photo more than she already had, she placed it in the glove box where it would be safe until she could get a better look at it.

She'd already been warned to mind her own business, but now someone was leaving her evidence? Shivers coursed over her as she locked the doors. She took a moment to gather her thoughts before she looked at the map again and saw where she'd taken the wrong turn. She merged back onto the road.

Ten minutes later, Lizzy parked in front of Tree Top Apartments, which made no sense since there was only one tree in the vicinity as far as she could tell. The apartment building looked older than dirt with its cracked stucco and peeling paint.

Lizzy followed the numbers and headed upstairs. Vivian's apartment was on the far corner. She knocked on the door and waited patiently. After a few minutes, she knocked again. The curtains were drawn tight. Nobody was home. She inhaled deeply, relieved that no weird smells were coming from the apartment.

Next she headed for the main office, which was empty.

Lizzy hit a bell.

A short, hunched-back man waddled in from another room, where she could hear a television blasting.

"Hi," she said. "I'm looking for Vivian Hardy in apartment 154A. I just knocked on her door but nobody answered."

"You're a brave woman," he said.

"What do you mean?"

"Anyone who knocks on Vivian Hardy's door is doing so at their own risk. The girl does not like to be disturbed and even pays rent in advance to ensure nobody bothers her."

"When was the last time you saw her?"

He shrugged. "Three weeks ago, maybe four."

"Are you kidding me?"

"Do I look like I'm kidding?"

Lizzy frowned.

He walked to a file cabinet across the room and waved Lizzy over. "Let me show you something."

Lizzy moved to his side and watched him open the cabinet labeled G through M. He shuffled through the drawer and pulled out the Hardy file. He opened the file and showed Lizzy a thick stack of formal letters written in perfect penmanship by Vivian herself.

Letter after letter was addressed to the landlord of Tree Top Apartments asking the landlord and staff not to allow anyone to bother her. Unless she called with a problem, he was not to call, and that included knocking on her door to see if she was OK.

"Can I see the file for a moment?"

He obliged, and Lizzy looked through the letters under the pretense of reading one after another. Instead, she took a good look at the contract that listed references, including Vivian's mother, Abigail Hardy, and her phone number and mailing address in Brooklyn, NY.

The phone rang and the landlord walked away, giving Lizzy time to grab a pen from her purse and write Mrs. Hardy's telephone number on her hand.

CHAPTER 28

A PICTURE IS WORTH A THOUSAND WORDS

Morning came much too fast. Lizzy walked sleepily into the kitchen, surprised to see coffee already brewing. Hayley was sitting on the living room floor petting Hannah. "I thought you were allergic to cats?"

"I am." Hayley dangled a string over the kitten's head, making Hannah twist and turn in an eager attempt to capture it.

"I never heard you come in last night," Lizzy said.

"Liar."

Lizzy smiled. "You're up early."

Hayley nodded and said, "I left something on the coffee table for you."

Forgoing the coffee for a moment, Lizzy made her way to the large envelope on the coffee table. She reached inside and pulled out a pile of pictures. Two dozen pictures at least: horrible, dirty, sickening pictures.

"Shit." Every picture was of a younger Frank Fullerton with his daughter, Carol. "Shit, shit. Shit. This is not good. Where did you get these?"

"Where do you think?"

"You broke into the man's house?"

Hayley shrugged. "Do you mean the sicko pervert's house? The window was left open."

"How? Last night?"

"Over the weekend," Hayley said matter-of-factly.

"You were babysitting all weekend."

"Jessica pissed me off. I needed to blow off some steam."

"Do you have any idea how much trouble we could get into if anyone found out?"

"I don't think about those things. Ruth Fullerton is running out of time. And since you're losing your mojo, I thought I'd help you out."

Losing my mojo? Lizzy shook her head. "What is wrong with you, Hayley? What's going on inside that head of yours?"

"What's wrong with you, Lizzy? What's going on in that head of yours?"

"Tit for tat," Lizzy said. "Is that it?"

"That's it."

"Have you talked to Linda Gates lately?"

"Have you?"

Lizzy left the pictures for now, went to the kitchen, and filled a mug with hot coffee. When she returned to the main room, she saw that Hayley had moved to the couch, one leg folded beneath the other.

Obviously, Hayley was angry about something and needed to blow off steam. Lizzy sat on the other end of the couch. "Tit for tat it is," Lizzy said. "I haven't seen Linda in over two weeks."

"I haven't seen her in three," Hayley said.

"I haven't seen Linda Gates because I've been busy."

"Ditto."

"I have been busy trying to keep my business running. And while I'm spinning around in my hamster wheel, I've let my personal life go to pot."

"You and Jared broke up?"

"No, nothing like that."

"So what happened with moving in with him?"

"I chickened out and told him I wasn't ready."

"And now you're regretting it or are you just upset about the hot next-door neighbor?"

"How did you—oh, Jessica."

Hayley nodded. "I never tagged you as the jealous type."

"That's because I'm not...at least I didn't think I was. I don't know what it is, but I don't like it...feeling insecure and wishy-washy."

"I believe it's called love."

Lizzy sipped her coffee. "Sounds like you have some experience in the field."

Hayley grunted. "If you ask me, love doesn't exist. They, whoever they are, say love is some sort of intangible thing—unconditional and almighty." Hayley shook her head in disgust. "Come on, really?"

There was a short pause before Hayley continued.

"Maybe I don't believe in love because human beings, overall, are such pricks."

Lizzy didn't know what to say to that, so she said nothing.

"Maybe I don't have the capacity to love, or maybe I just don't understand it. Love seems so stifling. Not my thing, I guess."

"Well, maybe someday one of us will be able to enlighten the other on the subject of love."

"Cool."

"About breaking into Frank's house..."

Hayley nodded, waited.

Lizzy couldn't hold it in. "Are you crazy?"

"Most people who know me would say yes."

"What would you say?"

"That you ask too many questions."

"Hayley, do you understand the danger you're putting yourself in every time you do something like holding a knife to a man's throat or breaking and entering?"

"I do."

"But you're not worried?"

"Not one bit."

Before Lizzy could continue her lecture, Hayley said, "Fire me if you want. But I want you to know that won't stop me from going after assholes like Frank Fullerton."

"So you've decided to become some sort of vigilante?"

"I don't think of myself as much of anything. But everybody likes to put a label on shit, so call me whatever makes you happy."

After escaping the evil grasp of Spiderman, Hayley had confided in Lizzy and told her that for the first time in a long while she wanted to live. But Lizzy was just now realizing that Hayley might possibly want to live for different reasons than Lizzy first thought. "Where have you been going late at night?"

"I thought you weren't going to try to be my mother."

"If I was your mother, I wouldn't give a shit where you were at night, would I?"

Hayley looked away.

"I'm sorry. That was uncalled for. It's just that I'm worried about you, that's all."

"Well, don't be."

Silence engulfed the room.

"Do you want me to move out of your apartment?" Hayley asked. "I would completely understand. Your place, your rules."

"No. I just want you to talk to me, Hayley."

"Why?"

"Because I want to help you."

Hayley stood and took her empty coffee mug to the kitchen sink. Then she grabbed her backpack, pulled the strap over her shoulder, and headed for the door. After unlocking the deadbolt, she looked over her shoulder at Lizzy. "You can't help me any more than you already have."

"Then just do me a favor and be careful. I don't want to see you end up getting in trouble for trying to do what's right, but going about it all wrong. You've got a natural instinct for investigative work. You could go far in this business. And don't ever forget that you're one of the smart ones, Hayley. So be smart."

Lizzy went to the door. "And thanks for the pictures," she called out before Hayley could get away.

* * *

Lizzy went to her bedroom and turned on her computer.

She had called Jared back last night, but they only had a moment to talk before his pager went off. He was working on a whopper of a case, something to do with money laundering by a federal judge in another state but with connections here in Sacramento. If convicted, the judge would be removed from office immediately.

Last night Lizzy had transferred Vivian's mother's telephone number from her hand to a notepad. She picked up the phone and called the number.

A woman's voice sounded on the other end of the line after the third ring. "Hello."

"Hello. My name is Lizzy Gardner, and I'm calling about Vivian Hardy. Is this her mother?"

"What now? Is she in the hospital again?"

Lizzy took that as a yes. "Does Vivian go to the hospital often?"

A ponderous sigh could be heard on the other end. "I have no idea. I just remember getting a call from one of those med centers once telling me my daughter needed someone to pick her up."

Lizzy could hear shuffling on the other end.

"That was over a year ago," the woman said. "I make notations on my calendar when she calls. It looks like we talked a few months ago."

"I went to her apartment and knocked several times," Lizzy told the woman. "There was no answer, and the landlord hasn't seen her in months."

"Vivian likes her privacy. You would too if you needed more than one fireman to get you from place to place."

"Firemen?"

"She has two bum knees, and when you're over three hundred pounds with bad knees, you need help. She won't listen to me. Never has, never will. What is it that you need exactly?"

"Apparently, Vivian had joined the Weight Watcher Warriors, an online weight loss group. She befriended a girl named Diane Kramer, who has been missing for some time."

"That name sounds familiar."

"Did you meet Diane?"

"No, no. I haven't made the trip to California to see Vivian, but I do remember her talking about a woman named Diane when she called last. She was worried about her. That in itself is uncharacteristic of Vivian, you know, to worry about anyone but herself, so the name stuck in my head."

Lizzy decided to give Mrs. Hardy time to think…see if she remembered anything else.

"If I remember correctly, Diane was even larger than Vivian. No," she amended, "I think it was the other way around. Anyhow, Vivian didn't like the way the woman's sister treated her, trying to push Diane into losing weight. I couldn't speak my mind, of course, because I agreed with the sister. But there's no helping someone that wants to eat their way to an early grave."

Suddenly Lizzy felt sorry for Vivian. "Do you remember anything else your daughter might have said last time the two of you spoke?"

"She did talk about joining a fat camp or something."

"Do you know where?"

"I don't. Wait…she said something about a mountain cabin. That's all I know."

"Do you remember if the cabin was located in California?"

"No, I don't remember, but I would assume so."

"If you remember anything else, would you mind if I left you my number so you can call me?"

"That would be fine."

Lizzy exchanged information with the woman, surprised when Mrs. Hardy didn't say another peep about her own daughter. Something like: "Would you let me know if you hear from Vivian?" Or "I'd appreciate a call if you hear anything about my daughter." Nothing.

Lizzy got off the phone and made notes that she filed away. Then she made a list:

Diane Kramer Missing Person Case
Give photo of Diane to police
Find Vivian Hardy
Talk to Andrea Kramer
Have a nice long chat with Anthony Melbourne
Send daily e-mails to WWW, the online group
Stay in touch with Debra Taphorn and Michael Denton

Carol Fullerton Cold Case
Ask Ruth Fullerton about Frank's relationship with his daughter
Hold off a few days before telling Detective Roth about the pictures
Have Jessica or Hayley follow Carol's friend, Ellen Woodson
Find out if Hayley heard anything re: Burning Man

There were three new messages from the WWW group. Nothing important. Lizzy looked at the clock. It was time to get ready for exercise. Instead of working out on the treadmill, she planned to give Melbourne's brain a workout. Following him around wasn't doing anybody any good. It was costing Andrea Kramer a lot of money for Lizzy to get toned.

Although Lizzy liked money as much as the next person, she preferred to do actual work for the money she earned. Besides, she was tired of doing push-ups and lunges. A hike here and there, a good ol' walk down the street, maybe even a bike ride might be all right, but exercising every day with an egomaniac health guru wasn't her thing.

She needed to take a lesson or two from Hayley. That girl would never waste her time doing something as stupid as working out every day in the hopes of learning one little tidbit about a case. No, Hayley might get carried away more often than not, but she knew how to take the bull by the horns and get the work done.

Hayley was absolutely right.

Lizzy was losing her mojo. Starting today, though, she planned to get it back. After taking the bloody photo of Diane Kramer to Detective Roth for analyzing, she needed to find a way to get into Vivian Hardy's apartment.

CHAPTER 29

PUMPED UP KICKS

If there was one thing Jessica didn't want to be when she grew up, it was a private investigator. After sitting in her car for three hours, her butt was sore and her neck was stiff. She had borrowed her mom's car and was parked a few houses away from Ellen Woodson's house.

Well, she reconsidered, if she ever *was* a private investigator instead of a psychologist or a criminologist, she would have to pay someone else to do surveillance…as Lizzy had done when she'd assigned her this tedious, boring job.

Why couldn't Hayley do this? What was Hayley doing in her free time? That's the person they should be watching, Jessica thought. They should be watching Hayley.

She'd been following Ellen Woodson in hopes that she would lead them to Carol. Today Ellen had gone home for lunch instead of to the mall like she'd done the other two days. A three-hour lunch seemed a bit much, and Jessica thought about leaving.

The good news was that while Jessica was sitting here, she'd gotten a head start on one of her classes that wouldn't begin for another few weeks. The professor had been kind enough to let her students know what their first assignment would be. Among other classes, Jessica would be taking Introduction to Criminal Justice and Society at California State University–Sacramento.

She put her book away, afraid she might fall asleep if she read another word about societal response to criminals. She drank from her water bottle and then turned up the music and tapped her fingers against the console in rhythm to "Pumped up Kicks" by Foster the People. She listened to the words and smiled when she realized she was listening to the CD Hayley had made for her.

Before Foster the People could sing the second verse, Ellen Woodson came out of her house rolling a piece of luggage behind her. The woman looked around suspiciously before opening her trunk and shoving the luggage inside.

Holy Moly! Jessica couldn't believe what she was seeing.

This was the longest lunch Ellen had taken so far. And now luggage?

Jessica was a glass-half-empty sort of person and she figured hell would have to freeze over before Ellen Woodson would do anything remotely out of her regularly scheduled day.

Trying not to get overly excited, Jessica kept her head back against the headrest and made sure not to make any sudden moves.

Although both sides of the street were lined with parked cars, as far as she could tell, her car was the only one with somebody in the driver's seat. If she made any fast moves, Ellen might see movement and then she would know they were on to her. The music suddenly sounded too loud, but there was no way she was going to risk leaning forward and turning the volume down. The moment Ellen Woodson shut her trunk and climbed in behind the wheel, Jessica felt safe enough to turn the music off. Her hands were shaking. She felt as if she was following a criminal instead of a harmless bank teller.

Ever since Jessica was shot six months ago, she'd been a little wary about investigative work. That had happened right after she'd started working for Lizzy. Thinking a math tutor was Spiderman, the serial killer roaming the streets of Sacramento at the time, Jessica had brought a gun into the math tutor's house. Instead of finding a serial killer, she'd found herself in the middle of a crazy sex scandal. One of two men shot her. The men, it turned out, spent their weekends searching for a poor lonely soul to dress up and play with. They threatened their victim with his life while forcing him to perform sexual acts. They filmed the whole thing and then, of course, turned around and sold the video to thousands of perverts around the world.

What was the world coming to? Jessica wondered as she started the car and merged onto the street, careful to stay well behind Ellen Woodson's car.

＊ ＊ ＊

"I'm glad you're home," Lizzy said the moment Hayley walked through the door of her apartment.

Hayley took a step back. "Why? What's going on?"

"I need to ask you for a favor."

"No, I'm not going to stop going out at night. And no, I'm not going to put away your dishes too. If it's about that candy dish I broke, I'm sorry. I didn't see it when I pulled out the coffee mug. You really need to organize your cupboards better."

"It's nothing like that," Lizzy said. "You broke my candy dish?"

"It really wasn't that nice anyhow. I wouldn't serve my best friend candy corn in that thing."

"Do you have a best friend?"

"No, but that's not the point. That dish was ugly. I already did you a favor."

Lizzy didn't care about the dish, and she knew Hayley felt bad. Besides, she had other things on her mind. "I need you to help me break into somebody's apartment," Lizzy blurted.

Hayley's eyes narrowed. "You just gave me a big lecture this morning about being smart, and now you're asking me to show you how to break and enter?"

"I know. It's horrible of me. And wrong. But I'm not asking you to do it, I'm just asking you to show me the way."

"You're serious?"

"Sadly, yes, I am. I've been trying to get in touch with Jared all day, hoping he could get me a fast-pass to getting a warrant, but he's working a case right now, and even if he had time to call me back, he certainly isn't going to have time to get me the warrant I need sooner rather than later. Legally the process could take fifteen minutes, depending on the circumstance. The problem is, Vivian Hardy could be in trouble, but she has signed dozens of documents that don't allow the landlord to enter her apartment. Besides, there are no smells coming out of the place."

"You mean dead body smells?"

Lizzy nodded. "Right. No scent of a decomposing body. The girl really likes her privacy. If she's inside and alive, I need to talk to her about Diane. She's my only hope. If she's not inside, I need to search her apartment for clues, and I don't think the police would allow me to have access were I to call them and convince them that Vivian might be in danger. I need to do this today. My body can't take another morning in the gym."

"Whoa, whoa, whoa," Hayley said. "You're talking way too fast, and you lost me at 'show me the way.'"

"Why don't I explain it all in the car? It's going to get dark soon."

"Dark is good," Hayley told her in a calming voice. "You don't break and enter in the daylight, Lizzy." Hayley shook her head. "You really are losing it. I knew it was getting bad, but not this bad."

Hayley shut the door and locked it. "First we need to dress in dark clothes, and I don't mean a ski mask and gloves, just dark jeans and a dark, normal-looking shirt. After we're dressed appropriately, you need to buy me a couple of tacos on our way to the apartment building because I'm starved."

* * *

If there was one thing Lizzy didn't like, it was the dark. Dark clothes, dark night, and the dark, decaying building didn't help matters.

This wasn't fun, but then why did Hayley look so damn calm? She was in her element, Lizzy thought, that's why.

"Which apartment?" Hayley asked after they parked the car.

"One fifty-four A. Upstairs, on the corner."

Lizzy watched Hayley unzip a slim, black pouch. She pulled out two metal picks. "This is a twisted tension wrench. I also like the short hook, another useful pick."

Lizzy nodded. Now was not the time to question Hayley on her abundance of breaking and entering equipment. "Come on. Follow me," Lizzy said. "I've knocked on the door twice. I know exactly where we need to go."

Two minutes later, they were standing outside the apartment. Lizzy was about to knock when Hayley stopped her. "What are you doing?" she whispered in her ear.

"I thought we should give Vivian one more chance to answer before we barge inside."

"If you want the neighbors to come out and see what we're up to, then go ahead and knock."

"Just do your thing," Lizzy said, frustrated. Before Lizzy could get any more nervous than she already was, Hayley used the tension wrench to open the door. She pulled Lizzy inside without a word and then quietly shut and locked the door.

"I'll look for the girl," Hayley whispered. "Use your flashlight and start looking for whatever it is you're looking for."

Lizzy shook her head. "I'm going with you. I need to make sure Vivian isn't hurt before I go snooping around her apartment."

Hayley was already walking off, leaving Lizzy to follow.

The place was small: one bedroom, one bathroom, a tiny kitchen, and an even tinier patio with one chair and one dead plant.

Hayley opened the bedroom closet, then went to the bathroom and checked the linen closet. There was also a closet containing a small washer and dryer, one on top of the other. Vivian was not there.

Lizzy headed back to the desk in the corner of the bedroom and began searching through drawers.

"The longer we take," Hayley told her, "the better our chances of being caught. I suggest you put anything you might want to look at in this bag." Hayley handed Lizzy a reusable grocery bag she'd found in the other room. "Just shove it all in there. If it'll make you feel better, you can send it all back to Vivian later or leave it at her doorstep in a few days."

Lizzy's cell phone vibrated.

"Don't answer your phone."

"It's Jessica. She's on surveillance. I have to take the call." She hit talk. "Jessica, what's going on? Where have you been? You're supposed to check in every hour."

"Lizzy, you're never going to believe this, but I've been following Ellen Woodson on the highway for three hours now. She took a three-hour lunch, but it turns out she was packing for a little trip."

"Where are you exactly?"

"I just passed a small airport. I'm on 99 headed south."

It was dark, but Lizzy could see Hayley stabbing a finger toward the exit.

"You're doing great," Lizzy said. "It's late, so it looks like you might end up having to get a hotel after you follow Ellen to her destination. Get the address and then head for a hotel and call me."

"Will do."

"I have to go now. Great work, Jessica. Call me back in an hour." She shut her cell phone and tucked it into her pocket.

"I'm leaving," Hayley said, her voice heated.

"Give me two more minutes."

There was a *rap tap tap* on the door.

"Shit."

Hayley disappeared for a minute and then came back. "Looks like nosey neighbors. Happy?"

Lizzy started piling every folder and file she could find into the bag. At the last minute, she grabbed the desk calendar and tucked it under her arm before following Hayley to the door.

"It's clear," Hayley said. "I'm going."

"It's too soon." But that didn't stop Hayley. Nothing stopped Hayley. Lizzy had no choice but to follow the girl or spend the night in Vivian's apartment. They were almost to the stairs when a woman called out. Hayley kept walking, but Lizzy was chicken shit and couldn't do it. She turned back to the woman. "Can I help you?"

"Are you Vivian's mother?"

"Yes," Lizzy said without hesitating, "yes, I am. Vivian's in the hospital with a ruptured appendix."

"Oh no. Is she going to be all right?"

"Surgery went well. The doctors are expecting a full recovery. We just stopped by to grab a few of her things that she requested."

"I'm so glad. Hank and I have been very worried about Vivian."

"No need. She's good. Thanks for your concern." Lizzy started walking backward. "I'll tell her that you and Hank send your sympathies."

"We would appreciate it." The woman smiled and waved.

Lizzy turned and jogged down the stairs and the rest of the way to the car.

Hayley was already behind the wheel. She wasn't taking any chances. "Give me your keys," Hayley said with her hand extended, the one with only four fingers held palm up as she waited for the keys. "Now."

Lizzy did as she said, although she didn't appreciate her tone or the idea of taking orders from the girl who had way too much attitude today.

Five minutes passed before Hayley said, "You are the worst burglar in the history of burglars. I hope you had a nice chat with the neighbors. Did you make sure she got a good look at you?"

"I'm pretty sure she could pick me out in a lineup," Lizzy confessed.

"You think this whole thing is funny, don't you?"

"I do now that we're safely in the getaway car."

"Don't ever ask me to do anything like that again," Hayley said. "At least not with you. I'll go alone next time. I don't know what I was thinking trying to teach you how to do something illegal. Goody two-shoes like you and Jessica are *not* cut out for this type of work."

"Goody two-shoes?"

"I don't want to talk to you right now."

Lizzy wanted to release some nervous laughter, but now wasn't the time. She was relieved that it was over. She even had a strange feeling of euphoria at having accomplished what she set out to do. "The neighbor woman was sweet," Lizzy said. "She was just worried about Vivian. She thought I was Vivian's mom, and so I went along with it."

Hayley didn't respond.

"You're right," Lizzy said. "I asked you to help me with something illegal and immoral and then I didn't follow orders. I could have gotten us both in a lot of trouble. I'm sorry. I truly am."

There was a police car in the far right lane. Lizzy saw Hayley hold her breath while the patrol car passed them by.

"I'm the one who should be apologizing," Hayley said after the police car made a right and disappeared. "I went to see my mom last week."

That explained Hayley's recent change of mood. "How was she?"

Hayley didn't answer right away and Lizzy didn't rush her.

"She was the same," Hayley finally said, her voice strained. "Exactly the same. She's living in filth and she doesn't want to change."

Lizzy sat quietly.

Hayley exhaled, keeping her eyes on the road in front of her. "I offered to take Mom to Narcotics Anonymous. I told her I would pick her up and attend the meetings with her, but she said she couldn't do it. She said she was weak and that I was the strong one."

"Stronger than most," Lizzy agreed.

"I'm not as strong as I pretend to be," Hayley said. "I lie awake at night fantasizing about revenge against every perverted monster out there. I'm all screwed up inside, Lizzy. I don't know what's happening to me, but it's not good. My thoughts are dark, and sometimes I feel like I'm being strangled from the inside out. I don't think I can overcome the darkness like you did."

"Hayley, you have only just begun to dig yourself out of the nightmare you've had to live. You have to fight it. It's way too early to think about giving in."

After a moment Lizzy added, "I still have nightmares. Spiderman is dead, and yet he's not. He's inside my head, but I'll never stop trying to get him out of there. More than anything, I want peace. I want you to have peace too. And people like Ruth Fullerton. We all have our demons. Sometimes I think it's not a matter of getting rid of our demons as much as it is learning to live with them."

* * *

Jessica looked at the clock. She had been driving for four hours and twenty-five minutes without a pit stop. More than anything, Jessica had to pee. For the past thirty minutes, she'd been wriggling in her seat. There was nothing she could do about it. There was no way she was going to lose Ellen. If that happened, her entire day would be one big waste of time.

Just as Jessica contemplated peeing in her pants, the left blinker on Ellen's car lit up.

Thank God.

A few miles back they had exited onto CA 58 East. It was dark now that they were no longer on a main road. It was impossible for Jessica to see the road signs.

Ellen was driving faster. She probably had to use the restroom too.

Jessica tried to memorize lefts and rights, but quickly gave that up, figuring she'd just have to write down the nearest address once they came to a stop.

About eight miles up the road, Ellen made a right onto a long dirt road. The sign was big enough that Jessica could make out the words: Livingston Farms. Jessica did not follow Ellen down the road. Instead, she drove straight ahead, made an illegal U-turn, and came back to the road. She turned off her lights and slowly made her way over the dirt road that appeared to be one long driveway.

Ellen's car was long gone, and that caused Jessica to panic. She sped up to about twenty mph until she saw a small farmhouse up ahead on the right. The road was narrow, but she pulled her car as far over to one side as she could before she shut off the engine. She crept quietly out of her car and hurried toward the nearest tree. Under any other circumstance, she never would have even considered leaving the car. But desperate times called for desperate measures.

The hoot of an owl sounded in the distance. Jessica took her time relieving herself. She felt like a new woman as she zipped her jeans and walked back to her car.

As soon as she climbed in behind the wheel, something sharp stabbed into the back of her head. "Get out of the car nice and slowly. Any fast moves and I'll blow your head off."

CHAPTER 30

DOCTOR, DOCTOR

"Could you leave the mirror alone and loosen the cuffs a little, sweetheart?"

Hayley ignored Dr. Daniel Williams, a physician who specialized in spinal injury medicine and rehabilitation. He was considered to be one of the best spinal doctors in the area, but like many men, doctors, lawyers, and politicians included, he had a weakness for illegal sex.

The reason Hayley had selected Dr. Williams as her victim, over dozens of other doctors who enjoyed the age-old practice of buying sex, was his attitude.

After cuffing Williams's hands to the swirly scrollwork of the cast iron bed, she moved on to tying thick leather straps around his ankles. Like Peter, Randy, and Brian, she'd been watching Dr. Daniel Williams for a few months now. She knew he brought the girls he picked up to this particular dump of a hotel. She'd visited the hotel more than once, and she already knew that the cast iron bed frames would be perfect for tying and cuffing.

While tightening the leather straps around his ankles, Hayley caught her reflection in the mirrored wall to her right. Seeing herself in a full-length mirror threw her off track. The black push-up bra beneath a see-through blouse together with the sequin miniskirt was enough to catch a lot of unwanted attention, but the skirt and bra weren't what Hayley was focused on. It was the short, spiky blonde wig, blue eye shadow, and funky four-inch wedges that made it impossible to look away. She could hardly believe the person looking back at her was actually her. She might have laughed, maybe even cried, if she thought she could get away with it.

But the man on tonight's menu wasn't drunk or drugged. She had to be careful. Unlike the others, this man did not know her, but that didn't mean he wouldn't be able to pick her out of a lineup if things went awry. And laughing or crying would only serve to give her away.

She had too much work to do to let a little lapse in judgment mess up her plans. She turned back to Williams and pulled on the strap around his ankle.

"Ouch. Damn it, sweetheart, you're going to hurt me if you're not careful there."

She brushed a finger over the bottom of his foot.

He tried to pull away but couldn't, which meant she'd done her job. He was secure.

"Stop that. And stop chewing that nasty gum."

She snapped, crackled, and popped just to piss him off.

"No, really," he said. "I'm serious."

She blew a bubble. A big one. *POP.*

"I'm done. That's it. Undo these cuffs and take off those straps. I'm not going to pay you either."

That look—she knew that look. It was the same smug look Brian used to give her every time he came into her room.

"Oh, come on," she said in a breathy voice. "Don't be such a baby. I thought you enjoyed a little S&M every once in a while."

"Not S&M, honey; B&D is more my style."

Hands on hips, she took a step back and looked at him long and hard. "Is that right? I didn't know there was a difference." The guy looked like Brad from the original *Rocky Horror Picture Show*. He even wore the same geeky glasses.

"My preferences fall toward bondage and discipline," he explained, "not sadism and masochism."

"Whatever."

He lifted a brow. "If you're a professional, shouldn't you know the difference?"

She grabbed the strap around his other ankle and yanked hard. "You're probably right," she told him.

"Do you have a name?"

She chewed her gum, blew a giant bubble, and then watched it slowly deflate.

The expression on his face turned from anger to worry. "Who are you?"

She walked across the room, picked up her backpack from the floor, and then came back to him and set her backpack on the edge of the bed. Reaching inside, she pulled out a roll of duct tape.

"I want to know what's going on," he said as he watched her rip off a piece of tape. "What are you doing?" he asked.

Using her free hand, she grabbed his neatly folded shirt from the chair nearby and used it to wipe his mouth before placing the duct tape over his smoothly shaven jaw. He was mumbling now, his eyes growing wider by the second.

She reached inside her backpack again and pulled out a black permanent marker and a soldering iron, which she plugged into the wall socket.

He didn't seem to like her soldering equipment at all. Oh well, he had serial killer Samuel Jones to thank for that idea.

His mumbling grew louder, but she wasn't worried. They got all kinds in this hotel; hearing moaning and groaning and other strange noises through the walls was nothing new.

She glanced at the good doctor's face.

Yeah, he was definitely seeing red now.

"Maybe," she told him, "this will teach you to stop thinking with your dick instead of your brain." She tapped her knuckles on his forehead. "Do you have a brain in there?"

She grabbed the permanent marker, climbed onto the bed, and straddled him while she wrote two words in big bold letters, centered and in all caps, above his navel: SICK FUCK. She ignored the panicked mumbles beneath the duct tape as he bucked and twisted.

She climbed down and then ripped the duct tape from his mouth.

"What do you want from me?" he begged.

She tucked her pen inside her backpack and pulled out a letter addressed to his wife and the CEO of the hospital where he worked. She held the letter in front of his face so he could read what it said.

"What would you do if your wife knew everything about you?" Hayley asked him when he finished reading the letter.

"Why are you doing this?"

"I am glad you asked," Hayley answered. "There is something I need you to get for me."

"What is it? Money? How much do you need?"

She pressed a finger into the middle of his chest and said, "Listen carefully. I need a syringe filled with an immobilizing drug and, of course, a hypodermic needle. Etorphine hydrochloride, haloperidol, immobilon, take your pick. The man I plan to inject is approximately five foot ten, 160 pounds. I need to put him out in under a minute…two at the most."

"Tranquilizing agents don't affect everyone the same," he said, his voice strained. "There's no way to detect whether or not you'll have the exact dose needed. It will take time to enter the bloodstream."

"Then make the dose high enough to do the job in under a minute."

"It could trigger respiratory problems. He could die."

"That's a risk I'm willing to take. Can you get me what I need or not?" She waved the letter in front of his face. "It's your call. You do realize that the CEO of your hospital despises creeps like you. Did you know the CEO's daughter was raped by their neighbor, a man he trusted?"

"I'll do it, but it's not going to be easy."

"I never expected it to be easy. Two days from now, not three days and not four," she warned. "In two days, when you take your brown bag lunch to Marshall Park on Twenty-Seventh Street, I want you to make a small detour from your regularly scheduled park bench to the bench closest to the horseshoe pit. It's impossible to miss, and nobody ever plays horseshoes on weekdays. Even if they do, they won't pay any attention to a doctor eating his lunch. Tape the bag you're going to leave for me to the bottom of the bench. If the syringe isn't there, I will be mailing the letters. And don't even think about trying to intercept the letters. I have your in-laws' address in Florida and the home address of every colleague you've ever worked with." She continued to look into his eyes, unblinking. "You don't want to piss me off any more than you already have."

Hayley stepped away from the bed. "I wrote everything down so you wouldn't forget." She held up a piece of paper and then folded it and tucked it in the pocket of his suit jacket that was hanging over the chair.

She continued to talk to him as she began to gather her things. "If you hadn't spent most of your life fucking young girls who had no interest in being fucked by you, girls who asked you to stop, underage girls who you drugged, then you wouldn't be here right now. You deserve to die. You really do."

"I have a family."

"Yeah, I know. Two girls and a boy. I also know that you've paid your own daughters a few too many visits in the middle of the night."

"I would never do such a thing."

She looked over her shoulder at him. "You're a liar."

"You don't know what you're talking about."

"I wish that were true," she said as she moved back to his side. "I saw you outside the Road Town Bar two weeks ago. You picked up two underage girls. I happened to run into those girls later, and they told me all about the sick things you do."

"They were whores. Why do you think they're on the streets?"

"You think it's because they want to sleep with ugly assholes like you?"

"Yes."

Her mouth tightened and her vision blurred as she ripped off a new piece of duct tape and slapped it over his mouth.

Anger rolled its devilish fingers around her heart, strangling whatever sense of normalcy she had left inside. Nothing had been the same since she'd visited her mom. Mom loved drugs more than she loved her own daughter. Life wasn't fair, she knew that, but she also knew that until she took care of the men who had ruined her mom's life, and her life, she wouldn't ever be able to move on.

"Every single one of those girls on the street," she ground out, "needs money to survive. There are a few girls out there who'd rather dole out blow jobs than work nine to five behind a desk, but many of those girls have been trafficked. If they don't bring their pimps back something in the form of green-backs, they get beaten to a pulp. Those pimps make sure the girls are addicted to drugs so that they will never leave. So that they'll believe they have no choice but to sleep with sick fucks like you."

Although branding these men was part of her ritual, tonight it all felt different. She didn't feel like herself. She grabbed the sol-dering iron and pulled the extension cord as far as it would allow, and then climbed up onto the bed and straddled him once again. She made sure he was looking at the tip of the soldering iron as she slowly moved it to his chest, using the permanent marker she'd already used as a guideline.

The doctor bucked and wriggled when the iron touched his soft white skin. His face turned blood red. The smell of burnt flesh no longer bothered her, which should have been her first clue that things might be getting out of hand.

She lifted the iron before finishing even half of the first letter. If she finished, he might not follow through with getting her what she needed. "You're one of the lucky ones, Dr. Williams," she said as she climbed off him and hopped off the bed.

He looked relieved to see her packing up her things. After everything was put away, she came to the side of the bed and hovered over him, her face only inches from his.

"Those girls didn't want you. You're a sick bastard, a pervert. Your daughters would be relieved to learn that their father was dead."

Afraid she was going to finish him off, his eyes widened in fear—exactly the reaction she was looking for. She pointed a finger at the tip of his nose. "You're not going to die tonight, Dr. Williams. But if you ever touch one of your daughters again or you don't follow through with getting me what I need, this won't be the last time we meet. And I can guarantee if I ever do feel the need to see you again, I will finish what I started."

CHAPTER 31

A TASTE OF FREEDOM

Sierra Mountains, Day 61

Vivian stared at the door to the cabin and watched it slowly creak open, surprised to see Melbourne's assistant.

What was she doing here? Why now?

The woman looked different than the last time she was here. Her hair was pulled back from her face and tied in a rubber band. Her face was red and she was breathing hard. Once again Vivian recognized her, but from where?

"What are you doing here?" Vivian asked, praying Jane might help her. The first time she'd met Melbourne's assistant was after she'd been in the cabin for one week. Jane had come alone. She'd said she only stopped by to check on her and make sure she was OK. Vivian had begged her to let her go, telling her she'd changed her mind, but it was obvious Jane had been brainwashed by Melbourne.

Vivian figured she'd be best served if she stayed calm and pretended everything was fine and dandy.

"How are you?" Jane asked.

"I'm ready to go home."

Jane smiled. "You look like you've already lost a lot of weight."

"I have, which is why I'm ready to go home."

"Soon," she said. "Very soon."

Jane took some things out of her backpack and took them to the kitchen. Next she went into the pantry.

Vivian held her breath.

Sure enough, Jane came out holding the plastic bags filled with water bottles and her journal. "Going somewhere?"

"Obviously not." Vivian rattled the chain beneath the covers.

Jane disappeared inside the pantry again. Vivian could hear her cleaning up the spilt oil and putting the water bottles back on the shelf. After that was done, Jane carried Vivian's journal and pen back to her bedside and set them on the table next to her.

She looked around. "Other than the mess you made in the pantry, the place looks clean."

"Yeah, your clean-freak boss did a fine job of sterilizing every nook and cranny."

Jane looked down her nose at Vivian. "So now we're seeing your true colors, aren't we? What happened to the sweet girl I met not too long ago? The young woman who was finally ready to stop stuffing her face and make a change once and for all?"

Vivian was done pretending. When the bitch finally stopped talking she said, "Look at you. Your ass is wider than Mount Everest, and yet I'm the one chained to the bed. That makes no sense to me."

Jane's eyes narrowed into tiny, scary slits.

The woman was actually a skinny bitch, but Vivian could tell she was insecure. "Where's the TV your boss promised me?" Nobody had ever promised Vivian a TV, but from the beginning, she'd hoped to stir up trouble at Melbourne's office.

The woman shook her head in much the same way Melbourne was fond of doing. Damn it. She knew that face. Where the hell had she met Jane before?

"You don't get it, do you, Vivian?"

"You're right, Jane. I don't get it. I've changed my mind about this whole thing. I am truly grateful for what you and your master have done for me. Now let me go, or I might just have to go straight to the police when I finally get out of here."

Jane crossed her arms against her chest. "You signed a contract. Consideration has been fully extended."

"I was told I would have a television—breach of contract."

"Sorry, there's nothing in the contract about you getting a television. Whoever mentioned a television was probably just trying to get you to the cabin—like using a big juicy bone to lead a dog outside."

"There's also nothing in the contract about me wearing a cuff and chain," Vivian said, ignoring the dog comment.

"You're wrong. The contract states that the client will be confined. Besides, you think they're going to care about any of that after they see that you signed a contract and paid thousands of dollars to do it? The only one who would be dragged to a cell and put behind bars is you."

"We'll see about that," Vivian growled. "Are you finished here? Because I would appreciate it if you would leave now."

Jane sighed as she went to the door and picked up her backpack. When she looked back at Vivian, her gaze fell on the mirror and on the fabric puddled in a heap on the floor.

Shit. Vivian held her breath again.

Jane's hand grasped the doorknob.

Vivian could literally taste freedom. She was so close to escaping.

But then Jane turned fully around and said, "Damn. I almost forgot." She unzipped the front section of her backpack and reached inside. Smiling, she held up a cuff: a fur-lined cuff that looked much smaller than the cuff Vivian had finally gotten out of.

Jane held the cuff outward at chest level as she came back toward the bed. "I need to replace your cuff, Vivian. You look like you've lost a lot of weight. It's time."

Vivian felt like the baby deer she'd seen through the kitchen window. Trapped. There was no way she was going to let Jane come near her. "Stay away from me."

"Don't make this any more difficult than it needs to be. You're on your way to living a happy and healthy life. Why mess it all up now? Your hormones are making you think irrationally."

"There's no way I'm going to let you put that cuff on me. Is this what happened to Diane?"

Jane blinked, trying her damndest to look nonplussed.

"She was here, wasn't she?"

"I've never heard the name. You'll have to talk to Anthony about all of that. Right now you need to stay calm."

"Why are you doing this to me?"

"You did this to yourself, Vivian. Why can't you people see that?"

As Jane moved toward her, Vivian readied herself for a fight. She refused to stay in this torture chamber for another hour. She might have lost a lot of weight, but she could still hold her own.

Jane reached for the blankets and pulled them off with a flick of her wrist. She looked from the empty cuff on the bed to Vivian's face.

"That's right," Vivian said. "I'm free." And then she lunged with all the viciousness of a grizzly bear.

They rolled across the floor, neither able to take full control of the other. Vivian had a wad of Jane's hair in her fist and she pulled so hard she felt a tuft of hair come loose.

Jane hardly seemed to notice. She still held the new cuff and she kept hitting Vivian with it, hitting her head, her arm, her hip, wherever the cuff would fall.

Jane was relentless and determined.

Why did she care so much? What was motivating Jane to fight to keep Vivian here? It made no sense.

Refusing to let her get the upper hand, Vivian summoned every bit of fight she had left inside and rolled over Jane, pinning her with her weight. She'd lost a lot of poundage, but she was no Kate Moss.

Vivian used her right hand to keep Jane from pummeling her further with the cuff.

Jane smiled at her, creeping Vivian out with a reaction that did not compute until Jane spit, hitting Vivian square in the eye and causing temporary blindness. "You bitch," Vivian cried out.

Her body angled now, Jane used her boots to repeatedly kick Vivian until Vivian managed to throw her weight on top of Jane once again. They were on the move, rolling across the floor toward the kitchen table.

Every time Jane took a swing at her, Vivian felt the fight leaving her. Her body felt bruised and weak. Lack of food wasn't helping her situation. She knocked into a chair. It toppled over.

Vivian's head hit the wood pedestal under the table, and that's when she stopped fighting back. She had nothing left.

The room was spinning now and Vivian couldn't hear anything. Her vision was blurred. As Vivian's eyesight returned, she saw something scrawled beneath the wood table. Words carved on the underside of the table in the same way someone might carve their initials in the trunk of a tree.

Three words: *Diane was here.*

The chains rattled. *Click. Click.*

Vivian didn't have to look at her feet to know what had just happened. She felt the familiar fur collar around her ankle, only snugger this time.

She was going to die here.

* * *

The mounds of paperwork, Lizzy realized, whether she was at the office or at home as she was now, were getting out of control. She had missed exercise this morning, but she didn't care.

So far, she'd managed to go through a few of Vivian's notebooks, mostly depressing journals about her life. Nothing concrete. Vivian mentioned Diane on more than one occasion, but it was all standard chitchat transferred to paper.

Therapeutic? Possibly. Helpful? Not really.

Lizzy glanced at the envelope Hayley had given her. She picked it up and pulled out the pictures of Frank and Carol. She hadn't had time to look at them until now. Looking at the pictures made her sad, made her understand what Hayley had been talking about last night.

The evil. The darkness.

It was always there.

People could pretend that everything came up roses if they said it enough times, but the darkness would always be there. Maybe not on their street or even in their neighborhood, but it was there…somewhere close, lurking, waiting.

One picture.

That was all it took. It was enough to make her want to lose her breakfast. Lizzy jumped to her feet. Clutching the envelope to her chest, she slipped her feet into a pair of sandals, grabbed her purse, and headed out the door. She left so fast, she didn't have time to leave a note telling Hayley where she was off to.

* * *

Ruth Fullerton looked much worse than the last time Lizzy had seen her. No pretty silk scarf covering her head, only tufts of hair here and there. Her skin was the same ashy color, but her eyes were much more defined—hollow and sunken.

There was no denying it now; Ruth was clearly running out of time. She was bedridden. A nurse took care of her until Frank returned home each night. At the moment, the nurse was in the other room watching a soap opera.

Lizzy had exchanged pleasantries with Ruth when she first entered the room. But now it was time for the *un*pleasantries.

"Ruth," Lizzy said, her voice lined with sadness, "why did you hire me?"

"I want closure," she answered, her voice raspy. "I need to know what happened to my daughter."

Lizzy sat in a chair next to Ruth's bed. Her elbows rested on top of her knees, her head bent forward, fingers sifting through her hair. She lifted her head, straightened, and looked deep into Ruth's eyes. "I think you know exactly what happened to your daughter."

Ruth looked seriously confused.

Lizzy hated to upset the woman, but there would be no lies coming out of Lizzy's mouth today. At least not in this room. Nothing but the truth, the sordid, awful truth.

"You're in denial, Ruth."

"Have you found her?"

"Not yet, but I think we're close." One call from Jessica and she'd know where to go, but Jessica hadn't called, and that wasn't helping Lizzy's shattered nerves.

Ruth was staring at the ceiling now.

With each breath Ruth took, Lizzy could see the rise and fall of her chest through the thin fabric of her nightgown. "I need you to tell me about Frank's relationship with Carol."

"He loved Carol with all of his heart."

Lizzy shook her head. "That's bullshit. All bullshit."

Silence. No rebuttal.

"He's a sick man," Lizzy told her, "and the worst part is I think you know it."

"Everything Frank ever did was out of love."

Lizzy's head fell forward, back into her hands. If Ruth Fullerton had known what Frank did to her daughter and did nothing to stop him, then Lizzy hoped the woman died right this very moment. "Your husband raped Carol. I have reasonable cause to believe he raped Carol on a regular basis. So consistently did he put his dirty, disgusting hands on that girl that there is no possible way *you* could not have known."

"Why are you doing this?" Ruth asked.

Lizzy shook her head in wonder. "Are you serious? Did you know that Frank was raping your daughter?"

"He would never do such a thing. Never."

Filled with rage, Lizzy picked up the envelope and whipped out a picture, the worst picture out of the pile, and handed it to the woman. "Then explain to me, Ruth, what the fuck he was doing with Carol in that picture!"

Ruth tossed the photo to the floor. "Where did you get that?"

"Your husband needs help. He took those pictures, Ruth. There are dozens more just like it." Lizzy handed her another picture, but Ruth wouldn't grasp it. She turned her head so she didn't have to see the truth.

"You knew what Frank was doing and you did nothing to stop him."

"I didn't know. I didn't know."

Ruth was crying now, and the nurse must have heard her because she walked into the room. "You need to leave," the nurse told Lizzy. "She needs her rest."

Lizzy picked up the picture Ruth had tossed to the floor. "I'm leaving, Ruth, and I won't be back until you call me and tell me you're ready to deal with the truth."

Ruth's eyes remained shut. She didn't move, but her chest still rose and fell with each breath.

She would call, Lizzy prayed. When Ruth Fullerton was ready, she would call.

CHAPTER 32

STRAWBERRY FIELDS FOREVER

Jessica woke to the sound of a rooster's crow. She had fallen asleep on a cot with a very thin, lumpy mattress. Her back and shoulders, her entire body, in fact, felt as if she'd been camping out on the hard ground for a week.

Her hands were tied behind her back, but she managed to sit up on the edge of the bed, her feet flat against the cold hardwood floor. She could hear voices in the other room. The voices had woken her.

"If you knew you were being followed, why did you come here? You could have driven to the market down the street, anywhere but here. What were you thinking?"

"I guess I wasn't."

The last voice was Ellen's. Jessica recognized her voice immediately.

"It's been a long week," Ellen said.

Tell me about it, Jessica thought.

"None of this has been easy on me," Ellen finished.

"How do you think Carol feels, putting you through years of being questioned?"

"Leave her alone, Dean," another woman's voice interrupted, a stern but gentle voice. "The only reason Ellen came on such short notice was because I asked her to. None of this is Ellen's fault."

"Are you saying it's my fault?" the man asked.

"I'm not saying anything of the sort. I just don't know why you had to put a gun to that girl's head and drag her into this. Like Carol told us over the phone, that girl in the other room works for a private investigator my mother hired. She's harmless. You need to let her go."

"You think that after twenty years of hiding out I'm going to let that nosy girl in there ruin everything?"

"We don't have a choice, Dean. Do you think that after twenty years of hiding out I'm going to let you go to jail for kidnapping? What's the plan? Keep her locked up for twenty years while we continue on our merry way?"

It was quiet for a moment. Jessica felt the color drain from her face at the thought of being locked in this tiny room for twenty years. She should be grateful they hadn't discussed murdering her and burying her under the fields of strawberries. That would suck.

"Let her go, Dean. We'll move. We'll pay someone to pack up our stuff. We'll get tickets to the Caribbean, anywhere but here. We'll start over. We did it before, we can do it again."

Jessica stood and went to the window. Carol was alive. But what was Carol so afraid of? What had she done to warrant hiding out for the rest of her life?

Outside Jessica could see endless strawberry fields, fruit trees, and newly tilled farmland ready for planting. She turned her back to the window and used her fingers to fiddle with the latch. Her eyes widened in surprise when the latch flipped open.

Slowly, trying not to make any noise, she pushed the window open, inch by inch. Once she had the window open far enough to fit her body through, she turned around and stuck her head out to see how far she'd have to drop. Not far at all. She needed to get her legs through the window and then jump once her head was clear of the window frame.

She could do this.

It was awkward to maneuver her legs one at a time, especially with her hands tied behind her back. But it worked. She fell to the ground. Soft dirt and dead flowers greeted her backside. She was definitely going to have a few bruises, but a few bruises were better than spending a day, let alone twenty years, in that room.

Without bothering to look around and see who might be watching, she started running.

A dog barked in the distance.

She didn't bother looking for her car. The odds of the keys being inside were slim. And the man had taken her cell phone last night, so she couldn't call anyone.

She ran over clods of dirt, trying not to sprain her ankle in the process.

Once she reached the dirt road, the rooster crowed again. She was out of breath, but that didn't stop her from running as fast as her legs would carry her.

At the end of the driveway, she saw a car pass by.

She glanced over her shoulder, wobbled to her left, but refused to slow down, especially after seeing a truck screech out of the driveway and head her way.

Her breathing was ragged. She felt as if she was sucking in dust instead of air.

There were fruit trees to her left and a high fence to her right. She had no choice but to keep running a straight path down the driveway.

If she could just get to the road, she could stop traffic and get help. As she gained momentum, all she heard was the roar of the engine behind her.

* * *

Thump, whirr, clink, thump.

"Great, just great." Lizzy needed her car to break down about as much as she needed a broken leg. "Damn," she said as she steered her car to the side of the road.

She was on a busy road and her car had died. Lovely. The back of her car stuck out just enough to block traffic. Cars honked before they finally got a clue and inched their way around her.

There was nothing she could do about it. She sat there for a moment, trying to think.

"It's OK," she told her car, patting the console as if it was an animal instead of a vehicle. She loved this car. She and Old Yeller had been through a lot together. But she already knew that Old Yeller's time was up.

Lizzy slid to the passenger side and climbed out. She had left the car in neutral and was trying to push it out of everyone's way when a woman came running over and gave her a helping hand. Lizzy didn't realize who had helped her until the job was done. "Jane?"

"Hi, Lizzy."

"Wow, great timing. Thank you so much for helping me out."

"Not a problem. I noticed that you weren't at the gym this morning."

Guilt crept up Lizzy's neck and into her face. "I know. I'm sorry. I should have called, but I had too many things to do today. The weird part is that I was just headed to the gym. I really need to talk to Melbourne."

"He might be gone by the time you get there," Jane said, gesturing toward Lizzy's car.

Lizzy frowned. "You could be right about that."

"Why don't you call a tow truck and we can sit over there and have coffee while you wait." Jane pointed to a coffee shop across the street.

"You don't have to wait with me. I'll be fine."

"No, I'd love to chat for a minute and get to know you. Anthony speaks very highly of you."

Lizzy laid a hand on her chest. "Are you sure he's talking about me?"

Jane nodded. "He's impressed with the way you've managed to overcome so much hardship in your life. Nothing better than reading about someone who figures out a way to move on with their life after being through so much. You're a true hero."

Lizzy really didn't know what to say to that. She certainly was no hero. Quite the opposite, in fact. But she was tired, exhausted really, and she could use a coffee with a triple shot of espresso.

"I hope I'm not overstepping any boundaries by talking about your past."

"No," Lizzy said. "It's fine." She opened the passenger door of her car and looked through the glove box for an emergency roadside number. There it was, right on top where she'd put it last. She made the call and then tossed her cell in her purse. "Ready?"

Jane found a table outside while Lizzy waited for their coffee orders. Something about Jane showing up at just the right time and then offering to have coffee with her niggled at her, but she decided to let it go.

Lizzy realized she was becoming paranoid and suspicious. No sleep tended to do that to a person. At least she had someone to keep her company while she waited for the tow truck.

"So what's your connection with Anthony, anyhow?" Jane asked.

Lizzy recalled what Hayley had said about Jane having a crush on Melbourne. She also remembered what Hayley had said about Melbourne feeding his assistant a cheeseburger and fries. Why would he lecture his clients and then turn around and feed the girl french fries?

"I'm sorry, is that too personal?"

"Not personal," Lizzy told her, "just a bit random, I guess. I have no connection with Anthony Melbourne. My sister, like millions of women out there, happens to be a huge fan of his, so I decided to sign us up for a few seminars and a retreat and get some much needed exercise too."

"I didn't see your sister in San Francisco," Jane said.

Was Jane keeping tabs on her? "My sister couldn't make it, so I decided to check out Melbourne's seminar for myself."

"And you were impressed?"

"Very," Lizzy lied.

"He mentioned that you asked him about Diane Kramer when you were at the Tahoe retreat."

"Sounds like the two of you talk a lot," Lizzy said.

"I'm his assistant. I need to know what's going on if I'm going to do the best job possible."

"I have two assistants. They have no idea I'm sitting here with a broken down car, and I have no idea where they are at this very moment."

Jane took a sip of her vanilla latte and then shook her head. "That's not good business." She looked at her phone and smiled. "Anthony just sent me a text. He's meeting with the mayor in twenty minutes."

When Jane leaned over to put her phone back into her purse, Lizzy saw two long scratches on the back of Jane's neck. "Ouch," Lizzy said, "looks like somebody scratched you. Does that hurt?"

Jane thought about it for a moment and then smiled. "Oh, those," she said pointing to her neck. "My niece is the culprit. She's only a year old and somebody, namely her mother, needs to cut her nails."

"I'll say." Lizzy wondered if Jane was lying. Every moment was more awkward than the last.

"You know, I really should head off," Jane said. "But there is one thing I need to get off my chest."

Lizzy arched a brow and waited.

"I know you're a private investigator."

"It's not a secret," Lizzy said.

"Did Andrea hire you to watch Anthony?"

Caught off guard, Lizzy didn't quite know what to say, so she remained quiet.

"You should know that not only did Andrea work out with Anthony Melbourne in the past, she used to work in his office and help him with his paperwork and filing. She's been infatuated with the man for years."

"She's married with three kids," Lizzy told her.

"Aren't they all?"

At a loss for words, Lizzy remained silent.

Jane reapplied her lipstick, and Lizzy noticed it was a familiar shade of red. She wanted to ask her if it was Cherry Bomb by CoverGirl, but apparently their conversation was over because Jane stood and grabbed her things. "Do you need a ride anywhere?"

"No, that's OK. You've done enough already. I'll get a ride to the auto shop and figure it out from there."

Lizzy stood too and offered Jane her hand. "Thanks again. I really appreciate you helping me get my car off the road."

Between the coffee and the purse, Jane's hands were full. She shrugged, smiled, and headed off, leaving Lizzy to wonder what the hell was going on.

Aren't they all? What did that mean?

Lizzy thought about running after Jane and asking her a few questions of her own. Instead, she decided to get the car situation taken care of and then pay Andrea a visit.

CHAPTER 33

HOME SWEET HOME

Two o'clock in the afternoon. Hayley couldn't remember the last time she'd slept so well. It was five in the morning by the time she'd gotten home last night.

The first two nights at Lizzy's place, she'd slept on the couch, but last night she opted for the bedroom Lizzy had set up for her. The room was small and filled with boxes, files mostly. Lizzy had a twin bed set up. The bed was the centerpiece of the room. The headboard had colorful tulips and roses painted on it.

She didn't like the idea of getting too comfortable. Neither did she like the idea of mooching off other people. Cathy had taken her in, and now Lizzy. Hayley needed to find a way to pay rent. She'd spent most of the money she'd made working for Lizzy on sturdy knives and other gadgets. That stuff wasn't cheap.

Sitting up, she rubbed the back of her neck as she thought about her mom. The fact that her mom refused to change made her sad, but it also cemented her resolve when it came to following through with her plans of revenge.

Despite the heavy sadness hovering over her, Hayley felt as if she was getting some closure as her big day drew near. As long as

Dr. Williams left the syringe at the park as instructed, she would be on schedule to take care of Brian once and for all.

The thought of ridding the world of that one particular man made her feel oddly refreshed. When it was all said and done, she could possibly end up in jail. She wasn't going to dress up in wigs and high heels for Brian. What he saw was what he would get.

Her mom might be sad about Brian's demise, but not for long. Hayley's hope was that her mom would become clean after Brian was gone for good. If her mom didn't have Brian hanging around, keeping her high on drugs and alcohol, she might have a fighting chance. And that's all that mattered to Hayley.

Jail wouldn't be so bad, Hayley figured. It couldn't be any worse than the time spent at home with Brian and his friends, or the time spent with her grandfather way back when, or the time spent with Spiderman.

She noticed that Lizzy had hung a new picture on the wall. It dangled slightly to the right. "Home Sweet Home."

She smiled.

There was nothing fake about Lizzy, and yet something about the picture didn't ring true: not that Lizzy didn't want it to be true, because she did. And sometimes that's all that mattered.

Hayley had told Lizzy she didn't know what love was, but that wasn't completely true. She loved her mom. And she loved Lizzy like a sister. She didn't have any siblings, but she figured the way she felt about Lizzy was probably the same way many siblings felt about one another. Lizzy was a good person. She always put everybody else first. She never thought about her own wants or needs. Even the Jared thing was more about Jared than Lizzy, Hayley figured. Lizzy didn't want to creep him out with her nightmares and crazy highs and lows. Lizzy was nice, but she was still screwed up. Anybody who knew her well enough could see that.

Maybe that's why Hayley liked her so much.

She glanced at the Home Sweet Home picture again and knew that was definitely why she liked Lizzy: she was one messed up lady who was trying so hard to be normal.

* * *

It didn't take Lizzy long to find Andrea Kramer's address in El Dorado Hills. It was interesting to Lizzy that Andrea didn't use her married name. The binder that Andrea had given her was chock-full of detailed information—on everyone except for Andrea herself.

The car Lizzy had rented while the auto shop looked at Old Yeller was nicer than she'd expected or wanted, but it was all they had left: a shiny new 2012 Cadillac CTS with navigation and everything else you could ever want in a car.

Lizzy drove straight from the rental shop to Andrea Kramer's house, a massive ten-thousand-square-foot mansion on the top of a hill overlooking Folsom Lake. The driveway was long, and visitors were kept at bay with a sturdy gate.

Leaning out her car window, she hit the button on the black box, hoping somebody would let her through.

"Hello?" came a timid voice from the box.

"Hi, this is Lizzy Gardner. I'm here to talk with Andrea Kramer."

"What are you doing here?"

Lizzy was confused by Andrea's tone of voice. She sounded angry. "You didn't leave me a telephone number where I could reach you," Lizzy explained, "but I was able to find your address."

"How did you find me?"

"I'm a private investigator, remember? I need to talk to you about your sister."

There was a buzzing sound and the gate slowly slid open. Lizzy drove the Cadillac up the driveway lined with tall, well-fertilized palm trees. Fountain. Check. Sprawling green grass and manicured hedges. Check. Pond with expensive fish swimming about. Check. Although she couldn't see the fish, she had a good imagination.

She pulled into one of five parking spaces, got out, and admired the view before heading for the stairs that led to the front door. As she climbed a ridiculous number of flagstone steps to a humongous front door made from imported rare wood, no doubt, she was surprised to find that she was still able to breathe. The workouts were actually doing some good.

Andrea greeted her at the door. Lizzy couldn't help but wonder if the woman slept in her Armani and then lay perfectly still so as not to ruin her perfectly coiffed hair. How did women like Andrea do it—always look so put together? She was lucky if she could get her laundry done.

"You really shouldn't be here," Andrea said, wringing her hands and looking around nervously.

Lizzy blew out some hot air. Today was another scorcher. "Should I come back later?"

"No, no. Come inside. My kids are playing across the street. They might see you."

Lizzy looked over her shoulder to make sure they weren't behind her. "Just tell them I'm an old friend stopping by to say hello." What was the big deal?

Andrea gestured again for Lizzy to come inside and quickly shut the door behind her. "I sent you a check yesterday. The money should arrive at your office by tomorrow."

"I didn't send you an invoice," Lizzy said, confused.

"Oh, please don't send me an invoice. No paperwork, if you don't mind. I believe I told you that my husband can't know about our exchange."

"I don't recall, but why is that?"

"He works in finance. He watches every penny."

"Your sister is missing. I would think with all of this," Lizzy said, motioning with her hands at the fifty-foot ceilings and expensive statues, "he might see it as money well spent."

"He never liked Diane. He wouldn't understand. Why don't you tell me why you're here so we can get this settled."

Get this settled? The woman clearly didn't like Lizzy being here. Lizzy looked around and saw no sign of life. No toys lying around. No big teenager shoes near the door or any sign at all that anyone else lived here. "Usually," Lizzy explained, "I meet with my clients once or twice a week to keep them apprised of what's going on with their case. The reason I came to see you, Andrea, is because following Anthony Melbourne is not producing results. I don't mind keeping an eye on him for a few hours every day, but I don't see any point in following him around twenty-four-seven."

"Do you know where he is now?"

"As in right this very minute?" Lizzy asked.

"Yes."

"I have no idea."

"Well then, it doesn't seem to me that you've been doing your job."

OK, now she was starting to piss Lizzy off. "I told you from the start that I have other work to do. Your missing sister is not my only case. Today I had other things that needed my attention, and then my car broke down. Thankfully, Melbourne's assistant happened to be driving by and sat with me while I waited for a tow truck. Thus the rental car and here I am."

"Jane helped you?"

"Yes, and she mentioned that you used to work out with Anthony Melbourne."

Andrea looked down her nose at Lizzy. "That's not a secret. I told you that I worked out with Anthony, remember?"

Lizzy scratched her head. Had she completely lost her memory? She couldn't remember Andrea ever saying anything about working out with Melbourne. "He trained you?"

"Yes." Andrea lowered her voice as if they weren't the only two people in the house. "The truth is I used to be as big as Diane. My husband insisted I lose the weight. He doesn't like Anthony Melbourne."

"Does your husband like anyone?"

Andrea ignored her. "Ever since I lost the weight, he's been jealous of other men, especially Anthony since he and I worked together for months, hours at a time."

"Did your husband have any reason to be jealous?"

"No, of course not. I love my husband dearly." Andrea looked at her gold Cartier watch. "You really do need to go. My husband should be home any minute."

Lizzy tried to talk fast. "I wanted to let you know that I'm not going to work out with Melbourne at the gym any longer. I'm going to cancel my membership tomorrow."

"Fine."

Surprised by Andrea's quick agreement, Lizzy said, "Andrea, is there anything else you're not telling me?"

She was wringing her hands again. "There is one thing. I've been receiving a lot of calls, day and night. When I pick up my phone I hear breathing and then the caller hangs up."

"And you think it might be Melbourne?"

She nodded. "After I got to my goal weight, I worked part-time for Anthony, but I'm afraid he was upset with me when I had to quit for the sake of my marriage. I think he might have done something to my sister to get back at me."

"I see," Lizzy said, but she didn't see at all. Andrea was acting strange. Although she had planned to tell Andrea about the photo she had found and that she thought she was being followed, she suddenly decided to keep it all to herself. "OK, then," Lizzy said, feeling tension between them, "I'll see what I can do."

Andrea sighed. "Since you're here, you might as well tell me about your weekend in Tahoe. Did Melbourne ever leave the retreat?"

Lizzy shook her head. "I had a direct view of his car from my room. He never left the lodge except to take us on a hike. If he had left, where do you suppose he might have gone to?"

Andrea sighed, clearly exasperated. "I've already told you. I think he's hiding something. He has secrets, and I hired you to find out what those secrets are."

Alrighty then. Lizzy clasped her hands together and nodded. For the first time since she'd met Andrea Kramer, though, she wondered what exactly the woman was up to. Was this some sort of wild goose chase?

"I guess we're finished here. Thank you for the update," Andrea said, clearly ready for their talk to end.

Lizzy headed for the door. "If I learn anything about your sister, how would you like me to contact you?"

Exasperated, Andrea turned about and walked quickly to the sprawling kitchen with the two refrigerators and two ovens. She jotted down a number and came back to hand Lizzy the scrap of paper. "If you learn anything new, call me at this number and leave a message if I don't answer."

Lizzy held up the paper. "Will do."

"Oh, and I wouldn't believe anything that Jane woman tells you."

"Why is that?"

"She's a little cuckoo, if you know what I mean?" Andrea made the little cuckoo motion people tended to do when they said the word, spinning her slender, well-manicured finger next to her ear.

Lizzy thought it was a little cuckoo that Andrea would bring up Jane at all.

Andrea was holding the door open, and Lizzy was afraid if she didn't get the hell out of there, she was going to feel the tip of Andrea's expensive shoe in her backside.

Glad to be leaving, Lizzy made a quick exit.

After clearing the gate at the bottom of the driveway, she waited for one of Andrea's neighbors to grab a ball that some kids had thrown into the middle of the road.

Lizzy rolled her window down so she could talk to the woman. "Which of those kids over there belong to Andrea Kramer?"

"Do you mean Andrea Smith?" the woman asked, pointing to the house Lizzy just left.

Lizzy nodded.

"Are you friends with Andrea?" the woman asked.

"We just met. She said her kids were playing at the neighbors, and I was just curious if maybe those were her kids over there."

The woman came closer to Lizzy's window. "I don't know if it's my place to tell you, but her husband left her recently and took the kids with him. I heard through the grapevine that he even went so far as to get a restraining order against her."

Lizzy was too stunned to say anything at all.

"I'm sorry if I said too much."

The kids across the street were yelling for their ball.

"No, not at all," Lizzy said. "It's good that I know. Next time I see her, I'll be able to tell her how sorry I am for all she's going through."

The woman nodded, but before she could get away Lizzy had one more question. "Do you have any idea what kind of car Andrea drives?"

"She drives a silver jaguar, but every once in a while I see her in the Expedition," the woman said before she ran back to the kids and handed them the ball.

Before Lizzy could let that information sink in, her phone rang. Hoping it was Jessica, she answered on the first ring.

"Lizzy Gardner?"

"This is her."

"It's Debra Taphorn. I think we should talk."

"I'll be there in twenty minutes."

CHAPTER 34

A VERY LONG DAY

Boredom seeped into every crevice of Hayley's being. For most of the day, she had played with the cat, watched a movie, and pondered on Brian's last moments in this world.

At the moment, she wondered what Lizzy had been doing all day since she usually checked in at least twice a day. Hopefully, Lizzy wasn't driving around breaking and entering just for the hell of it. Lizzy had looked as if she'd enjoyed the process entirely too much. Maybe she was in jail and had already used her only call. Except Hayley knew that that's not how it worked. Back when she thought Brian was an OK guy, he'd gotten a DUI and she and her mom had gone to the jail to pick him up. They had to wait until morning when they could hire a bail bondsman to put up the money to get him out. He'd called at least six times, which had cost her mom a pretty penny considering she had to give the voice recorder a credit card number before they would connect Brian from his cell. He said there was a payphone inside the holding cell.

Hayley sighed, figuring she might very well find out how all of that worked soon enough. Her next thought was about Jessica. Jessica had been on surveillance duty yesterday and Hayley couldn't help but wonder how that was going. Jessica was smarter than many, but she wasn't even close to being the shiniest tool in the shed. Sure, she had a few clever ideas every once in a while, but that was about it.

And then there was Brittany Warner. She thought of Brittany as a sister. After being abducted by Spiderman, Brittany's newfound fame had helped to make her dreams of becoming a cheerleader come true. Suddenly she was popular and everyone wanted to be her friend. Nobody else knew about all of the confusing thoughts running through Brittany's head. The mind was a powerful thing; it tried to control people with random thoughts throughout the day.

Hayley had read Erica Taggert's *A Better World*. She could easily memorize whole passages without trying, which always made school easy for her. Erica Taggert was a spiritual teacher and a thoughtful thinker. One of her ideas that Hayley had latched onto was that a person's thoughts were separate from the person. A constant stream of negative thoughts could easily become debilitating. But to become aware of those thoughts and to know that one's thoughts are not who they are can be freeing.

Hayley sighed.

All good feelings were swept away as she went over a mental list of what she needed to do to take care of Brian once and for all.

1) Find a way to distract bodyguard camped outside Brian's house
2) Get syringe into Brian's house without him seeing it
3) Make Brian believe I miss him

Her cell phone rang, breaking her concentration. It was the woman she'd talked to about Burning Man. She asked the woman to hold while she went to the desk in Lizzy's bedroom. Then she sat down and wrote down the names of the people on the committee in 1989. After thanking the woman for her help, she hung up the phone. There were six names in all.

She turned on Lizzy's computer. She would try to find out where they lived and hopefully get a phone number. If she could talk to anyone on the list, her first question would be whether they ever owned or drove a Buick.

While she waited for the computer to warm up, her gaze fell on the pile of papers and journals that Lizzy had stolen from Vivian's apartment. After she researched the names on the Burning Man list, she figured she could help Lizzy out by reading Vivian's journals. Suddenly she had a lot of work to do.

* * *

The drive to Debra Taphorn's apartment building was surprisingly nice. The seat in the Cadillac was cushiony and the air conditioner worked a little too well, making Lizzy shiver despite the fact that the temperature outside was still in the nineties.

She wasn't used to being comfortable while driving. Her hair wasn't stringy and wet, no sweat dripping down her spine. She could get used to this.

She made a right into the same parking lot where she'd been left a warning last time she was here. She parked close to the building, hoping that would stop someone from scribbling another note on her windshield.

Had that been a random warning?

Lizzy got out of the car and headed for Debra's apartment. If Andrea drove an Expedition, she thought, that would mean she was more than likely the one who had been following her. What was Andrea up to?

Debra Taphorn opened the door on the second knock. Her greeting was friendlier than Andrea's, but despite being the one who had called Lizzy here, Debra didn't look thrilled to see her either.

"I've fixed us some iced tea," Debra said. "It's all set up in the living room."

Without bothering to remove her shoes, Lizzy followed her inside. She took a seat on one end of the couch, glad she wasn't hot and sticky. "What's going on?"

Debra poured the tea, complete with lemon wedge, and handed Lizzy a cold glass.

The iced tea tasted lemony and refreshing. "This is very good. Thank you."

Debra took a seat on one of two cushiony chairs facing the couch. "You're probably wondering why I called you here."

Lizzy nodded and waited.

"I couldn't sleep last night. I have no interest in having the feds get involved, but you must understand that I signed a confidentiality agreement with Anthony Melbourne when I signed up for his Extreme Exercise Program. I lost over one hundred pounds and I've never been happier. The regimen was difficult and even scary at times. I would never recommend it to friends. Even if I wanted to recommend the program, I'm not allowed."

"He doesn't want recommendations?" Lizzy asked. "He never promoted you as the poster child for before and after?"

"No," Debra said. "It's not like that at all. He handpicks the people he thinks he can help. He's a very passionate man. He truly cares about his clients. Every once in a while he checks up on me to see how I'm doing."

"Really. Melbourne calls you to check up on you?"

"Anthony has called me once or twice. Sometimes his assistant will call."

Jane certainly got around, Lizzy thought.

"Before I can tell you much more I need a guarantee from you that I won't be sued. I run a very lucrative weight loss center. My clients can find me in my office twelve hours a day, ready to help them reach their weight loss goals."

"Like Weight Watchers?"

"No, not exactly. I don't offer meals. I am considered a consultant. My clients can call me at any time. I get calls in the middle of the night and sometimes I need to talk them down from the ledge, in a sense. Many times they call when they're tempted to binge."

Lizzy nodded.

"I can't afford to have my story get out to the public. I would lose my reputation if my clients knew what I had to do to lose the weight."

"What did you have to do exactly?"

"Are you willing to sign a document stating that you will not go public with what I am about to tell you?"

Lizzy nodded. "I'll sign anything you want."

Debra had already typed up a one-page agreement. Lizzy wasn't worried about signing it. She had no plans to go public with anything Debra told her. Her lips were sealed. She signed and dated the agreement. "OK," Lizzy said, "now what?"

"Now I'm going to tell you about Anthony Melbourne's well-kept secret. The morning he and Jane picked me up, I had a small suitcase packed with my favorite books, CDs, iPod, anything I might need for a long vacation."

"How long were you planning on being away?"

"I knew it could be anywhere from two to four months."

"That's a long time."

Debra nodded. "They told me to dress comfortably. I wore shorts and a T-shirt. It was summertime, not quite as hot as it is today, but the point is I didn't need to bring much. It wasn't long before we stopped for gas. At that point, which was about an hour into the trip, Jane asked me to put on a blindfold. I didn't like the idea because I'm claustrophobic, but she said if I didn't cooperate we would need to return home."

That didn't surprise Lizzy.

"The tone of Jane's voice, and Anthony Melbourne's sudden inability to speak, caught me off guard. I began to worry about what I had signed up for, but I put the blindfold on and I did whatever I was told. It all seemed suddenly very serious."

"Did they ask you to do anything else?"

She shook her head. "I'm almost certain I was drugged."

"How?"

"Jane must have switched my water bottle because suddenly she was telling me I needed to drink more water or I was going to get dehydrated. She hadn't told me to drink water until after the blindfold was on."

"That is strange."

"I must have dozed off within fifteen minutes of drinking the water," Debra went on. "I never fall asleep in a car while someone else is driving. But that day—I passed out immediately."

"So you never saw where they took you?"

"Funny you should ask. Right before I dozed off I had the sensation of going in circles. I don't know if Anthony Melbourne was actually driving in circles or if he had made a U-turn. I have an inkling that he was trying to throw me off. You know, as to which way we were headed."

"They thought of everything," Lizzy said.

Debra nodded. "While I was sleeping, though, my blindfold must have slipped to the side in such a way that I could see out of the corner of my left eye. Just barely. Enough to see a sign for a lodge as I was coming to."

"At that point do you know how long you had been in the car?"

Debra shook her head.

"Do you remember the name of the lodge?"

"No, I'm sorry. It was a wood sign and there were flowers painted on it. Daisies, I believe."

"Can you draw a picture for me?"

"Sure. After seeing the sign, we made a right turn. It was all windy uphill from there on. I remember feeling nauseous before I passed out again. If you think any of that was weird, wait until you hear the rest."

Thirty minutes later, Debra finished her story.

It was hard for Lizzy to believe that the same woman who had been chained, cuffed at the ankle for three months, left with enough food to feed an army, but expected to ignore a ridiculous number of temptations, was sitting here now, telling Lizzy she was not only grateful for the journey but thankful to have had the opportunity.

Despite spending thousands of dollars to be in Melbourne's secret program, her life had not been the same since. And she insisted that was a good thing. Not only did she look terrific, she now had a thriving business and a loving fiancé.

Debra Taphorn was happy.

CHAPTER 35

GOOD NEWS AND BAD NEWS

"I have good news and I have bad news," Hayley told Lizzy the moment she walked into her apartment.

"This has been the longest day of my life," Lizzy said. "Please tell me because I couldn't make a guess if you paid me."

Hayley followed Lizzy to the kitchen, talking as they went. "I have the name of a man who not only helped plan Burning Man back when Carol Fullerton disappeared, he also drove a Buick. His name is Dean Chandler. I haven't been able to find an address or a telephone number, but I was hoping you could talk to Jared and have him run a report on the man."

"That is great news," Lizzy agreed.

"Not only that," Hayley went on, "I also read every single one of Vivian's journals and notes."

Lizzy poured herself a glass of cold water from the fridge.

"Man, that Vivian woman likes to make notations about everything. She even writes about bugs that crawl by. And she had a lot to say about the neighbor you met."

Lizzy winced. "She doesn't like that sweet old lady?"

"Not one bit. But forget about the neighbors for now. According to Vivian's journal, she hadn't heard from her friend Diane Kramer,

T. R. RAGAN

so she drove to Diane's house. That was over six months ago. When she arrived, Diane was getting into a car. According to Vivian's notes, there was only one person in the car besides Diane. It was a man—a muscular man. Vivian decided to follow them. Unfortunately, an hour later, she ran out of gas and lost Diane. For weeks she was angry with her friend for leaving without telling anyone, but after failing to hear from Diane, her anger grew to concern."

"Damn," Lizzy said as she put her empty glass in the sink. Believing Hayley was finished she said, "I talked to Debra Taphorn again today. She never met Diane, but she's been through some sort of crazy secret weight program of Melbourne's. Although this is all to be kept confidential, she paid thousands of dollars to be cuffed and chained at the ankle for three months. I guess Melbourne handpicks the people for his program. He takes them to a secluded mountain cabin complete with treadmill, kitchen, and enough food to last a dozen people for months."

"It's a weight loss thing, right?"

Lizzy nodded.

"Then why all the food?"

"According to Debra, he wants his clients to learn to live with the temptations. Debra said it worked for her. Although she was scared at times, she's glad she did it."

"Are you going to call the police?"

"No. Not yet. Melbourne hasn't admitted to anything, and Debra has no idea what direction they were going when they took her to the cabin. She saw a sign for some sort of lodge. There were flowers painted on the sign. I asked her to draw a picture, but do you have any idea how many lodges there are in California? Anyhow, after the sign with the flowers, they made an immediate right. It was all long and winding roads after that. North, south, east, I have no idea where to start." Lizzy sighed. "I feel helpless.

Diane Kramer has been missing for too long. If she was a part of the program, why hasn't she come home? And now Vivian is missing too. It can't be a coincidence."

"Well, you haven't heard the good news yet."

"Give it to me."

"Vivian wrote down the name of the highway. They were headed east on Interstate 80. Vivian made it as far as Gold Run, past Colfax."

Lizzy's phone vibrated and she picked it up.

"Lizzy, it's me, Jessica."

"Thank God. Are you OK?"

"I've been to hell and back. I want a raise."

* * *

It was early the next morning when all three of them, Lizzy, Hayley, and Jessica, sat in the front room in Lizzy's apartment. They all looked equally haggard—complete with puffy eyes and pale faces.

Last night, Hayley and Lizzy had driven for hours in order to meet with Jessica. After hearing what had happened to her, Lizzy didn't want Jessica driving home alone. Hayley had driven Lizzy's rental car back while Lizzy and Jessica followed behind in the Honda. They returned to the apartment after three in the morning, and all three of them found it hard to sleep, thus the early morning meeting.

Jessica passed around orange juice that nobody bothered drinking.

Dean Chandler, the man who had picked Carol Fullerton up on the highway over twenty years ago, was sitting in jail in Kern County for kidnapping Jessica. Although Jessica wasn't keen on pressing charges, especially after getting the chance to talk to Carol in person and hearing about her reasons for running away, she had agreed with Lizzy to start the process until they knew exactly what was going on.

Apparently, Carol had not met Dean Chandler until that same fateful day she disappeared. Why Dean felt the need to kidnap Jessica made no sense to Lizzy. Carol tried to explain to Jessica that her husband had panicked. Dean and Carol had been hiding for so long that the idea of being found out was beyond his reasoning at the time.

Ellen Woodson, it turned out, had been keeping Carol's secret for a very long time. Ellen, being a good friend—maybe too good considering her own life seemed to have suffered because of her secret—had vowed never to tell anyone of Carol's whereabouts. The two women had been corresponding with each other on a regular basis for over twenty years.

Jessica sat down and was now looking through the pictures Hayley had stolen from Frank's home office. She grunted and huffed as she sifted through the photos one at a time. "Poor Carol," she said.

"Did Ruth admit that she knew what was going on?" Hayley asked.

Lizzy shook her head. "She didn't admit to anything, but she knew what was going on. No matter what, she knew enough. She's in denial. Either way, their time is up. I need to hand these pictures over to the police and let them take care of Frank."

Lizzy looked at Jessica. "Did you tell Carol that her mother was dying and wanted to see her?"

Jessica nodded. "I don't think that's going to happen. I've never seen such raw hatred before; almost as if all the bad stuff that went on had happened to Carol only yesterday."

"I don't blame her," Hayley said. "It doesn't sound like Ruth Fullerton deserves to see her daughter one last time."

"My first time solving a real case," Jessica said, "and I feel like crap for doing it. Some things are better left dead and buried."

"I don't agree," Lizzy said. "Nothing but good comes from letting out the truth, or seeing the truth in Ruth's case. I still hope Carol will say good-bye to her mom and give herself closure too. After she does that, she and Dean should be able to go on with their lives without hiding from the world. It couldn't have been easy for either of them, hiding for so long."

Disgusted, Jessica put the pictures away and was now staring at her iPhone, the one the police had retrieved from Dean Chandler. "Did you see the newest headline this morning in the *Sac Bee?*" Jessica asked.

Both Lizzy and Hayley shook their heads.

"Some guy named Peter was arrested on drug and sex trafficking charges. They found him after he went on a wild rampage beating every hooker he could get his hands on. Apparently someone used some sort of hot iron to carve letters into his chest and he was not happy about it."

"What was on his chest? Some sort of cryptic message?" Hayley asked.

"No, not cryptic at all. The message was straightforward and to the point: 'Sick Fuck.'"

Lizzy pointed a finger at Jessica. "I wonder if it was that same guy you found on the Internet. The man on the street corner who was caught on video?"

Jessica shook her head. "Two different instances. This Peter incident happened at least a week before the one we witnessed on the Internet. In fact, the reporter mentions both incidents." She looked straight at Hayley and said, "He thinks Sacramento has a 'Seeker of Revenge' on its hands."

CHAPTER 36

EXERCISE CAN BE DEADLY

Lizzy didn't feel good about leaving Hayley and Jessica in her apartment alone, just the two of them, but she didn't have much choice. Besides, they looked as if they were warming up to each other. Truthfully, neither of them talked to the other any longer, which Lizzy figured was a good start.

For days now, Lizzy had been meaning to stop by her sister's house and let her know she wouldn't be working out every morning. But once again that would have to wait. First she planned to have a long talk with Melbourne and Jane. She had tried to do things Andrea's way, but following Melbourne around wasn't getting them anywhere. And clearly Andrea wasn't being truthful with her.

It was time to sit down with Melbourne and ask the same questions the police had probably already asked him. Diane Kramer and Vivian Hardy could be in danger, and it was time for Melbourne to fess up.

It was seven in the morning.

The rest of Melbourne's posse usually arrived around seven thirty, even though class didn't start until eight.

There were two cars parked outside, she noticed as she made her way to the front entrance. She walked inside. It was eerily quiet. The lights in the gym and the equipment had yet to be turned on. "Hello?" she called out.

Nobody answered. She felt a prickling unease starting at the back of her neck. Something was very wrong. Listening for any sound at all, she reached over her shoulder, feeling for her Glock. She unsnapped the strap and pulled out her gun.

Pressing onward, she walked slowly in the direction of Melbourne's office. About ten feet in front of his office was Jane's desk…and blood, lots of blood. Lizzy took a few steps backward so that she could peer into the gym, looking for movement in the shadows, making sure nobody was hiding in the dark.

Convinced nobody was hiding in the gym, she took a closer look at the blood on the floor. From the looks of it, something had been dragged across the blood and into Melbourne's office. Following the bloody path, she walked slowly through the open door and blew out some built-up tension at the horrid sight before her.

Anthony Melbourne lay dead on the floor. Jane was dead too, her head resting against his chest.

Lizzy examined the room. There was a closet. Her heart beat faster.

She took quiet steps toward the closet door.

With her gun readied, she used her left hand to pull open the door. The door knob hit the wall with a bang.

The closet was empty.

Turning back to the gruesome sight, she guessed that Melbourne had been in his office, perhaps sitting at his desk, when the killer walked in. From the looks of it, he came to his feet right before he was bludgeoned with one of two marble bookends that now lay on the floor in the corner of the room. He'd also been stabbed multiple times in every part of his body. The killer had made use of every utensil he or she could find in Melbourne's office. His engraved letter opener protruded from his left eye, the M on the handle clearly visible. A pencil had been stabbed through his neck. Every picture on his wall was either cracked or had been tossed in the garbage. And then there was Jane, lying in his arms.

Lizzy's gaze followed the bloody path back out Melbourne's office door. When people walked through the front entrance of the gym, the first desk they came to before arriving at Melbourne's office door, was Jane's.

Jane must have arrived just as the killer was done with Melbourne. The killer didn't waste any time finishing Jane off too. Jane's purse lay in the middle of the floor next to the biggest blood stain near her desk. Jane hadn't had time to put her purse away. She was taken down before she could figure out what was going on.

After the killer left, Jane must have dragged herself into Melbourne's office where she died with her head resting against his shoulder, tucked innocently in the crook of his arm as if they were both just taking a nap.

Lizzy walked back to where Jane's purse lay and noticed a cell phone inside. Jane could have called 911. Instead, she chose to spend her last moments in Melbourne's arms.

It dawned on Lizzy then.

She knew the killer personally. Her head snapped up and she looked outside toward the parking lot. "Andrea," she said. "You bitch."

* * *

After calling Detective Roth and waiting for him to arrive at the crime scene, Lizzy spent the next two hours answering questions.

Finally she told Roth she would either be at home or he could reach her on her cell if the police had further questions.

Lizzy drove as fast as she could. She had filled up the shiny new Cadillac with gas and now she was making calls as she went.

She called Jessica first. "Jessica, I'm headed east on Interstate 80 toward Nevada. Is Hayley there?"

"No. She said she was going out to get something to eat, but that was hours ago. She hasn't come back. Where have you been? I thought you were coming back to the apartment this afternoon."

"I went to the gym to have a talk with Melbourne and Jane. They're both dead. Murdered."

Jessica gasped.

"I need you to do me a favor, Jessica. There are pictures on my desk in my bedroom. Hand-drawn pictures of a lodge with flowers painted on it, daisies, I think. The actual sign is four feet by four feet. The problem is I don't know the name of the lodge. I need you to get on the computer and do a search, find anything at all that looks like the picture on my desk. If you find something, I need you to call me back on my cell. It could be life or death."

"OK," Jessica said. "Anything else I can do?"

"Detective Roth should be coming by to pick up the pictures of Frank and Carol Fullerton. I need you to give him the envelope."

"Does he know how the pictures were obtained?" Jessica asked.

"No. And at this point I don't see any reason why we should tell him. If he asks, just tell him you have no idea."

"Lizzy, I know you probably need to go, but I've wanted to talk to you about Hayley. I'm worried about her."

"So am I," Lizzy said. "So am I. But there isn't a whole lot we can do today. Let's help one person at a time. I'm afraid Vivian Hardy could be in a lot of trouble."

"What about Diane Kramer?"

"If I can find Vivian, I'm hoping Diane is there too. Just keep your fingers crossed and call me if you find anything."

* * *

Hayley pulled over to the side of the road. She looked at her map. X marked the spot. She was close. Very close. A left on Hickory and then one more right turn and she would arrive at her final destination.

Tonight was the night.

For months, Hayley had been planning for this night.

The other guys she visited had deserved more than they got, but Brian would pay the ultimate price for all of them. Brian would pay for what he had done to her and her mother.

Hayley's gaze fell on her nine fingers gripping the steering wheel of Jessica's car. She looked at the stub where her tenth finger used to be and realized she rarely gave Spiderman a first or second thought. Her therapist, the lady Lizzy insisted she talk to on a regular basis, was convinced that the missing digit was a constant reminder of that time in Hayley's life. But the missing digit didn't bother Hayley at all. It was the feelings within, the hidden mental shit that nobody could see, that made Hayley feel as if she might go crazy if she didn't find an outlet for the pent-up anger she held inside. Her anger had nothing to do with Spiderman or her missing pinky finger and had everything to do with Brian. He was a cold-blooded creature who deserved to die.

Brian had taken her body and her spirit and had destroyed the essence of her humanity. Years ago, Hayley had sought help at a rape crisis center. The woman who had greeted her and taken her in was kind and patient. She was pleased by Hayley's ability to acknowledge the hurt and anger she felt toward her assailant. Hayley had spent two weeks talking with other rape victims. Ninety percent of the girls believed it was inappropriate to have feelings of hatred and vindictiveness for their assailant. These girls were trapped in a world of guilt that made no sense to Hayley. The people at the center were not aware that Hayley's nightmare was ongoing...a weekly, if not daily, ritual.

Hayley was sure she would never stop seeing Brian's face hovering above hers, his breathing uneven, his stench unbearable. Even back then, Hayley knew how this would end. She just hadn't known when it would happen.

Until now. It was time.

She inhaled deeply as she merged back onto the street.

She had left Lizzy's apartment hours ago. After finding the brown paper bag taped under the bench at Marshall Park, she'd sat and waited for the sun to set. Lizzy and Jessica had been calling her all day, forcing her to turn off her cell phone. She had work to do.

Despite the hour, there were a few lost souls wandering the streets. No gangs hanging out tonight. No Bloods or Crips on the street corner looking for trouble.

The fewer people, the better.

She made a left off Florin. On the corner, there was a two-story apartment building that looked abandoned. She made a right on Alita Road: a row of tract homes with unkempt yards, broken windows, and graffiti.

There it was.

Brian's house. The best looking house in the neighborhood, painted in neutral colors, with a fenced-in front yard and lots of trees. She wasn't sure if Brian's bodyguard would be in attendance tonight, but there he was. Seeing the muscled man had been hit and miss when she did her drive-bys. But she had covered all her bases, which was exactly why she was wearing the same outfit she'd worn for Dr. Williams.

After passing Brian's house, Hayley pulled up to the curb in front of the vacant house next door and shut off the engine. She got out and pretended to examine the back tire. When that was done, she opened the trunk and bent over, making sure Brian's bodyguard had a good view of her assets.

"What's the problem?" she heard the bodyguard ask.

She turned toward the approaching man. "I have a flat tire," she said, feigning exasperation.

"Do you have a cell phone?"

"Yes."

"Why don't you call a tow truck?"

She held up the tire iron in her hand. "I'm in a hurry and that would take forever. I'll figure it out." She went to look at the flat tire. She had let out just enough air earlier to make it look flat.

"Looks like you ran over a nail."

"Yeah, looks like it."

"You're going to need a jack."

"This is my friend's car," she said, leaning her hip against the car in a seductive pose. "Do you know where the jack would be stored?" She chewed on her bottom lip.

He let his eyes roam over her, his smile broadening. He glanced over his shoulder at Brian's house, and then looked at her again. "I'll help you out, but it's going to cost you."

He didn't need to say another word. She knew exactly what he meant in terms of payment. "Sure, OK, but I don't have a lot of time."

"Five minutes of my time and five minutes of yours."

She smiled. "Sounds fair to me."

He chuckled and then leaned into the trunk in search of the jack.

Hayley lifted the tire iron and swung hard. She was ready to strike twice, but one good swing was all it took. Working fast, she grunted and heaved until she had the lower half of his body tucked neatly into the trunk. She grabbed the duct tape from her bag and wrapped it around his mouth. Her heart raced as she ripped the tape and then wrapped his ankles and his wrists. She shut the trunk and then slid in behind the wheel. She made a circle and parked her car closer to the apartment complex where few cars were parked. She jumped in the backseat, kicked off the heels, pulled off her skirt and blouse, and slid on her pants and skull T-shirt. Next she pulled off the fake eyelashes, using the lining of the skirt to wipe off her eye makeup and lipstick.

She slid on her shoes and didn't bother to tie the laces before she grabbed her backpack. She grabbed the bottle of Jose Cuervo that she'd taken from Cathy's liquor cabinet. She held the bottle up, making sure nobody would be able to tell that the liquor had been tainted. It looked perfect. She'd also found a miniature bottle of scotch, the kind of bottle they used to serve alcohol on airplanes. She unscrewed the cap and swallowed a mouthful, letting the alcohol drizzle down her chin and neck. She took another mouthful, then gargled and spit the rest outside on the street. She rubbed alcohol-covered hands through her hair. Working quickly, she leaned back into the car and grabbed the package from Dr. Williams. After carefully unwrapping the contents, she used a piece of duct tape to secure the needle in place.

She had rehearsed this night so many times, she felt as if she could do it in her sleep.

269

She shoved the roll of duct tape into her pack and then looked around the inside of the car, making sure she had everything she needed. Securing her backpack over her right shoulder, she grabbed the tequila and left the car behind.

The gibbous moon shed enough light to lead Hayley around the side of Brian's house without tripping over anything. She crept past a row of misshapen garbage canisters.

The garage door was ajar.

A shuffling noise inside the garage caused her to freeze. With her back against a stucco wall, she closed her eyes and waited. Footsteps. Shit. She couldn't move now. Whoever was in the garage was close. Could they see her?

She could smell smoke. Whoever was in the garage was smoking. Her heart rate soared. She was too close to finishing off Brian to be caught now. The cigarette was tossed just outside the door. A booted toe appeared and snuffed the cigarette bud. The door closed and Hayley took in a breath.

That was close.

She crept around to the backyard. There was a covered hot tub and a lot of dead plants. Someone had started a garden, because even in the dark, Hayley could see what looked like a couple of Roma tomatoes hanging off the vine.

She counted the windows on the house: One. Two. Three. Lizzy had access to a lot of county records. Hayley probably could have Googled the house plans; either way she knew Brian owned the house and that the third window belonged to the master bedroom. Logic told her that Brian slept in the master bedroom. Logic also told her that this was the room where Brian would take her.

She set her backpack on the ground directly beneath the window, figuring she'd be able to lean out the window later and grab her things when the time came.

She returned to the front of the house, inhaled another deep breath of fresh air, and headed for the front entry.

It was finally time for her long-awaited reunion with Brian.

CHAPTER 37

A LONG AND WINDING ROAD

Lizzy had been driving around for six hours, taking any and every long, winding road that led to a mountain cabin. She'd knocked on a few doors, peeked through windows, made a lot of calls, and talked to more than a few townspeople in and around the Reno, Nevada, area, asking if they knew of a lodge with a painted sign.

It was getting dark and she had yet to find one wooden sign with flowers painted on it. She had just filled up her gas tank for the third time when she picked up her phone on the first ring.

"I found it! The sign Debra drew matches this exactly. It's the Evergreen Lodge. The reason Debra couldn't see the name of the lodge is because the letters are painted the same brown as the wood. Everything else on the sign is white."

Lizzy pulled to the side of the gas station parking lot where people could put air in their tires. She put the car in park and hit the menu button on the navigation system. "What's the address?"

Jessica gave her the address and Lizzy punched in some numbers, messed up, and started over again until she got the hang of the navigation system. She finally managed to type in the street name and number, knowing she would still have her work cut out for her once she found the street.

"Have you heard from Hayley?" Jessica asked.

"No. I've been calling all day. I think she shut her phone off," Lizzy said.

Jessica sighed. "I never should have lent her my mother's car."

"If you need to get home, call Cathy. I'm sure she'd be glad to pick you up and take you wherever you need to go."

"That's OK. I'm fine. Hannah and I will keep each other company until Hayley returns. Call me if you find the cabin."

"I will," Lizzy said. "Call me if you hear from Hayley."

It took Lizzy twenty minutes to find the sign. She made the right turn as instructed and followed the narrow, winding road. She took it slow, keeping an eye out as she drove. The cabins were few and far between.

Debra had said they drove for a while before finally stopping. Lizzy figured she would head for the top of the mountain and work her way down. She'd already called Detective Roth, who was not happy that she'd headed to the mountains without telling him where she was going. Although he was annoyed with her, she could also tell that he wasn't surprised. He was a nice man with two grown children and a wife who kept his dinner warm. He was satisfied with his life, and it showed. With all the murder and mayhem, they were becoming fast friends.

Lizzy pulled over and lowered her window when she saw a woman getting groceries from her trunk. "Excuse me. I'm looking for a secluded cabin on this very street that I believe is owned by Anthony Melbourne. Do you know where that might be?"

"I don't recognize the name, but if you go to the top," the woman offered, "there are three more cabins. The one on the top is brand new. Before you get to the top, though, a few miles up

the road, in fact, you'll see a turnoff. It doesn't look like much, but there's a long trail. The kids and I take walks over there every once in a while, but the path dead-ends. At that point, at least in the daylight, if you look uphill you can see the roof of a small cabin in the middle of the woods. We've never bothered to go all the way to see who lives there, but since I've never heard of the name Melbourne, perhaps that's his cabin." She shrugged. "Sorry I can't be of more help than that."

"You have been a huge help. Thanks."

The woman continued unpacking as Lizzy drove off. After a few miles, just as the woman had described, there was a turn-off. Lizzy grabbed her cell phone, figuring she could use the free flashlight application to see where the hell she was going. She stepped out of the car. The temperature had dropped drastically; Sacramento would still be hot and sultry. Not so in Nevada.

* * *

Sierra Mountains, Day 72

Vivian sat on the bed, her foot propped on a pillow before her. The knife in her hand was the sharpest knife she could find. It had a good, heavy weight to it, and the blade was sharp. She looked at her foot and examined it closely to determine where the best place would be to cut through skin and bone.

She had already ripped a sheet into strips of cloth. She would use a few of those as a tourniquet. There was no alcohol to drink, which would have been nice under the circumstances.

Cutting through bone was not going to be easy, but she had found a meat tenderizer that she planned to use to break the bone if need be. She would have to cut through tendons and muscle.

Severing the nerve would hurt the most. Other people had amputated their arms and legs to free themselves. There was no reason why she couldn't do the same.

She had been thinking about it for days. Planning, gathering tools. She could do this. She had no choice, she told herself.

Diane was dead. The scrawled note beneath the tabletop said it all. *Diane had been here.* And nobody had seen her since.

Vivian had thought it strange that Melbourne had accepted her into the program so quickly, but now she knew why. She had called him more than once. She had asked too many questions. She knew too much.

What bothered Vivian most these past few days was that she'd realized what a waste her life had been. She was smart. She should have gone to a doctor and found a way to work with her weight and her loneliness.

Others had done it.

After getting help, Vivian could have gone to school and made something of herself. Lots of people had controlling mothers who drove them up the wall. Many young girls had lost their fathers at an impressionable age.

Vivian should have told her mom to leave her alone. She never should have taken her mom's word as gospel. Vivian had done nothing wrong. She wasn't a failure. She was strong and she would prove it.

Trapped in a cabin in the middle of nowhere, she thought, and now suddenly everything seemed clear. Timing was everything.

The cabin was only slightly bigger than her apartment. She rarely went outside when she was home, but as soon as she'd been cuffed and chained, she'd wanted nothing more than her freedom. Melbourne didn't realize he might have found a cure for much more than weight loss. Isolate people by force and suddenly they want to live and see the world!

She laughed: a bitter laugh, but still a laugh.

Ready to be free, she took hold of the knife and held it steady, the blade hovering over her flesh at the smallest part of her ankle. She could do this, she told herself.

Before she made her first slice, the door to the cabin swung open.

Quickly she used the blanket to cover her leg, the knife, and the strips of cloth. No footsteps or rattling of a key had warned her that somebody was coming.

It was Jane.

And yet for the first time, she realized it wasn't Jane at all. She knew that face. She and Diane used Skype when they chatted. No wonder she had recognized the woman the first time she paid her a visit. The woman standing before her had the same blue eyes, the same face as her friend, Diane.

It was Diane's sister, Andrea Kramer.

"What have you done with Diane? Where is she?"

* * *

Andrea set her backpack on the floor. She sighed and took a seat on the edge of the pull-out bed. Vivian Hardy looked a hundred times better than she had when she first came to the cabin. "You look great. It's such a pity that you're not going to be able to show off your weight loss to your friends and family."

"I could care less about my weight loss," Vivian said. "Even when I joined WWW, where I met Diane, I only wanted to lose a few pounds. More than anything, I wanted to make new friends."

"Aren't you glad you met Diane?" Andrea asked with disdain. "If you'd never met her, you wouldn't be in this predicament, now would you?"

"Diane cared about everybody she ever met. She was the best friend I ever had."

Andrea shot to her feet in a flash. "You don't have to preach to me about all of Diane's wonderful attributes. Her friends called her an angel sent from heaven, which is why I did her a favor by sending her back to the place where she belongs."

"You killed your own sister! I tried to warn Diane about you, but she wouldn't listen. There wasn't anything in this world that she wouldn't do for you."

"Diane was fat. She was selfish and she was weak."

"She was the most compassionate being I've ever met in my life."

Andrea couldn't bear to listen to such mindless chatter. She went to the kitchen, shuffled through the drawers, and came back into the room with a butcher knife. Somebody needed to shut the fat bitch up once and for all.

CHAPTER 38

FIRST TIME FOR EVERYTHING

Hayley knocked on the front door again, louder this time. The loser who opened the door was approximately the same width and height as Brian, but that's where the resemblance ended.

"I need to talk to Brian," Hayley said.

"Where is Tango?" the guy asked.

She shrugged and then squeezed her way past him when he stepped outside to take a look around.

Hayley walked into the living room and found herself standing before Brian and one of his many woman friends. They sat side by side on a well-used beige couch playing video games, both pointing their controllers at the television.

The woman with long brown hair stopped what she was doing and looked at Hayley. She looked stoned out of her mind. Brian looked more like a rock star than a drug dealer with his thin, muscled body and black, spiky hair.

It took a moment longer for Brian to look up at her. His head tilted to the side as he said, "What the fuck?"

Hayley set the bottle of tequila she'd brought on the table in front of them. She pretended to sway as she raked her fingers through already tangled hair. "I had nowhere else to go."

"Where the fuck is Tango?"

"Your boy at the door asked about him too. Who's Tango?"

Brian shouted the name Mike, telling him to find Tango so he could have a talk with the man.

Hayley figured Tango must be the guy in the trunk of Jessica's car. It had taken every bit of strength she had to get the lower half of Tango's body into the trunk. Dead weight was heavier than shit.

Keeping her expression deadpan with just enough innocence wasn't easy. She looked at Brian and said, "Can we talk?"

"I've heard things about you. If you have something to say to me, say it."

She straightened and looked at the woman. "In front of your friend?"

"You've never been the shy type."

She swallowed, wondering how her plan could possibly work with three against one. Mike, the guy who had answered the door, came back inside and took a seat. "Tango must have run to the store," he told Brian. "He'll be back." He grabbed the tequila Hayley had brought and drank from the bottle.

The woman elbowed the guy and told him to save some for the rest of them.

Unfortunately, Brian wasn't taking the bait.

Lizzy's words played through her mind...*you're one of the smart ones, Hayley*. She didn't feel too smart at the moment. She had to think fast.

Brian relaxed a little and released a bored sigh. "What's the problem, Hayley?"

With everything to lose, Hayley began unzipping her jeans, slowly, as if she were going to do a strip tease for Brian and his friends. "When you're fucked at such a young age," Hayley said in the sexiest voice she could muster, "it screws with your mind, and pretty soon you don't care who you're screwing as long as you're doing someone." She let out a crazy laugh. "Remember what you used to tell me about your dick?"

The girl with the luxurious hair got a chuckle out of that. She used her elbow to jab the other guy. "Turn off that crap. I want to know what Brian used to say about his dick."

The room was silent. All eyes were on Hayley.

Brian came to his feet and threw his gaming controller on his empty seat. "Looks like I'll have to take care of this in private after all."

A couple of steps brought him to Hayley's side. He grabbed the back of her neck and began to steer her out of the room, toward the hallway.

"Where are you going?" the woman asked.

"Don't you be jealous, sweetie. This will only take a minute." He snickered and then looked at his friend. "And there's plenty to go around."

Brian pulled Hayley down the hall and into a bedroom to the left. Unlike Peter Peter Pumpkin Eater, Brian's room was remarkably tidy. But he took her to the wrong room.

Shit!

Brian shut the door behind him and then leaned against the door and crossed his arms. "So why are you really here?"

Hayley stepped farther into the room and closer to the bed before she turned back to face him. "I've missed you." She slipped off her shoes and then took off her pants too. No miniskirt or wig needed tonight.

No disguises.

Just Hayley and Brian.

Standing at the end of the bed in a lacy pair of thong underwear and her favorite T-shirt, complete with bleached stains and holes, she waited for him to attack.

Nothing happened, and that worried her.

He scratched his bony shoulder. "I heard about what happened to you from your mom. I guess spending time with a killer made you see how good you had it, huh?"

"Yeah, you could say that."

"It's a good thing you came," he said. "Your mom owes me a lot of money. She's had to fuck all of my friends and then some just to keep from groveling in the streets."

Let it go, she told herself. "So? You got any ropes, cuffs, whips…anything at all?"

He smiled. "Wow, Spiderman must have really did a number on you."

She spread her legs a few inches, hoping to entice him to come forward. "You think I'm here to pay you back for fucking me whenever you wanted without my permission?"

"Let's just say I like to be prepared for any unforeseen events."

She smiled. "I'm not the only one who has changed."

"News gets around fast," he said. "I know what you've been doing in the middle of the night when most people are sleeping."

"Don't know what you're talking about, but I'll tell you this. Spending a few days with a serial killer made me see that you weren't so bad after all." She rubbed her neck as if it was getting hot.

"Is that so?" he asked. "I thought you hated me."

"I thought so too."

He locked the door, and then turned and practically lunged for her, catching her off guard. He used his body to pin her against the closet door, his facial expression a maze of hard, angry lines.

Nothing was going as planned.

Brian was sober, for one thing. And he was angry with her... as if she was the one who had somehow ruined his already fucked-up life.

"Raise your arms above your head."

"Why?"

"Just do it."

Tentatively she raised both arms, glad she was backed up against the closet door, praying he wouldn't see what was taped to her back beneath her shirt.

Brian patted her down as if he were a TSA agent at airport security, giving Hayley time to think about Lizzy and how much faith Lizzy had in her. Lizzy had taken her in and even gave her room to breathe. She treated Hayley as an equal. More often than not, she overheard Lizzy telling others how smart Hayley was and how she'd overcome so much in such a short time.

If only she knew.

Jessica knew.

Jessica had superhero abilities. Laser beams for eyes that could see right into her brain and decipher what she was thinking. Sometimes Jessica seemed to know what Hayley was going to do before Hayley knew. It was downright scary. And yet Hayley sensed that Jessica cared about her too.

Hayley wasn't used to having so many people care about her. Lizzy, Jessica, Cathy, Brittany. Hell, even Jared asked about her whenever he called Lizzy.

Brian took his time patting her down. His fingers felt way too familiar, callused and dry, making her feel dirty.

Hayley felt a tear roll down the side of her face. If she'd taken the time to jot down twenty things that might happen tonight, crying would not have been on the list.

Tonight was the finale, her last hurrah, the night she'd been waiting for. Tonight she would finally get her revenge: sweet, sweet revenge. She would free herself of the nightmares that had been haunting her dreams since the day Brian first walked into her room and took what didn't belong to him.

"Are you crying? You fucking come to *my* house, disturb my Grand Theft Auto game, drag me into my bedroom, and now the bitch is going to cry. Unbelievable."

He looked Hayley in the eyes, unblinking. She could smell his stale breath and feel his calloused hand through the cotton of her shirt as he massaged her breast.

She couldn't stop shaking. Another first. Quaking in fear was not her style. But she was sure as hell shaking now.

He was a monster, and she'd come to kill the monster once and for all. So what was the problem?

She'd come to Brian's house to take care of unfinished business, and yet her feet might as well be nailed to the floor. She couldn't move. It took everything she had inside of her just to hold in another heavy sob.

"Jesus. I can't fuck you if you're going to cry like a baby." He weaved his fingers through his hair and then turned and made his way to the bedside table. He pulled a pack of cigarettes from a carton. "Funny," he said. "The apple doesn't fall far from the tree after all."

Hayley tasted the saltiness of her tears on her lips as she reached a shaky hand behind and beneath her T-shirt. She couldn't find the tape. She swallowed a lump of metallic-lined panic just as her fingers brushed over the edge. Slowly, noiselessly, she lifted the corner of the tape until she felt the needle. With the needle in her hand, she used her thumb to flick off the rubber tip. "Did my mother cry?" she asked the monster.

Still shaking, but finding some semblance of control, she took short, methodical steps his way, the needle tucked in her hand, hidden behind her back as she moved toward him, watching his profile.

He packed the cigarettes against his open palm and then used his teeth to pull open the plastic strip on top. "The bitch cried every single night." The corners of his eyes crinkled when he smiled.

Hayley inhaled right before she plunged the needle into his arm. The needle went deep…cleanly and smoothly into his skin.

Brian looked from the needle in his arm to her face, clearly surprised that she'd somehow pulled a fast one on him.

There was no time to make sure she hadn't hit a vein. Not like she gave a shit.

He was going down fast.

She pulled out the needle and tossed the empty syringe on the floor. She'd never given anyone an injection before.

First time for everything.

CHAPTER 39

NOTHING WORSE THAN THE DARK

The downhill part of the trail had been easy, but the uphill part had already left Lizzy breathless. A few weeks at the gym, it seemed, had done her absolutely no good.

Detective Roth was right. She should have waited for backup. Why did she always find herself alone in the dark? There was nothing she hated worse than being alone in the dark.

She reached over her shoulder and touched her Glock. Despite the cool air, her palms were sweaty. Every once in a while the flashlight on her phone would go out and she had to hit a few buttons to get it to light her way again.

Eerie shadows and strange noises came at her from every direction. Her heart rate jumped. Keeping her eyes glued to the forest floor in front of her, she decided to concentrate on her breathing. Each breath came out in cold bursts of white fog as she kept a steady pace. Every so often she stopped and looked around, making sure she hadn't passed by a distant cabin.

Her flashlight app went out again, leaving her in the pitch dark.

A rustling of leaves caught her full attention. She stopped where she was, careful not to make a sound, glad the light had gone out, leaving her camouflaged between myriad trees and dead branches.

Even the crickets stopped chirping.

A twig snapped nearby, startling Lizzy. She grabbed her Glock and held it straight ahead. With the thumb of her free hand, she pushed the button on her phone. The bright light shone a few feet ahead where she saw a shadowy figure running through the woods.

Lizzy smelled smoke.

She looked in the direction the shadowy figure had come. In the distance, she saw a bright light. Fire.

Whoever had run off was in familiar territory and knew exactly where they were going; the dark figure was long gone, disappearing behind a copse of trees.

Lizzy looked back toward the fire. The flames had already doubled in size. She ran uphill as fast as her legs could manage. That damn treadmill was finally paying off.

* * *

Getting Brian from the floor to the bed had been easier than she'd thought it would be. Brian wasn't nearly as heavy as Tango, and Hayley was thankful for that. Now that she'd secured Brian to the bed, she dressed quickly. Quietly she opened the window, climbed out, and found her backpack beneath the window to her left, right where she had left it. Back in the room with Brian, she secured the window and then watched him for a moment. He was naked and vulnerable, tied with ropes and duct taped to the bed, arranged a little differently than Dr. Williams and Peter had been. She didn't have time to lollygag. She needed to work fast.

After plugging in the soldering iron, she pulled out her knife kit and examined the contents: a classic tactical hunting knife with reverse serration; her Remington three-piece skinner set for big game; and her personal favorite, a radical gut hook with four-inch blade, designed for maximum performance.

She reached out and touched each knife, figuring she had at least twenty minutes before one of his friends came to and got curious. Hopefully, they had drunk all of the tainted tequila she brought for them.

She looked longingly at her choice of knives and finally selected the four-inch gut hook. Moving closer to the bed, she looked into Brian's eyes as she held the cold blade to his throat. He was awake now and he was mumbling beneath the tape over his mouth.

For a fleeting moment, she hated the way she felt. The urge to slice open his carotid artery and watch the blood seep from his pale flesh was nearly too great to resist. She pressed the knife to his skin and watched the blade as it slid across the thin skin, pressing hard enough to make blood appear and make him squirm.

She inhaled a breath of moldy, shitty air and pulled away. "Guess what? You were right. I came here tonight to make you pay for every shitty thing you ever did to my mom and me. Tonight you're going to die. But first I want you to think about what you've done."

She set the knife down and grabbed the soldering iron. She climbed on top of him, surprised at how calm he managed to stay. He wasn't bucking and fighting her like the others. He said a few words beneath the duct tape and then fell quiet, his eyes watching her every move.

The craziest part was he looked as if he was enjoying every moment. Brian knew exactly what he was doing. He didn't need words to use reverse psychology on her. He was trying to guilt her with his eyes. By the time she finished burning the first word into his flesh, the gleam in his eyes matched that of the devil. "I forgot," she said. "You don't like tattoos and body piercings, do you?"

He didn't acknowledge her, but his eyes still bored into her, not blinking.

"Just two words, Brian. No big deal. I'll make sure you're barechested while you lie in your coffin so that when your friends pay their respects they can see your new tattoo: Child Rapist," she said, so he'd know the words she'd seared across his chest.

* * *

Vivian woke to the smell of smoke.

She was on the floor, bleeding from stab wounds, mostly to the legs and arms. She'd fought Andrea Kramer, surprising her with a knife of her own. But Andrea was taller and stronger, and she'd gotten the best of Vivian.

Most of the wounds were not as deep as the one in Vivian's leg. The knife had come at Vivian over and over until she'd finally feigned her death. Only then had Andrea stopped attacking. With blood everywhere, Andrea must have decided the only way to get rid of the evidence was to burn the place down.

The smoke was thick, making it difficult to breathe. Vivian dragged herself toward the door, but the chain wouldn't allow her to reach the knob. The kitchen was lit up, popping and crackling as the blaze spread. Flames flickered, gulping up oxygen and coming Vivian's way.

"Is anybody in there?"

Vivian wasn't sure if she'd imagined the voice coming from outside, but she shouted back just in case someone was there. "I'm in here!"

"Get away from the door," the voice yelled back.

Vivian crawled toward the window and away from the flames and the door.

Gunfire sounded. Three shots fired in all before the door was kicked open. The woman who entered was slight in frame, her face and body haloed by flames that reached the ceiling behind her. Vivian still weighed close to two hundred pounds. There was no way this woman would be able to get her out of here.

The blaze spread quickly. The smoke was thicker than ever.

Vivian could hardly see. She had nothing left. She couldn't crawl, let alone breathe. As she realized her last moments were upon her, she watched a smoky shadow yank the blanket from the bed. Before Vivian knew what the woman was up to, Vivian felt her body being rolled onto the blanket and dragged toward the door until the chain stopped her from going any farther.

The woman cursed as she whipped out her gun, firing at the chain at close range. The chain snapped apart.

Vivian's ears rang from the gunshot. She felt a fiery heat against her face as the flames drew close.

And then she felt a tug.

The woman was stronger than she looked. She pulled the blanket with Vivian on top of it through a wall of fire and smoke. The last thing Vivian remembered was the way each wood step felt pounding against her head as she was dragged outside and down the stairs.

* * *

By the time Hayley was done burning the message onto Brian's chest, much of her anger had subsided. That had never happened before, and she didn't like it one bit.

Despite his being determined to watch her every move, Brian had drifted in and out of consciousness.

He was awake now.

She slid off the bed, unplugged the iron, and went back to the side of the bed to look at her knives. Which one, she wondered, should she use to cut out his heart?

She ripped the tape from his mouth in case he wanted to say any last words. He chose to remain silent, which annoyed her more than it should have.

"You're going to die, Brian. Any messages you want me to relay to family and friends?"

Nothing.

She took hold of the knife with the longest blade. Once she cut into him, a voice in her head warned her, she would be a killer and there would be no going back.

She shifted her weight from one foot to the other. She had come to terms with the idea of being a killer a long time ago. That was the plan. Stick to it. Since when did she ever second-guess herself?

"Having second thoughts?" Brian asked.

Her mouth tightened as she put the sharp tip of the blade over the area where his heart lay beneath flesh.

It wasn't the blood that would bother her. It was the taking of a life. But he wasn't human. He was a monster. He deserved to die.

She was angry with herself for being so fucking pitiful. The idea that she might not be able to kill the monster had never once entered her mind over the past few months. Not once.

Her hands shook. She couldn't do it. She exhaled and began packing the knives away.

If she couldn't kill the monster, she'd have to think of another way to get him away from her mother. Maybe she could save some money and take her mom to another country where they would live for the rest of their lives—somewhere remote—a place where Brian would never find them no matter how hard or how long he looked.

She packed up the rest of her belongings. By the time she was at the door ready to go, Brian had found his voice.

"The first place I'm going when I get out of here is to your mom's house. The old, ugly bitch is going to pay for her daughter's bad deeds. I'm going to use the ax out in the shed to cut her head clean off. It's much sharper than those toy knives you carry around."

A bubble of rage worked its way up Hayley's throat, leaving a bitter taste. He was a big talker, and she knew he was full of shit, but the fact that he could say those things while she still had full control was too much. He wouldn't shut up.

The rage built quickly, filling her head until she could hardly see straight. Reaching into her backpack, she pulled out her knives and grabbed the hunting knife. Her fury continued to build upon his every word.

As Brian continued to ramble on about all the awful things he would do to her mother, she turned toward him, the knife held in front of her as she walked back to him.

Looking into his eyes, letting him know she wasn't afraid of him, she grabbed his shriveled penis with her left hand and pulled and stretched. After one clean sweep of the knife, his penis was no longer attached to his ugly, skinny body.

He was shouting now, screaming at the top of his lungs. Much better, she thought, because she no longer had any clue what he was saying.

Blood spurted, covering the bed and his body, but he wouldn't shut the fuck up so she went to his side, and when he opened his mouth to call her one more name she'd heard a million times before, she shoved his bloody penis inside his mouth. "There. Chew on that for a while, dickhead."

* * *

It was morning and Lizzy hadn't slept in nearly forty-eight hours. She stood outside Andrea Kramer's house in El Dorado Hills and watched as Andrea was read her rights.

Detective Roth stood at Lizzy's side, talking on the phone. After he hung up he said, "They found Diane's body, what was left of it, buried in the woods not far from the cabin."

"Murder?"

"Looks that way. Multiple stab wounds. They'll be running tests for a few days. I'll call you when I have the results."

Lizzy nodded, thankful to have met Detective Roth. He had a round face. Multiple laugh lines and deep dimples gave him character. He was quick to smile and easy to like.

"Why the hell did Andrea Kramer hire you in the first place?" Roth asked her.

"Andrea was sure that all the evidence she gave me would point to Melbourne. If she couldn't have him, she wanted him to spend the rest of his life in jail. When she realized I wasn't going to take Melbourne down without sufficient evidence, she decided to take matters into her own hands. After her husband left her and took the kids, I think she snapped. Jane just happened to be in the wrong place at the wrong time."

He nodded. "What about Melbourne's secret program?"

"I think he truly believed he was providing a service for women who he thought couldn't help themselves."

"So he wasn't in cahoots with Andrea?"

"I don't think so. I would bet he knew Andrea was in love with him, but he had no idea how dangerous she was."

Detective Roth was called away.

As Andrea was led down the stairs, Lizzy stayed at her side. "Why did you kill Diane?" Lizzy asked.

"I didn't kill her. Melbourne and his floozy assistant have hidden her away somewhere, I'm sure of it."

"You killed your sister and buried her in the woods."

"I would never do such a thing. I was always trying to help my sister. She wanted so badly to be beautiful like me. When we were little we looked like twins. But then Mom died and Diane wouldn't stop stuffing her face."

"You said you gained a lot of weight too. You did the very same thing. You ate because you were sad."

"I was nothing like Diane. I realized I had a problem and I took care of it."

"She loved you, Andrea. She thought you walked on water, and you killed her."

"I already told you I didn't kill her. She could be lounging on the beach in Hawaii for all we know."

"Give it up, Andrea. They found her body. Multiple stab wounds."

Andrea's face paled. "You have no proof."

"How did you get those cuts on your arms?"

"Trimming the rose bushes," she ground out.

"Vivian's in the hospital," Lizzy told her. "The doctors say she's going to pull through. The police are waiting to talk to her."

Andrea's face turned an ugly shade of red. "Anthony Melbourne is the killer and you know it. I handed you the evidence on a silver platter, but you were too stupid to see what was right in front of you."

"That's enough from you," Detective Roth said as he joined them, his voice a bored drawl. "Put her in the car."

Lizzy's phone rang. She clicked a button and put the phone to her ear.

"It's me, Jessica. The reporters are swarming the office and I can't get through the door."

"How did they find out about Andrea already?" Lizzy asked.

"They didn't. It's Hayley. She's been arrested. They're saying that Hayley is the same girl that you and I saw in that crazy video on the Internet. It's all over the news. What are we going to do?"

CHAPTER 40

THE REUNION

"Why didn't you stop him, Mom?"

"I didn't know."

"You knew," Carol said. "More than once I saw you standing outside the door peeking in. If the father of my children ever touched one hair on their bodies, I would never just go on as if nothing had happened. I wouldn't still be living with him either. I would have killed him. I would have stabbed him, driven a knife straight through his heart."

A long stretch of silence followed.

When Carol had called the hospital, the doctor had told her that her mother would be lucky if she made it to the end of the month.

Her mother looked older and yet the same. Carol couldn't help but wonder if she was born like that…dead, without any spark. "Why are you still with him, Mom?"

"I didn't know how to leave him."

Carol looked away.

"Not everyone is as strong as you, Carol."

"Didn't you ever, just once, want to pack up and leave?"

"Where would I have gone?"

"Anywhere. To the dump. Who the fuck cares? To the fucking dump. Better to live *in* garbage than with it."

The door to the hospital room opened. It was Frank. He looked from Carol to Ruth.

"What the hell is going on here?"

"Get the fuck out of here," Carol told the man whom she would never again call father.

"What is she doing here? What is going on, Ruth?"

"I'm saying good-bye to my daughter."

"Get out…now," Carol said, her voice calm yet firm, a deadly glint in her eyes.

He pointed a finger at Carol. "If you think you can talk to your father that way, you are profoundly mistaken. I'm not going anywhere."

Carol reached into her purse and pulled out a pistol. She cocked it and aimed the barrel at Frank's chest. "Wrong again, Frank. One more step and you're going straight to hell. No passing Go. I should have shot you twenty-one years ago."

"Ruth, tell her to put the gun down."

Ruth let her head fall back onto the pillow. "I'm sorry, Carol. So sorry. You were right about everything…except I could never have stabbed him through the heart."

"Why not?" Carol asked.

"Because he doesn't have one." Ruth looked at Frank. "Go away, Frank. I'm tired. I already talked to Detective Roth. He has the pictures you took. He's waiting for you back home. Tell him hello for me, Frank, will you?"

CHAPTER 41

ONE WEEK LATER

For the past thirty minutes, Lizzy had talked to her therapist nonstop, getting it all out. Once she was finished, her shoulders fell. She looked at Linda Gates and waited to see what she had to say.

"It's not your fault that Hayley is in jail."

Lizzy exhaled. "This time, Linda, it is my fault. For months, I've seen obvious signs that something was wrong. Hayley hasn't been herself. My other assistant pointed it out more than once. I knew Hayley was out walking the streets at night, but I took her at her word and never imagined she was seeking revenge. Every single one of those men deserved to be punished, but Hayley is the one who will pay the price."

"What is it exactly that you think you could have done?"

"I could have been there for her. Instead, I swept it all under the rug, figuring I'd deal with Hayley once I tied up a few of the cases I was working on."

"If you were there for her, would she have listened?"

Lizzy shook her head. "No, she would have gotten angry and left the apartment."

Linda nodded.

"But that's not the point."

"What is the point?"

"The point is I didn't try hard enough."

"So this isn't about Hayley," Linda said. "It's about you."

Lizzy thought about that for a moment. Once again, Linda was right. She looked at her therapist, the woman she'd been confiding in for fourteen years. "Are you trying to tell me that I can't save everyone?"

Linda nodded.

"And I can't take on guilt every time someone close to me makes bad choices?"

Linda kept on nodding.

They had been down this road a million times before. The good news was that Lizzy caught on a little faster each time. "What about Jared?"

Linda angled her head just so. "What about him?"

"Why am I so afraid of moving in with him?"

"Because you're a very smart woman. You've been living alone for a long time and you want to make sure he's the right man for you before you make a big commitment such as moving in."

"Wow," Lizzy said. "I didn't see that coming."

Linda chuckled. "I have confidence in you, Lizzy. I've always told you that you're a smart one, and you've never let me down; so keep being smart. When you're ready to fully commit to Jared, I'm sure you'll have no problem moving in with him and accepting him for who he is."

"What about telling him I love him?"

"What about it?"

"I feel sick to my stomach every time he says the words."

"Why?"

"Because I feel guilty for not saying the words back."

"Do you think Jared expects you to say the words back to him?"

The answer came easily. "No," Lizzy said. "I'm sure he doesn't. He loves me for who I am, the good and the bad. If I never said the L word, he would be fine with it."

"You'll say the words when the time is right and when you feel it in here." Linda put a hand over her heart.

Lizzy knew she was right. "I'm sorry I missed so many appointments."

"Don't be. You were busy."

"It must be nice to have all the answers," Lizzy said.

Linda smiled.

* * *

"Are you sure you don't want to stay for dinner?" Lizzy asked Jessica.

"And be a third wheel?"

Lizzy rolled her eyes.

"The truth is," Jessica said, "I have a date with Casey. He's taking me out for a hamburger and a movie."

"Well, good for you." Lizzy could tell she had something else on her mind. "Go ahead, Jessica, say it. I'm all ears, and Jared won't be arriving for a few more minutes."

"It's about Hayley. I'm worried about her."

Lizzy stopped chopping carrots for a moment. "I thought you two didn't like each other?"

"We don't see eye to eye for the most part," Jessica said, "but I like her. And I think she likes me too, although she would never admit it." Jessica smiled. "I know this is wrong of me to say, but I'm proud of Hayley. She didn't kill anyone. I know she must have wanted to kill those men, but she didn't. She used restraint, and that's not something I thought I'd ever say about Hayley Hansen."

Lizzy nodded in understanding. "Jared's going to make sure she has a good defense lawyer."

"I'm glad." After a moment Jessica added, "I heard that Farrell is suing after all."

"Don't worry about him. We have pictures of your bruises. I saw the welts with my own eyes. He's not going to get away with it. The company that hired me to watch Farrell is backing us up one hundred percent."

A knock at the door put an end to their conversation. Jessica grabbed her purse, looked through the peephole, and opened the door. "Hi, Jared."

"Hi, Jessica. I heard you did some great work with the Fullerton case."

"Yeah, it wasn't easy, but I found Carol. Speaking of which, your girlfriend owes me a raise."

He chuckled. "I'll have a talk with her."

"See you both later," Jessica said. "Enjoy your evening."

Jared shut the door, locked it, and then headed straight for Lizzy. Without a word, he took her into his arms and kissed her soundly. "I missed you," he whispered into her ear.

"I'm glad you're home," Lizzy said. "It's been a rough couple of weeks."

"I don't like being away from you. Move in with me, Lizzy." He took hold of her hand and kept his gaze on hers. "We're going to have good days and bad days. There might even be days you wished you never met me. You might refuse to talk to me or look at me, but I'm never going to let you go to bed mad. I'll keep you up all night, reminding you of all the reasons you love me. Years from now, when we're old and gray, when our kids have grown and moved away, we'll look back and think fondly on all the good times and we'll laugh at the bad times and then we'll cry tears of happiness, just because."

Lizzy laughed. He had just quoted a passage from the movie *Romancing Rachel*. "You memorized that for me?"

"Nobody but you."

"I love you, Jared Shayne. I really do love you."

"Don't tease me," he said.

"I'm not teasing. And it's not just because you quoted such a wonderful passage from my favorite movie." She stood on her tippy-toes and kissed his cheek and then his nose and his chin. "I love you."

She looked away for a moment, her eyes wide with wonder. She inhaled. "I feel OK." She looked at him again. "Telling you I love you feels good."

"I love you too, Lizzy Gardner," he said, holding her tight again. "You know that I do."

Meow.

Smiling, Jared bent down and picked up the kitten. "How did Peter Pan get here? I thought he was at my house."

"Her name is Hannah."

He wrinkled his nose. "Hannah?"

"Don't ask. It's a done deal."

He set Hannah back on the ground, wrapped Lizzy in his arms, and kissed her neck.

To love and be loved, Lizzy thought, knowing she was one of the lucky ones.

* * *

Two days later, Lizzy followed Jared into the front entrance of the California Division of Juvenile Justice. Usually visitors were not allowed to visit until after thirty days, but Jared had pulled some strings so she would get a chance to see Hayley.

After checking ID, they were asked to leave their cell phones and other personal belongings at the front desk. A final check and a frisk allowed them to follow an unarmed guard to the Level 2 facilities where Hayley was being kept. Firearms were allowed only outside of the institution. The DJJ was a division of the California Department of Corrections and Rehabilitation where education and treatment services were provided for some of California's most serious youth offenders, ranging in age from twelve to twenty-five. According to the reports Lizzy read, teens with mental health problems were failing to be rehabilitated. The place felt cold and smelled sterile. It made Lizzy sick to think that Hayley was somewhere inside.

The most serious offenders were locked down for twenty-three hours a day. Not as punishment, the institution said, but as a means to keep the teens safe.

They followed the guard down a long, narrow hallway, where the only sound was the click of their heels. It was early. Most of the incarcerated youths were still asleep. Hayley didn't sleep much, which bothered Lizzy further, since she wondered what Hayley would do to keep herself busy.

They entered a room that resembled a school cafeteria. A guard stood at a door on the other side of the room. The guard next to them said they had ten minutes. Then he stepped back, arms stiff behind him, and waited quietly.

Hayley sat alone at a long table in the center of the room.

When Lizzy had first met Hayley, she had black, spiky hair. Her hair was layered now, flyaway pieces framing a pale, heart-shaped face. Most of the black had grown out, revealing her natural color, a rich, dark chocolate, the same color as her eyes. All of her piercings had been removed. She wore a one-piece brown uniform. She was not cuffed. No chains around her ankles. For that, Lizzy was thankful.

Lizzy looked at Jared, who gestured for her to take the lead. He followed behind and took a seat at the same table, but sat quietly a few seats away. Earlier he'd made it clear that he would be right there if she needed him.

Hayley's hands rested on the table, one on top of the other, the stub of her pinky finger clearly visible.

Lizzy put her hands on top of Hayley's and looked into her eyes.

"Don't you be sad," Hayley said.

Lizzy smiled. "Everything's going to be OK. Jared's going to help me get you out of here."

"Assault with a deadly weapon is considered a felony," Hayley told her. "It's punishable by up to four years in state prison. That's not counting fines up to ten thousand dollars, which we both know you can't afford."

Lizzy looked at Jared. He nodded his agreement with her assessment of the situation. As usual, Hayley had done her homework.

A moment of silence passed before Lizzy said, "I left some books for you at the front. They'll give them to you after they check everything. There's also an iPod from Jessica. She said it was old and she wanted to get a new one anyway."

Hayley smiled. "I hope she downloaded some decent music. Have you ever heard the crap she listens to?"

Lizzy forced another smile. She could hear the strain in Hayley's voice as she put on a strong front.

"I know I disappointed you," Hayley said, her tone serious. "I'm sorry about that, but I'm not sorry for anything I've done."

"You didn't kill that man. I'm thankful for that."

"I wanted to. My intention was to finish Brian off once and for all. I cannot and will not lie about that. That man does not deserve to be living and breathing."

A sigh escaped Lizzy.

"You don't need to worry about me. I realize this place has a bad reputation. Ninety percent of those released from this place end up in adult prison. It's overcrowded. The food sucks and the suicide rate is high. But you still don't have any reason to worry about me. I'll be fine."

"Time is up," the guard said.

"Is there anything you need?" Lizzy asked. "Anything I can send you before we get a court date set up?"

"Nope," Hayley said. "I'm good."

Jared stood and waited for Lizzy.

"By the way," Hayley added, "I heard you saved Vivian. I guess you didn't lose your mojo after all."

Lizzy squeezed both of her hands since they weren't allowed to embrace each other.

Hayley looked at Jared and thanked him for finding a way to visit. He told her to hang tough.

As the guard led them out, Lizzy looked over her shoulder, but Hayley had already disappeared through the door across the room.

The building was empty and quiet. Despite the dreary gloom weighing heavily on Lizzy's psyche, the depressing darkness inside of her blossomed right then and there into single-minded resolve. This was not the ending. It was only the beginning. She would do a thorough investigation, and she would utilize every contact she'd ever made to find out everything she could about the men Hayley had singled out for retribution. And then she would stop at nothing until Hayley was back home where she belonged.

ACKNOWLEDGMENTS

I have been writing for twenty years now. The encouragement and support I have received from family members has been the key to my success. There were times when I came very close to giving up on my dreams, but my mother-in-law, Pat Ragan, along with my sister, Cathy Katz, had read all of my books, and they would not let me give up. My husband, Joe, often reminded me that if writing made me happy, then I should do it for the love of writing and nothing else. My children never once complained about the time I spent glued to my computer. Instead, they celebrated my highs and offered sympathy during my lows. My support group includes my mom and dad, sisters, brothers-in-law, a wonderful father-in-law, and lots of nieces and nephews.

I love you all.

ABOUT THE AUTHOR

T. R. Ragan grew up in a family of five girls in Lafayette, California. An avid traveler, her wanderings have carried her to Ireland, the Netherlands, China, Thailand, and Nepal, where she narrowly survived being chased by a killer elephant. Before devoting herself to writing fiction, she worked as a legal secretary for a large corporation. She is the author of *Abducted*, the first Lizzy Gardner book. Writing under the name Theresa Ragan, she is also the author of *Return of the Rose*, *A Knight in Central Park*, *Taming Mad Max*, *Finding Kate Huntley*, and *Having My Baby*. She and her family live in Sacramento.